BATMAN

INFERNO

By Alex Irvine
(published by Ballantine Books)

ONE KING, ONE SOLDIER
THE NARROWS
BATMAN: INFERNO

BATMAN

INFERNO

ALEX IRVINE

Batman created by Bob Kane

BALLANTINE BOOKS • NEW YORK

To everyone
who has ever written a Batman story,
for making me a fan

ACKNOWLEDGMENTS

Thanks to Chris Cerasi at DC Comics and Keith Clayton at Del Rey, for their sharp eyes; to Mom, for the sweet toy Batmobiles; to Sam Hamm, for advice and a timely copy of *Blind Justice;* to T. Davidsohn, for arguments about the Bat-psyche; and to Lindsay, for keeping me on track.

BATMAN

INFERNO

BULL'S-EYE

Rafael del Toro, *Gotham Gazette* Columnist

Far be it from me—well, usually—to start a public dustup within the happy little *Gazette* family, but last week's little bit of (you'll pardon the pun) auto-eroticism put me right over the edge. The *Gazette*'s esteemed automotive columnist, you'll recall, published what was billed as a think piece on Batman's car—Batman's car!—wondering what kind of power train it had, what kind of suspension, whether the costumed crackpot had gotten hold of military-grade materials for its apparently bulletproof exterior, and so on.

And this was on Page One, above the fold, the same day that Carmine Falcone's goons turned the Gotham Superior Courthouse into their own personal shooting gallery, with judges as the little duckies going back and forth until they got plinked.

Priorities, people.

I've got an idea. If we're going to call this guy Batman, let's be consistent. Why bother to figure out what kind of car he's driving? It's the Batcar, on a Batchassis powered by a Batmotor, with top-of-the-line Batsprings and an aftermarket Batexhaust that every auto enthusiast between here and Detroit would kill his mother to have. He wears a Batsuit with a Batcape, and he goes home to a Bathouse where there's a Batwife and Batkids and a Batdog. He captures villains with little metal things? Okay, those are Batarangs, and he swings from building to building with a Batgrappler. Hell, let's brand the whole thing. Make a TV show about it, refurbish some of the old factories in Chinatown so they can turn out Bat-toys for little kids who want to grow up to be sociopathic vigilantes. That's urban renewal.

I think you've got the point by now, right? Calling this lunatic Batman is just feeding into whatever grandiose weirdness he has in his head already. Unless we're all ready for Gotham City to become Battown (it's already Batsh*t crazy, if you ask me), then we need to reel in this whole Bat-phenomenon before everyone goes right off the Bat-deep Bat-end.

And with that, I return you to your regularly scheduled obsession with costumed maniacs. Carmine, if you want to shoot me, I'll be at the rewrite desk.

July 26, 9:09 AM

Bruce Wayne has never figured himself for a power-tool enthusiast, but the fact is hard to deny. He blames Lucius Fox, which is a dodge, like blaming Tsunetomo for his love of physical discipline as expressed through the martial arts. It has always been there, latent. Waiting for the shriek of the lathe and the brutal seduction of the pneumatic drill. Today it's the jackhammer, pulverizing a bulge in the cave wall. Smoothing, leveling, squaring. He will bring order and regularity to the cave the way he brought order and regularity to his fear: through planning, diligence, and the necessary application of force. Where millennia of water had meandered and eroded and precipitated, leaving an organic and irregular labyrinth, a few weeks of work will yield a haven, a completed base of operations from which a man with the right kind of courage and dedication could save his city from those who would corrupt it and do it harm.

He wants as much of the cave to remain natural as is possible. Once he cleared and squared enough space for a laboratory, workshop, training area, and garage, that was enough; now he's in the finishing stages. Too much work, too much hammering and blasting and drilling, might displace the bats that were the reason for his coming here. As they were the collective reason for so much else. Bruce has already redone the cave's wiring twice to accommodate the additions he's made since deciding to create this hideaway two years ago, and if he goes ahead and adds all the facilities he has in mind, he'll have to do it again. Right now the computer workstation is in a level spot surrounded by stalagmites, the metalworking area nestles in an alcove that still stinks of guano, and he can't do any materials testing because he needs a climate-controlled room. Good thing I'm a billionaire playboy, he thinks. If I had a real job, I'd never have time to get all this done.

As soon as the jackhammer's echo dies away into the depths of the cave, Alfred is there. "Why don't you take a break, Master Bruce?"

"Alfred, you know I can't," Bruce says. "I need to get this squared off before the reception tonight."

"If I may be so bold," Alfred says mildly, "the cave will be exactly where you left it."

"Yes, it will. And tomorrow it will be a portfolio review, or a charity appearance, or a stockholders' meeting that will get in the way, and this will be just a cave until I come down here when I don't want to and get this done. Or are you suggesting I should put the job out to bid?"

The idea of a gang of Gotham's finest hard hats banging around under the foundations of Wayne Manor brings a smile even to Alfred's studiously impassive face.

"Surely not," he says. "But you must realize when you have brought your crew to the last of its strength." Alfred snaps a handkerchief out of his pocket and dabs at his forehead and the corners of his eyes. "If you'll excuse me, Master Bruce, I believe I will enjoy a break for both of us."

"Be my guest," Bruce says.

Alfred sits in the swivel chair in front of the bank of monitors near the elevator and leans it all the way back, resting a hand over his eyes. Bruce starts to go back to work, but out of all the thoughts about Tsunetomo and grand schemes for the cave, the morning's "Bull's-Eye" column creeps into the front of his mind and won't leave.

He leans the jackhammer against the cave wall. "You read the paper this morning, Alfred?"

"I'm quite sure you know the answer to that question, Master Bruce."

"So what do you think? Should I start to license Bat-gear? Or maybe I should get a Bat-wife first, and have some Bat-kids so I can sell pictures of them in the maternity ward to the gossip rags. Sound like a good idea to you?"

"It seems to me," says Alfred, "that the very fact of your marriage would keep the gossip rags in rapture for years. Whether your betrothed was a bat or not."

Bruce laughs. "True. Wonder if it's time for another Bruce-Wayne-jilts-socialite scandal. Think that would goose the stock price a little?"

"I highly doubt that shareholder value is dependent on your amorous escapades," Alfred says.

"Still, if there's any chance I could do the company some good . . ."

Alfred gives him a sidelong look. "I shall consult the social register," he says. "Surely there is a lass remaining who has not yet been victimized by your charms."

"That's the spirit," Bruce says. "When you find her, invite her to whatever the thing is tonight."

"The thing, as you so casually put it, is a charity event for Wayne Enterprises' Cystic Fibrosis Foundation."

Bruce starts clearing rubble into a bin. It doesn't match training on a glacier with Tibetan warrior-monks, but it's hard physical work and he falls into the rhythm of it, feeling muscle and ligament flex and lengthen, hearing the air in his lungs and the steady backbeat of his heart. There is music in the body, if you know to listen for it—a more metaphysical thought than Bruce Wayne usually allows himself to indulge in, but when you've decided to devote your life to breaking your body and your mind against the tide of evil and corruption that constantly threatens Gotham City, there is something centering about plain mundane labor. Especially when you can do it in a cave that's constantly fifty-seven degrees instead of the ninety-plus summer heat baking the city.

He has just topped the bin off and lifted the handles to wheel it back to a depression in the back of the main cave when Alfred calls, "Master Bruce. I believe you'll be interested in this."

"What's that, Alfred?" Bruce thought Alfred was asleep. He should have known better.

"If I'm not mistaken, a situation has arisen that requires the . . . informal . . . services you have of late

provided our fair city. May I suggest you have a look
yourself?"

Butler-speak, Bruce thinks. Much too late to cure
Alfred of it, but he has a passing impulse to endow a
charity for the education of butlers in idiomatic regular
English. "Be right there."

TAKING THEM TO TRASK
Duane Trask, *Gotham Globe*

Gotham City's favorite billionaire playboy was up to his usual shenanigans last night, pulling a no-show at an event he'd been splashing his face all over for the past three months. The Cystic Fibrosis Foundation of Greater Gotham soldiered on, but if you were a student of body language, you might have noticed that organizers spent a lot of time peering toward the door in hopes that our boy would make an appearance.

Unconfirmed reports suggest that Bruce Wayne was canoodling with real estate scion(ess?) Tiffany Haskell while Gotham's mucketiest mucks paid a thousand dollars a plate to eat foie gras and listen to has-been movie stars talk about The Need for a Cure. Whether the reason for Brucie's absence was Tiffany's charms or simple inability to put his mouth where his money is, the fact is that he has an ongoing problem with following through on the commitments he makes for other people.

Must be nice to be able to do that and get away with it.

Must be even nicer to be able to do that and still look at yourself in the mirror the next morning. . . .

July 26, 10:17 PM

The fire has bridged two tenements in Otisburg. From a rooftop near the fire—but not too near, he's learned that lesson—Enfer watches the firefighters and waits for the first of them to enter one of the buildings. He shouldn't indulge this temptation—it's what got him caught the last time—but if he were any good at resisting temptation, he wouldn't be where he is. Not that he regrets being where he is, although the road has been painful at times . . .

He loses his train of thought as the first of the deck guns starts up and steam explodes from the burning upper floors of the southern building. It's burning faster than the one to the north, and the boys are also laying water curtains down the alleys on either side of the fire. Enfer starts to worry that they're going to go surround-and-drown; that's not what he wants. From a pocket of his coat he takes a transmitter. He'll give them a couple of minutes, and if they don't go interior by then, he's going to change the rules of engagement. The timing of the whole enterprise is important. If the firemen don't cooperate and Batman doesn't show up, Enfer is going to have a little problem on his hands with a certain Dr. Crane—and that's the last thing in the world he wants. Just the thought of Crane sets a tiny part of his brain squirming, even though he's done pretty well at papering over the worst of his Arkham memories with a carefully cultivated vengefulness directed at Gotham City's ambivalently regarded hero: Batman.

Like a mantra, Enfer says under his breath: *None of this would have happened if it weren't for you.* He plans to repeat the words out loud, just before he torches the costume right off the oh-so-roastable flesh underneath it.

The smell of the chemical dump in the Atlas Mountains reminds him that he's getting excited, losing track of the plan. It leaks out of him when he gets agitated, as if his body has assimilated the chemicals that blew up around him that day and turned them into pheromones. Checking his watch, Enfer sees that the three companies of firefighters have opted for the surround-and-drown approach. Worse yet, it appears to be working. Pantywaists, he thinks. Why not just wait for it to rain? Surround-and-drown is the suburban strip-mall approach. Urban firefighters are supposed to go interior, supposed to be killing each other to get the nozzle, to make the stop.

So: he flicks a switch on the transmitter, and a despairing scream peals out of a broken window on the fourth floor of the northern building. *Heeelllp meeee . . .*

That does the trick. Enfer watches with a professional's eye as an interior team deploys. He waits for the six of them to get inside the building, and then he starts counting, figuring twenty seconds for each floor in full gear. One of the aerials backs closer to the northern building and raises its ladder between the structure and a close string of electrical wires; before it's come to rest against the wall below the broken window, one of the firemen is halfway up it. Brave souls, Enfer thinks. Such brave souls. When his count reaches eighty, he toggles another switch on the transmitter, and every window on the third floor blows out in a magnificent halo of flame. The force of the explosion flings the man off the ladder; trailing smoke, he tumbles in a long arc and lands flat on his back in the middle of Bjornsson Street. A pair of paramedics is converging on the spot before he hits the ground.

Another two men are already on their way up the ladder, and the deck guns swivel around toward the northern building, pouring water in the windows facing the street. Already there's water coming out the front door of the building, but while water is the best way to ensure that you kill a fire, it's also the slowest, and it only works if you can put enough of it on a fire to get the fire to waste all its energy vaporizing water instead of carbonizing tenements.

This is what you get, you courageous self-righteous backstabbing bastards, he thinks. Did you think you could just humiliate me, turn me into a scapegoat? Did you think you could just call me crazy, and that would be the end of it?

Two more aerials are maneuvering into position, from companies in adjacent districts. Here's where the timing is tricky. If Enfer has planned right and caught a break, it'll take the rescue teams long enough to get to the trapped men that a certain person will hear of the crisis and respond. If he hasn't, then at least he's gotten the first part of his revenge. Either way, it's a pretty good day—but he wants the Batman. Torching a bunch of brave stupid smoke-eaters is something he can do any-time. Wonder if any of them has spotted the speaker setup, he thinks. Might be a more interesting game if they figure out that they're being hunted. He decides to make the setup more obvious next time he does this, which—he thinks as he's checking his watch again—is going to be soon.

At T plus seven minutes Enfer feels a charge of elation at the sight of that unmistakable black cape fanning out in the night air. There he is, swinging down from God knows where to land with perfect grace on one of the ladders; almost too quick to follow, he's in the building, and then out again on one of the other ladders with a sooty body in a fireman's carry. He hands off the injured man and leaps back up—God, he's fast—into the build-ing.

Come on, hero, Enfer is thinking. He pulls his face mask down and buckles it, then runs through the rest of what he's come to think of as his pre-Batman checklist. Escape route: check. Little Easter Egg for Batman in case of pursuit: check. Big Easter Egg in case of capture: check, oh check.

With a sharp *chunk,* a gas-fired spike buries itself in the sandstone wall just below his feet. Showtime, he thinks, and sees Batman swinging in a wide arc away from the corner of the northern tenement. Smooth; he's got some kind of spool on the other side of the wire, and it snaps him in a long S-curve across the face of the building Enfer's using as his lookout. He rises and, just as he's reached the point of stillness at the crest of his swing, lets go of the wire and does a perfect somersault onto the other corner of the roof.

Now all there is between Batman and Enfer is a hundred feet of gravel-covered tar, and by the time Enfer has that thought the distance is fifty feet. He fans a group of what he calls Cherry Bombs across the gravel between them and hops over the rooftop parapet onto the fire escape as they go off at Batman's feet. He wants to look back; in fact it's killing him that he can't watch the effects of either the Cherry Bombs or the show he's put on across the street. But if there's one thing his demo training taught him, it's adherence to procedure, and he's had this plan in place for too long to start freelancing now. He's chosen Otisburg because it's convenient for the next stage, although what he really wanted was to do the whole thing in an empty department store near Crime Alley, where Batman seems to appear quite a bit. Maybe next time . . .

Right now the thing to do is stay a step ahead of Batman, who's coming down the fire escape a lot faster than Enfer has managed so far. When he gets to the third floor, Enfer jumps, then glances up to see how much of a head start he's got—only to find that Batman, three flights above him, has also jumped. Only a maniac would jump from a sixth-floor fire escape, he thinks, and corrects himself almost instantly as Batman fans out his cape and it miraculously stiffens, guiding him down like a hang glider. The upside of this nifty maneuver is that Enfer falls faster, and—*oof!*—is out of the alley and around the corner onto Bjornsson before Batman hits the ground.

The compulsion to stop and admire his handiwork across the street is almost too strong to resist, but Enfer keeps his legs pumping. If ever there was a time not to gawk, this is it. The firefighters are shouting at him, and he wonders if he knows any of them. Then he's pounding up Armory Street over the Hill and toward the northernmost Gotham River docks. He's always been fast, and the smell coming out of his clothes means he's started to metabolize some of the chemicals his body somehow learned to produce after what he's come to think of as his Chemical Baptism last year. One of these days he's going to find a discreet chemist—he wonders in passing if any Arkham residents are chemists—and see what it is, exactly, his body has started to make.

Whatever it is, he likes it. It makes him strong. It makes him fast. It makes him burn.

He crests the Hill and picks up even more speed on the way down. Ahead, he sees pleasure boats out for evening cruises, along with a single tug heading downstream. He crosses Ridgeview Boulevard against traffic, juking around cars like a running back for the Knights, and as soon as he's across he leaves another string of Cherry Bombs just to slow Batman down a little. He hears them go off with their signature little *whoosh*es, and hears a growl from Batman, who is closer than Enfer would like. Timing, timing, he's thinking . . .

And then he's out onto Pier 29, vaulting over the chain-hung gate and flipping Joysticks over his shoulder. How he loves the Joysticks, the way they light up and go spinning off into the air with that little whistle he built in for effect. Ah—there it is, like a dozen tiny train whistles. Enfer glances over his shoulder and sees Batman swiping at the Joysticks like King Kong on the Empire State Building, but just as he's starting to take real pleasure from the effect, the Joysticks are already burning out and Batman has slapped some of them to the ground, where they shatter in showers of sparks.

Enfer backs to the edge of the pier and glances down and behind him. Black water, ripples ridged in the orange of the sun setting out beyond the airport.

"I'm a little too old for fireworks," Batman says.

Enfer looks back and sees the vigilante less than ten feet from him. How different from the last time we did this, he thinks. I was almost beneath his notice then, trussed like a hog while he was on his way somewhere else and left on the sidewalk for the police to discover. This time I get the full villain treatment: pursuit, even banter! Or what passes for banter coming from Batman, who's not much of a conversationalist.

"Oh, come on," he says. "You must have enjoyed the show at least a little, or you wouldn't have come all this way to watch the ending."

"I came to make sure you answer for those firefighters," Batman says.

"Ah, justice," Enfer says. "We've all got our ideas about that. Justice, Batman, is—as you know—not the same thing to all people."

"Spare me," Batman says.

"Wonderful sight," Enfer says, still looking at the glow in the sky.

And now it's time to set the final part of this little plan

in motion. Enfer strikes a pose, looking out over the Hill at the glow of the fire burning a few blocks on the other side. How he loves the way the smoke catches the flashing lights of the fire trucks. "Allow me to introduce myself," he says. "I am called Enfer, and I have a message to convey to you. It goes something like this: *D'immenses dragons noirs se seraient jetés sur Vous, et vous auraient soufflé des flammes dans le cou . . .*"

Batman rolls his eyes, the whites visible for a moment through the holes in his mask.

"An affectation. Cuff me, Batman," Enfer says. "You do cuff villains, don't you? In addition to the common criminals?"

He holds his arms out, the right a little in front of the left, figuring that if Batman is right-handed, he'll use his left hand to hold Enfer's wrist while opening whatever Bat-cuff he's using with his right. And sure enough, Batman does exactly that. *If I had nerves there, that would hurt,* Enfer thinks as Batman clips a matte-black manacle over his right wrist. *Of course, it's his fault I don't.* He's trying to hold back a smile. *Just like last time, it's night and there are fires yet to birth and this costumed freak is imposing his will. You're just one man, Enfer* thinks. *You don't have any right.*

While Batman's hands are still occupied, one on Enfer's right wrist and the other snapping the manacle shut, Enfer jerks his right shoulder back and the arm separates cleanly at the joint, dropping to thump against Batman's left foot. In the same motion, Enfer leaps backward, somersaulting over the edge of the pier. For a paralyzing moment he feels Batman's fingers brush the edge of his wrist, but even Gotham's finest vigilante is only so fast, and as Enfer is completing his somersault, his feet just cracking against the surface of the Gotham River, he sees Batman drop the arm and duck into his cape before the entire end of the pier disappears in a mushrooming tower of flame.

3

July 27, 1:49 AM

The great virtue of pain is that it gives you something to surmount, to attack and vanquish. As an internal enemy, it keeps you in shape for the external battles. Bruce sprawls across a worktable, shivering as Alfred smears ointment across the burns on his legs. He deflected most of the blast with the cloak, but fire has a way of finding gaps, and the skin of his legs is blistered even though the suit survived without a mark. He makes a note to prioritize thermal insulation at the next redesign. Lucius will probably have some interesting ideas.

"Giant black dragons," he mutters.

"Beg pardon, Master Bruce?"

"He said something to me in French, right before his arm came off," Bruce says. "Something about giant black dragons breathing flames on my neck." And then he coughs, because his throat does feel like he's been getting mouth-to-mouth from a dragon.

Bruce sits up on the edge of the table and hops to the

floor, deliberately moving as if his legs don't hurt. Fake
it till you make it, he's read more than once. As Alfred
starts hanging up the suit and replenishing the gear in
Batman's utility belt, Bruce fires up the computer and
runs a series of phrase searches involving black dragons.
After culling several million references to various role-
playing games, he comes up with several references to
a poem. *Great black dragons with smoking tongues /
Would have blown red flames on your neck . . .* He
brings the entire poem up and reads it, absorbing its odd
religious fervor that coexists uneasily with a vivid section imagining how much worse the tortures of Jesus
Christ could have been. Enfer's quote came from that
section.

Bruce is no literary critic, but he is made more than a
little uneasy by a lunatic arsonist quoting poems about
the potential torments of the son of God at him. "Alfred," he says. "Have a look at this."

"Blaise Cendrars," Alfred reads. "A bit transparent,
don't you think?"

"Help me out here, Alfred. You remember what a
great French student I was."

"Well, apart from the obvious bilingual pun in the
first name, the surname means 'cinder,' more or less."

"Hm." Bruce hasn't even read the title of the poem or
seen who wrote it. "It's polyglot, anyway. An arsonist
named Cinder . . ."

He runs a search on the poet and comes up with more
poems, a wide selection of capsule biographies, an even
wider selection of essays, and a couple of portraits done
by Modigliani. Pulling one of the biographies, Bruce
scans it with Alfred reading over his shoulder. Born

in 1887 in Switzerland under the name Frédéric Sauser;
childhood stays in Egypt and Italy, probably England and
France as well, followed by stints in Germany and Rus-
sia, then France and Switzerland and Belgium and New
York. ("Bit of a wanderer," Alfred comments—a little
archly, Bruce thinks.) Back to Europe for a couple of
years before the war swept him up and . . .

"How about that," Bruce says.

Alfred, nodding: "Indeed."

. . . cost him his right arm in 1915, at the battle of
Navarin Farm in Champagne.

There is more after that, about this or that poem or
this or that woman, but Bruce has seen what he needs.
"Wasn't . . ." He runs another quick search. "Hm. The
town where he was born, La Chaux-de-Fonds. It was
the center of the Swiss watchmaking industry, but it's
also where Kropotkin came from."

"Watches and anarchists. So it's not terribly shocking
that our man has a bit of a fetish for both timers and
things that go boom," Alfred says.

"No, it's not. Seems like they always identify with
someone," Bruce muses aloud. "But this is the first one
who's thought he was a poet."

"Much less a maimed poet," Alfred says.

Bruce chuckles. "I was about to say all poets are
maimed, but if I remember correctly, you once gave
me five hundred lines for a comment I made about
poets."

" 'I will not indulge in juvenile disdain of my literary betters,' " Alfred quotes. "Was it only five hundred?"

"You'd remember better than I would."

"Quite. Well, Master Bruce. Let's get you resting, shall we? If you're to hunt down a mad arsonist who fancies himself a poet, you're going to need your strength."

You mean if Batman's going to hunt him down, Bruce thinks. Already he is itching to put the suit back on, become one more shadow in nocturnal Gotham City. Not for the first time, he has the notion that he is the costume, that Batman is more real than Bruce Wayne . . . that, to make a long story short, the long germination begun when Thomas and Martha Wayne lay dying in Crime Alley is now complete, and Bruce Wayne has been transformed into Batman more completely than his daily show of dissipation and profligacy can really disguise.

Bruce Wayne, for example, would be thinking right now that his legs hurt like a son of a bitch.

"Ouch," Bruce says, just to keep his mind straight. He's begun to realize over the past year that he is going to have to work to keep Batman cordoned off where he belongs: down here in the cave and on the nighttime Gotham City streets. One more exercise of will, he thinks; pain only exists when I want it to, and Batman only exists when I let him.

These thoughts occupy him on the elevator ride up from the cave to the third floor of Wayne Manor, where Bruce finds his lightest pair of pajamas. It's barely after two, but Enfer is gone and—Bruce guesses—will wait to turn up again until he has a new arm. It probably won't take long.

Tomorrow, Bruce thinks. Tomorrow I'll make excuses for the reception I missed, whatever it was for, and I'll give Lucius Fox a call, and I'll see if I can't make some kind of high-profile faux pas with a local celebrity bimbo. It's been a while since I did that. Have to keep up appearances. He crawls into bed, takes a deep breath, and lets himself hurt.

GCFD LOSES TWO IN SUSPICIOUS BLAZE
Gavin O'Connor, *Gotham Globe*

Two Gotham City firefighters died, and three others were hospitalized, when an Otisburg tenement fire unexpectedly spread to a second building and jumped floors in the first, trapping firefighters between floors. An all-out rescue effort succeeded in rescuing all but Francisco Giordano, 41, and Evan Gilbert, 33, whose bodies were only recovered after the fire was brought under control in the early hours of this morning.

The names of the injured were not released, and doctors at Gotham Central Receiving Hospital were not available for comment.

Batman was also spotted at the scene and according to witnesses was responsible for rescuing at least one of the survivors before pursuing a possible arsonist. "He came down the ladder and then, zoom, he was gone up to the roof of the building across the street," said witness Andrew Norster. "I saw another guy up on the roof there, but I thought he was just another fireman. He looked like one."

The fire department refused to comment on the possibility of arson, pending the results of their investigation. "We've lost two of our own tonight," said GCFD spokeswoman Erin McNamara. "It's not a time for speculation."

But several witnesses corroborated Norster's sighting of a figure on the rooftop across Bjornsson Street, possibly wearing firefighting garb. Gotham City police detectives arrived at the scene shortly after ten o'clock but refused comment. . . .

July 27, 4:30 PM

He flashes his city inspector's badge at the gates of Arkham Asylum and is rewarded with a momentary flash of panic on the guard's face. Muttering into the phone, the guard will not meet his eye; he hangs up and opens the gate without another word. In the oppressive afternoon heat, the asylum broods inside its ring of stone and sweeping spotlights. There is, as always, ample parking. Few of the inmates entertain visitors, and the staff is skeletal, to say nothing of—ahem—idiosyncratic. Many of them live on the grounds, and most of those might with some justice be incarcerated there rather than employed.

He shoulders his satchel and walks up the granite steps. The director is waiting just inside the main front doors. "This is highly irregular," he says.

"City codes, Doctor Crane. We're under no obligation to announce inspections."

"Apparently courtesy isn't one of your obligations, either."

"Honestly, Doctor Crane. An inspection with advance notice isn't much of an inspection, is it?"

Crane steps right up into his face. "And just what is the implication of that statement? Are you suggesting that because I insist on basic professional courtesy, there is something I need to hide about my practice here?"

In the offices adjoining the receiving lobby, Arkham staff surreptitiously take in the little drama. "Doctor Crane," the inspector says (he is enjoying his role a great deal). "Basic professional courtesy might also require that you allow me to do the job the people of Gotham City expect me to do."

"The people of Gotham City," spits Jonathan Crane, "don't know that you exist. They need me to heal these people, and your little surprise here is taking me away from valuable work."

"The sooner I do what I came here to do, the sooner you can resume your work. Now, Doctor, the first thing we ought to do is a walk-through. Are you able to do it, or are you too busy? Is there someone you'd like to delegate?"

He's smiling as he says it, and Jonathan Crane is, as the inspector's mother would have said, mad enough to spit nails. "I will do it myself," he says. "And when it is done, I will be on the phone to your director."

"Be my guest," the inspector says. Crane turns on his heel and walks fast through the door into the interior of the asylum.

Thirty minutes later the walk-through is done. The inspector has noted a number of minor violations, including substandard hygiene maintenance in staff restrooms and failure to maintain clear sight lines in hallways accessing inmate facilities. Dr. Crane has, as expected, protested each citation vociferously. Along the way, in those moments when Dr. Crane's attention was briefly directed elsewhere by calls from his staff, the inspector has also left a number of calling cards, to be deployed at the correct moment—and he has indulged in a single act of particular mischief, because in the inspector's opinion Dr. Jonathan Crane is in dire need of being taken down a peg. Or two.

Soon enough, he tells himself. They walk past the therapy rooms, and the inspector idly flips one of the padlocks and lets it clang back against the hasp. "Please refrain from your pranks," Dr. Crane snaps.

If you only knew, the inspector thinks. They pass an open utility closet, and as Dr. Crane fumes outside, the inspector searches through it and emerges. "Very good," he says. He has left another calling card inside.

They reach Crane's office and retire behind the locked door. A broad smile breaks across Crane's face. "You should have been an actor," he says.

"I thought I just was," the inspector says. They shake hands. "Ahh, home," the inspector says.

"Good to be back, is it?" Crane sits at his desk and neatens a stack of files.

"It's always interesting to be here when you know you can leave," the inspector says.

"I can't leave. I really can't. The work is much too absorbing." Still smiling, Crane changes the subject. "I hate to talk business so abruptly, but how's the business going with our nocturnal vigilante?"

"Perfect, so far," the inspector says. "I left an impression on him, that's for sure. It shouldn't be too difficult to keep him hot on the trail now."

"It never is. But this is a tiger by the tail, Freddy. I've got a lot invested in you."

The inspector refuses to rise to this bait. He will not think about Batman at this moment. Military training taught him to compartmentalize, to focus on the task at hand. Right now he is playing a role, which is similar to the role Dr. Crane believes he is playing, but not—as the doctor will soon find out—identical.

"If you didn't kill him, he'll be scheming," Dr. Crane goes on. "That's what he does. He thinks, and plans, and schemes. Unhealthily. The work of this deranged mind is a tumor in the body of this city. It must be cut out. What Gotham needs is proper control vested in the proper channels, not costumed maniacs with overdeveloped ideas about absolute right and wrong. That's no way to live in the world."

"You don't need to preach to me, Doctor. You told me what you needed, and I'm doing it. Let's leave it at that?"

"Dear me, no gratitude?" Crane leans forward over his desk, and something about the way the light catches the planes of his face gets the inspector thinking about the time he spent in those therapy rooms. He begins to sweat, and to lose his grasp of the role. It is all he can do to keep his finger away from the switch that will deploy the little calling cards he's left in his wake. Control, he tells himself. The steady hand.

"We have an agreement, Doctor. I would prefer if we kept our interaction professional."

The inspector's measured tone doesn't fool Crane for a second. The doctor sees that he's made his point. He leans back and says, "Of course. Shall I sign your report?"

"I'll leave a copy here. Go ahead and mail it in after you've had a chance to look it over."

"Oh, my," Crane says. "Courtesy returns. Are you short of resources for your mission?"

"Thanks, Doctor Crane," the inspector says. "We'll see you soon."

"I certainly hope so," Crane is saying as the inspector closes the door behind him. His heart is pounding and his shirt sticks to the small of his back. He can't get back out the front door fast enough, and he can't even wait until he's through the gate before his fingers find the switch and deploy the calling cards. As he heads south over the Trigate Bridge in the direction of Gotham University, fires are blooming all over Arkham Asylum, and the inspector is thinking: Now we'll see who's working on whose plan, Doctor Crane. You'll get your Batman, but I've got something I want, too.

EXTRA!: ARKHAM ABLAZE
Gillian O'Connor,
Special to the *Gotham Gazette*

A large fire is burning on the grounds of Arkham Asylum. Preliminary reports indicate that the fire is out of control and that the facility is in the process of being evacuated. Gotham City police and fire officials are uncertain what is to be done with the asylum's population while the fire is brought under control, and it is also unclear how many inmates might have used the fire as cover for escape attempts. Gotham City police have cordoned off all approaches to the island, but already reports are spreading through the city that various inmates have been spotted in nearby neighborhoods.

We'll keep you updated on this breaking story as it develops. . . .

5

July 27, 5:57 PM

When the city inspector—who looked awwwfully familiar, as the saying goes—went by and slipped the lock on
his door, the Joker was sure it was a trap. No sirree Bob,
he thought at the time. You don't think I've heard that
one before? Once there was an asylum inmate who
found his door open . . . the punch line involves guards
and boot heels and missing teeth, and that's the best-case
scenario. Could be a little trap to encourage Arkhamites
(Arkhamoids? Arkhamizens?) to misbehave so Doctor
Feelgood can practice whatever it is he does behind the
big steel padlocks around the corner. So the Joker is
content to sit there and collect whatever best-behavior
points might be due him when a guard comes by and notices that he hasn't gone rabbiting for the door even
though he knows it's unlocked.

Content, that is, until he smells smoke.

Now, fire is one of those things that's only funny if
it happens to someone else. Back before his brief and
disastrous—although life-changing!—stint as Little Red
Robbing Hood, a certain failing stand-up comedian ac-

quired a keen understanding of the fact that most humor is sublimated hostility, and that very few people are able to laugh genuinely when the joke is on them. Himself, he sure isn't about to laugh if good old Arkham Asylum is about to burn down around his ears.

So it's to the door and out, and if that means boot heels and missing teeth, well, he'll just learn to whistle through the gaps.

The hallway is your proverbial Chinese fire drill. Guards run one way, medical staff another. The Joker is happy to see that he's not the only inmate unexpectedly at liberty, and even happier—giggly, if the truth be told—to note that the guards have not the slightest interest in either putting him back in his cell or performing any impromptu shoe-leather dentistry.

Hm, he thinks, remembering the inspector. Have we met? I could swear I've seen you before . . .

Bits of an old show tune flicker through his memory, and he's about to start whistling along when flames whoosh out of a utility closet and set an inmate known as Broccoli Jim on fire. "Whooo!" the Joker says. "Combustible florets, ladies and gentlemen, the very latest in convenience for your cannibalistic kitchen!"

There's an explosion somewhere and all the fire alarms, which could hardly be blamed for overreacting, go off at once. The Joker hotfoots it (*hahahaha*) in the direction of the main door, burns rubber (*hohohohoho*) in the other direction when part of the lobby ceiling falls in, and blazes down the stairs into the basement when it becomes clear even to such an architecturally challenged person as himself that there's no way out on the ground. Rumors, though—

—and isn't it about time that someone gave rumors

their due? "Broccoli rumors, creeping like flame," the Joker sings, to the tune of the song whose words he can't remember, "tell me the way to get back in the game . . ." He does a little soft-shoe down the basement stairs, landing with a flourish. "The game, glorious ga-a-a-ame . . . of villainy!"

And the chorus swings in: *Let's hear it for rumors, for sources anonymous! For dark innuendo, and all things synonymous!*

(There's this door, see, waaayy down in one of the sub-basements. Four, I think . . .)

Was it Broccoli Jim who said that? He can't remember, but he fondly commends Jim's by-now-carbonized florets to the afterlife. He's rounding the landing between the third and fourth sub-basements. *Wonder if I'm under sea level,* he thinks, and now it's an old spiritual in his head. "I'm only go-o-ing under Gotham," he sings as his heels click down on the floor of the fourth sub-basement. "I'm only go-o-ing under home . . ."

Well. *Here I am,* he thinks. A door. He opens it. The room on the other side is dark and smells like a plumber's handkerchief. "My goodness," the Joker says in mock disgust. "I fear standards of personal hygiene are compromised here in the fourth sub-basement." With great drama he smells the underarms of his jumpsuit. "Me, of course, being a most educational counter-example. What's this?"

A door, is what it is, locked with one of those wheel things that he remembers from movies about submarines. "A hatch!" he exclaims with delight. "Crash dive! Ah-ooooo-gahh!"

The wheel is rusted solid, but the Joker has come much too far, endured Doctor Feelgood and the simian guards and even the wretched odors of the sub-basements. He has no intention of asphyxiating now. He puts, as the saying goes, his back into it, and the hatch mechanism gives a little. It's getting hotter down here, and there's a distant crashing sound as something up-stairs collapses. Nope, he thinks; no asphyxiation, no crushing under burning rubble. If I'm crushed under burning rubble, how will I ever send a thank-you note to whoever unlocked my door? Wrenching the hatch open, he leaps through, and here's where his enthusiasm has run away with him a little, since he bangs both kneecaps on an iron railing and goes straight over, instead of down the little stair that he sees as he falls past it. The impact hurts, okay, but he springs right up—never let 'em see you sweat—and says, "Ta daa! What! Six point eight? Come on."

"Russian judge," he answers himself, and skips off down the tunnel with whose floor he has recently be-come acquainted. Granite bricks. That means old. Old, if he's lucky, and he has been a very lucky ducky today, means forgotten. And forgotten means that he might just get to try his act on Gotham one more time. "Vil-lainy!" he says, with full-on jazz hands. Then he's run-ning, he's so excited; running and laughing, and he skids to a halt at a rusting iron grate and realizes that if he continues to be a lucky ducky, he'll get another chance at that strange and humorless creature everyone has been calling the Batman, whom he last encountered at the end of the reservoir debacle.

What a day.

And not even swimming down an old discharge pipe, wading through a containment lagoon at the D'Angelo

Wastewater Plant, and diving off the top of a chain-link fence into the fuh-reezing waters of the Gotham River can dampen his enthusiasm for this day. No sir. Not when there are helicopters fruitlessly spraying retardant foam on the blazing ruins of Arkham Asylum. (The idea of retardant foam, as it occurs to him in the middle of the river, very nearly makes him laugh hard enough to drown. As if the occupants of Arkham Asylum need any more retarding.) He wants to go upriver, get some distance between him and the various forces of law and order, maybe figure out who it was that let him loose. Or not. Doesn't matter. What matters is that he's swimming, and—uh-oh.

As if he's tripped an alarm, suddenly there are GCPD boats everywhere. And me without my pig nose, the Joker thinks and ducks under the water. So much for heading upstream. Plan B is to disappear into the city, although this is no mean feat for a man of his distinctive—to say nothing of distinguished—appearance. He surfaces near the north shore of Aparo Park, across from the line of piers that marks the northwest corner of . . . well, whatever the island used to be called before it was Gotham City. Probably something dour and Swedish. A lit-up clock face on a nearby church tower, equally dour and Swedish, pegs the time as almost midnight. Wringing out the sleeves of his jumpsuit, the Joker mock-tips his imaginary hat to the surprised lovers and recreational chemists who inhabit this part of the park during this part of the day. Well, during any part of the day, really. "Toodle-oo!" he calls to them and makes tracks along the Sprang River Bikeway, heading for the overhung—and, it must be added, generally hungover—tangle of Old Gotham.

But he never gets there, and if the Joker were an introspective man, which he is sometimes but not right now, he might think that the various obstacles that have presented themselves today were telling him something. As it is, he is merely out of sorts. Ill-humored, even, although that doesn't last for long.

The situation is this: he isn't the only Arkhamite indulging his yearning to breathe free. As a result, the GCPD, those detestable legbreakers, are everywhere. Right before the Joker's very eyes four of them take down a midget anarchist psychopath (the terms each meant only in a descriptive, and certainly not a pejorative, sense) known as Coup D'Tot. While they're getting their workout, the Joker starts to fade into the background, moving slowly lest he draw their attention. He's not prepared for direct confrontation, not yet. There are stockpiles to be accessed, cronies and sidekicks to be notified. Then and only then will he pick up where he left off last year. Yikes, and there's Batman, wouldn't you know it—but he's all of a sudden *fighting with the police!* The Joker nearly has an aneurysm trying not to laugh. It doesn't work, and he runs as fast as he can, letting the first really good laugh he's had in months trail away behind him as he cuts out of the park and zigzags his way through the side streets and alleys of Burnley. Along the way he decides that underground wasn't such a bad place to be after all. He's been watching workout videos in Arkham, and his newly toned muscles have no trouble at all loosening a manhole cover. Quick, quick, he's down into the sewers again, and every time he has a chance to keep going down he takes it.

After some time he realizes that one of the holes he's wriggled through connects not tunnel to tunnel but tunnel to cave. "My goodness," he says. It's a good thing he can see a little in the dark, or this entire adventure would have been a miscalculation. As it turns out, though, it's about the best thing he could have done. An engineer must have bored too close to a cave, and time did the rest. "I spelunk!" the Joker cackles.

Indeed he does. What a day.

INFERNO
Vicki Vale, *Gotham Gazette*

In an act of arson unprecedented even in Gotham City's troubled history, more than three dozen fires were set across Coventry and the Upper East Side last night, killing dozens of people and destroying several Gotham landmarks.

The first and largest of the blazes destroyed Arkham Asylum [see sidebar for a chronology of Arkham disasters and escapes], killing an unknown number of inmates and sparking a citywide manhunt for those who escaped. At this time, most escapees are said to have been apprehended, but neither the GCPD nor Arkham officials could estimate how many might remain at large.

Police department spokesman Jason Dodge suggested that only a handful of escapees were still on Gotham streets. "Based on the preliminary reports we're getting from Arkham, we think we've got almost all of them," he said. Dodge declined to give specifics, or to offer a concrete timeline for the release of all information about escapees.

"That's going to be up to Doctor Crane and the mayor's office," he said.

Dr. Jonathan Crane, reached by telephone late last night, said he had no idea how long it would be before asylum staff were able to compile a final list of the dead. "Until the buildings are safe to enter," he said, "we're stuck with estimates just like you are. And at a time like this, our focus should be on the survivors."

Finding out exactly how many of those survivors there are, however, is a top priority of local neighborhood activists. "I do hope Doctor Crane recognizes the importance of this information to the peace of mind of the average Gotham citizen," said Kathryn Smith of the SOS (South of Sprang) Neighborhood Association. "Hearing that Two-Face or the Joker is definitely off the streets will let us all sleep better at night."

Another question emerging in the wake of last night's disaster is whether a single person was responsible, and if so whether it was the same person who two nights ago set a fire in Otisburg that killed two Gotham City firefighters. The GCPD's Dodge wouldn't speculate, saying only that "fire department and police investigators are working closely to identify and arrest the person or persons responsible for this horrific act."

As in the case of the previous fire, Batman was observed at the scene. Various witnesses credit him with rescuing numerous people from fires, as well as personally recapturing a number of Arkham escapees. According to other eyewitness reports, Batman also engaged in a running battle with a mysterious figure in what might have been a firefighter's uniform. Conflicting reports suggest that this person was seen in the neighborhood of several of the fires immediately before they started, and there are unconfirmed allegations that he was seen at Aparo Park just before a car registered to Arkham Asylum exploded outside the park's Hillside gate. . . .

6

July 28, 10:17 PM

Out of the last twenty-four hours, Captain James Gordon has slept maybe three. He was up all night with the baby because Barbara's been fighting a cold, he forgot to eat breakfast, and most of his day disappeared in a tar pit of reports and meetings with the commissioner's flunkies. Now there are escaped Arkham loonies all over Gotham, and every cop in the city is on twenty-four-hour shifts until they're rounded up. They've gotten maybe half of them already, though it's hard to tell because with the fire still burning there's no way to know exactly how many escaped and how many died. Dr. Crane isn't being much help, either, and as usual Gordon has to spend half his energy threatening and cajoling the members of the force to do their jobs. Meanwhile the city is rife with lunatics. But nobody cares.

And on top of it all, there's this new maniac starting fires everywhere, and killing firefighters on top of that. Gotham City had no shortage of arsonists before, but now there's definitely a surplus. And this new one is a real piece of work, or so say the reports coming in from Batman. Knows his demolitions and incendiaries, and on top of it thinks he's a French poet. How Batman knows all this is, like most things associated with him, uncertain. Gordon isn't sure he wants to know, since his impression is that you either know everything about Batman or content yourself with nothing. Right now he's happier with nothing, as long as Batman keeps on doing what he's been doing. Gotham City likes having him around, and the mayor and Commissioner Piskura hate him, so as far as Captain James Gordon is concerned— not that anyone would ask—Batman is a welcome addition to the city's roster of the disaffected and extralegal.

A uniformed cop calls, "Hey, Captain."

Gordon gets up and goes to the desk.

"There's not too many of them left," the uniform says. He's not from Gordon's district, or what used to be Gordon's district, so Gordon doesn't know him. And if he's like most of the GCPD he doesn't want to know Gordon, so Gordon doesn't ask his name.

"That we know of," Gordon says.

"Sure, but sightings are starting to repeat, and we're getting less of them. So I think we're getting on top of it. Now if we could just catch this guy starting all the fires, we'd be all set. Wonder why your buddy in the cape doesn't get on that."

Suddenly Gordon figures out what's going on: the uniform is carrying someone's water, and that someone wants Batman to quit helping catch the loonies and go do something more difficult, more dangerous, and less visible. Like catch this mysterious poet-arsonist. And this someone figures Gordon can order Batman around.

"Whoever's errand boy you are, tell him to talk to me

himself next time," he tells the uniform. It's not smart, but Gordon already has a reputation for bullheaded idiocy among his fellow cops. What he can't figure out is why this Batman character has chosen him. It's one thing to believe you're the only honest man in a corrupt and decaying police force, but when a vigilante like Batman seems to agree, that puts your self-assessment in a whole different light. Does Batman think they're partners? Or are they just two men with a common interest but differing approaches? The commissioner and his underlings don't care; the important thing to them is that they've got a thorn named Jim Gordon getting in their collective side, and he is sympathetic if not actually in cahoots with the Goody Two-shoes in the cape and boots.

Thinking of this makes Gordon wish he had a better way to get in touch with Batman than what they have currently, which is that every so often he gets cryptic communications from a variety of anonymous email addresses. He knows Batman's out there somewhere, but . . .

His cell phone rings. He snaps it open. "Jim Gordon."

"Captain."

Speak of the devil, Gordon thinks—and on the heels of that thought comes the odd realization that he recognizes Batman's voice almost as readily as any other. "Call me back in two minutes," he says, and hangs up.

Two minutes later he's outside police headquarters, around the corner past the parking garage. He's smoked a cigarette almost to the filter already. The phone rings.

"There's some sentiment around here that you should leave the Arkham problem to the PD and go get this Enfer character," he says.

"I heard," Batman says.

Now, this Gordon doesn't like a bit. Whether they're on the same side or not, he doesn't want anyone bugging HQ. "Do me a favor," he says, and then stops. The truth is, he's wanted ears inside HQ himself more than once.

"What favor?"

"Never mind," Gordon says. "Actually, no. Don't never mind. Is there a good way for you to let me in on what you hear from in there?"

"Your computer there isn't secure," Batman says. "And I'm not sure this phone is, either."

"I'm guessing you have another idea."

"I might. But let's talk about it another time. Two-Face is waiting for you on the fifty-yard line at the stadium."

Harvey, Gordon wants to say. *His name is Harvey Dent.*

But it isn't, not anymore. Not since the holiday business. "Okay, thanks," he says.

"And I've spotted four new fires in the last fifteen minutes," Batman adds. "I think if you get a chopper up over Arkham, you'll find something interesting."

The connection breaks with a *pop,* and Gordon lights another cigarette. When it's done, he turns right instead of left, getting into his car and heading for the airport.

It takes some cajoling, as well as the standard badge-waving, but eventually Gordon is able to get a chopper for a run over the city. "I can't get too close to the nuthatch, though," the pilot says in Gordon's earphones. "Way it's burning, there's bound to be all kinds of up-drafts."

"I just need a good look at all of the fires together," Gordon says. They lift off, and he can see the Gotham cityscape speckled with orange. What is it about this place that draws them? he wonders. If he were a religious man, he'd be inclined to think that Gotham's ongoing plague of villainous crackpots was some kind of payback for the city's endemic vice, but that's a medieval attitude. More likely, he thinks, it's just that they all feel at home here. It's a pretty good place to be a violent criminal.

Despite my best efforts.

He hears Barbara's voice in his head: *That's no way to think.* And she's right. He does more than most of them, and if it never feels like quite enough, well, Jim Gordon has to be man enough not to let his tendency to feel inadequate get in the way of good police work. Feeling sorry for yourself doesn't catch the bad guys.

"I'm going to go north and come down," the pilot says. "That the way you want to look from?"

"Let's start with that." They're *thup-thup-thup*ping west over the Mooney Bridge, which is stop-and-go even at this time of night. The lights of police boats flash on the Gotham River to the south, and there are searchlights everywhere.

"Looks like some of the crazies decided to swim for it," the pilot says. "Me, I wouldn't get in that water even to get out of Arkham."

For some reason the water comment gets Gordon thinking about the Joker, who introduced himself to Gotham City by trying to poison the reservoir. He hates himself for it, but he's kind of hoping that the Joker didn't get out of Arkham. He might never know in any case, since Jonathan Crane doesn't look to be getting any more cooperative. *If I didn't have enough on my* plate with the allegedly sane parts of the city, he thinks, I'd take a closer look at that guy.

"Don't think the water's that bad anymore," he says.

"You can have it," the pilot says. They bank a little southward. Somewhere below them, under sixty or seventy feet of water and another several yards of silt and rock, are the county railroad tunnels; Gordon can see the air intakes on the shore at the western end of Amusement Mile. Going due south now, they pass over Knights Stadium.

"How much higher can you go?" Gordon asks.

The pilot doesn't answer, but they start climbing. Soon Gordon can see the whole city and the fires spreading across its midsection just south of the Sprang River. While he watches, two more burst into life. And then two more. And then an entire string of them, one after another, in the shape of a V maybe six blocks long. He waves the pilot forward, and the helicopter leans into its acceleration. More fires bloom between the lines of the V, and then to the west still more.

There aren't enough firefighters in Gotham City to handle all of these, Gordon thinks. He makes a call to HQ, outlining what he sees and telling whoever will listen that if they want the Coventry neighborhood to be anything more than ashes in the morning, they need to start calling in firefighting help from anyone who will respond. He hangs up before they can question him or make a remark about Batman.

That's an H, he thinks as the fires to the west of the V fill in. He racks his brains for words that have an HV in the middle, even though he's not ready to believe that anyone would .actually use fires to spell out a word across Gotham City.

Then, still farther to the west, on the edge of the Upper East Side, another line of fires sparkles to life. "Take us around to the south," Gordon commands the pilot, and as they fly directly over the fires he can see the massed strength of GCFD doing their valiant best to contain the blazes that make up the V. More ladder companies are screaming up from the southern parts of the city, and off to his right Gordon can see flashing red lights on the Trigate and Brown bridges. Help from the suburbs. The westernmost line of fires resolves itself into a second V—Roman numerals? Was there an H?—and then, as the pilot swings the helicopter around to face north, Gordon realizes he's been simultaneously wrong and terribly right.

Not V's. A's. With an H in between.

And the first letter is the blazing wreck of Arkham Asylum, which viewed from here is another H.

HAHA

Jesus, Gordon thinks. The Joker.

7

July 28, 11:16 PM

Months—*months*—he's been waiting to put this plan into action, and now that it's happening Enfer is on top of the world. Arkham Asylum is a bonfire, which all by itself would be enough to put him in a good mood, and the microdot transponder he stuck to the card he slid under the Joker's door appears to be in good working order. Speaking of the Joker, he appears to be well on his way to safety, and Enfer has been rehearsing their first meeting since the moment he conceived of this idea. They're kindred spirits, really, he and the Joker. They should be working together, complementing each other's strengths. As for me, Enfer thinks, I like a good joke. Who doesn't? *And I bet you're a man who likes a nice warm fire,* he'll say to the Joker when they meet.

Which will be as soon as Enfer is sure that the last se-ries of charges has gone off correctly. He's in a rooftop garden on the Upper East Side, just off the traffic circle at the northwest corner of Robinson Park. The owner doesn't know he's there, and in point of fact never will. Enfer looks around, his last charge of the evening cradled in one arm. He wants to get this last one exactly right, ceremonially right. Potted plant? Silly. Jacuzzi? Probably not the best idea, since even though the thermite handles water pretty well, this last exclamation point is the last thing in the world he wants to mess up right now. The thing to do, he concludes reluctantly, is lay it at the top of the heating duct that runs right along that beautifully combustible hardwood floor in the master suite. It'll take a little longer to be visible from the air, but that has to be balanced against the artistic imperative to keep it burning.

Singing a little ditty under his breath—*everything is catching, yes, everything is catching on fire*—he sets the charge and primes it, then waves to the owner on the way out. When he's stepping out of the service elevator into a hallway that leads to the building's loading door, he checks his watch. Right on schedule. Then he checks the transponder.

Hm. The Joker appears to be in the river. That wasn't part of the plan. Enfer picks up his pace, getting into a car driven by a recent Arkham graduate now employed as a chauffeur for Dr. Crane on an informal basis. The driver's name is something like Willy or Billy, Enfer doesn't know and couldn't care less. "Okay, Billy," he says.

"Okay," Billy answers.

Enfer has another look at the transponder's location. Either the Joker is moving toward Aparo Park or he's been eaten by a fish that's headed that way.

"Aparo Park," Enfer says.

"Aparko Par," Billy says. *Don't mind him,* Enfer imagines saying to the Joker. *You know how some of Doctor Crane's therapies can take hold.*

He starts flipping switches as they drive, and across Gotham City his little greeting begins to take shape. Enfer can't see it, though, because traffic is miserable what with fire trucks and ambulances flying everywhere. Oh, if he could only follow one of them and watch . . . or be on one of them . . .

That snaps him back to reality. There was then, and there's now, he admonishes himself. The Gotham City Fire Department had their chance, and look what they did. And, he adds—maybe out loud, he's not sure, but Billy gives no sign of having heard anything—*how many of them would rather be doing just what you're doing right now?*

He imagines interviewing a group of firefighters. How many of you guys would like to meet the Joker? Yeah? Pretty good living, this villain business. You get in with the right people and you can go a long way. Plus—with a knowing wink—the perks aren't bad.

It's when he starts imagining their responses that Enfer's mood whipsaws from jovial to blackly homicidal, and now instead of wanting to follow the fire trucks he's wishing he'd left little greeting cards at every single point of every single letter. He'll do it, too, just as soon as he and the Joker get together. First they'll have to take care of Crane, though, because as of this evening he and Crane are no longer working together, and Crane isn't all that sympathetic to former employees or former patients who look for other lines of work. Oh—and if he's planning to take care of Crane, he ought to be covering his tracks as of, say, right now.

They're pulling into the Aparo Park surface lot, traffic having improved quite a bit once they got across the river into Burnley. "Thanks, Billy," Enfer says.

"Thanks."

"Why don't you go find Doctor Crane and see what he wants you to do?"

"Frane Doctor Kind," Billy says, which is the funniest thing Enfer's heard all day, and because Billy was nice enough to add this bit of hilarity to the proceedings, Enfer waits a full five minutes longer than he'd planned before setting off the half a dozen Cherry Bombs he's left under the driver's seat of the car.

That obstacle cleared, Enfer straightens his coat and glances one last time at the GPS tracker. Then out of the corner of his eye he sees the Joker, strutting down the Sprang River Bikeway as if he's the king of Gotham City (the Beau Brummel of Fifth Avenue, Cendrars would have said). Enfer starts to walk after him. He doesn't want to make his approach immediately; there's a rise in the path that crests a bluff in a mile and a half or so, and until then Enfer is content to walk and see if he can learn something from the Joker. This is the man, after all, who not only set a new standard in Gotham villainy but also brought out the absolute best in Batman. Enfer imagines—and hopes—that if his display tonight hasn't drawn Batman's interest, the Joker's liberty surely will. What is it about you, he silently asks the Joker, that so provokes our common enemy? Does he hate jokes? It seems he must, although didn't he roll his eyes when I quoted Cendrars? That was a humorous response. Hm. They would consider it together.

There's a sudden ruckus on the path as a midget in a top hat and black overcoat bursts from the brush on the river side of the bikeway, closely pursued by four of Gotham's Finest. They jump him and give him the kind of beating you expect from GCPD: exuberant yet clini-

cal, savage yet somehow artistic. The fracas draws
Enfer's attention away from the Joker for long enough
that he doesn't see that party's quick disappearance;
then, when he's despairingly looked back from the place
where the Joker was to the scene of the midget's Close
Encounter of the Nightstick Kind . . . there's Batman.

Arguing vehemently with the cops about their treatment of a psycho midget from Arkham Asylum.

You have to admire him, Enfer thinks. A bad cop is as
much Batman's enemy as the Joker is, or as I am, and because of that he'll never win. He must know this. Is that
courage, to fight a battle you know you have to lose? Or
just a poorly expressed suicidal tendency?

The cops are giving it right back. Enfer is a little too
far away to hear the details, but he does get the impression that the cops would dispute his characterization of
them and Batman as members of the same team. One of
them, in fact, goes so far as to stand right up to the
Caped Crusader (as the newspapers have taken to calling
him) and say, "It was up to me, you'd be right there in
Arkham with the rest of the freaks. While it was burning."

With that the cop turns around and gives the prone
midget a kick, just for good measure, and before it even
happens Enfer has already envisioned the unearthly reflexes of Batman, his body pivoting smoothly around its
center of gravity to deliver a sweeping kick exactly to
the point of the cop's chin. He's down like all of his
bones turned to water, and the other three draw their
guns, and as the gunfire erupts Batman is suddenly a
shadow among them. Two more go down, and the last
of the four is doing the smart thing by going for his
radio. Enfer is rooted to the spot, watching the show,

and it's only the Joker's echoing hilarity that snaps him out of it. Batman is looking up; he's heard it, too. Time for a fully committed diversion.

At the top of his lungs, in the most jovial tone he can manage, Enfer shouts, "Batman! *Derrière ce rideau de flammes on aperçoit des grandes ombres qui se tordent et s'abattent, non?*"

And Batman is coming at him, and Enfer has time to lob a Char Broiler over his head into the midst of the four cops and their unfortunate collar. Can't have word getting out about Batman fighting Gotham PD, Enfer thinks as he goes sprinting off back toward Aparo Park. The *boom* of the Char Broiler almost—but not quite—drowns out the screams of the five men it incinerates. We've got to keep our reputations unsullied, whether that means bad unsullied by good or the other way around. I'm the bad guy here, and Batman's the good guy. We need to keep that clear.

"Like the favor I did you?" he shouts over his shoulder. "You need me, you know."

"What I need," Batman says, "is to get my hands on your other arm and break it off, too."

Then they're both running too hard to talk anymore.

8

July 29, 4:36 AM

The spelunking adventure, it must be said, has lost its initial attraction, or any attraction. This is no place for me, the Joker complains to himself. Squeezing through wet stone seams, slogging through mud, ruining my jumpsuit . . . all of this is fine for some, but not a man of my tastes and upbringing.

Which last phrase cracks him up, because the version of his pre-Joker existence that he's chosen to remember doesn't involve much taste or much upbringing. He's wheezing his way through a narrow crack in the cave, trying to stop laughing . . . well, not trying very hard, when . . .

Uh-oh.

There's something moving in the dark.

"What's so funny?"

The voice is so deep and so rough that the Joker feels as if he can feel each individual peak and valley in the sound waves hitting his eardrums. "Ah, um, well," he says, "it's hard to explain. One of those you-had-to-be-there kind of jokes. First thing you learn doing stand-up is that none of your audience was ever there."

There's a pause. Then that voice again. "Where?"

"There. If, for example, I were to tell someone about this meeting—assuming something funny happens, which is nearly always the case, wouldn't you agree?—they wouldn't find it funny in the same way because they weren't here. So the trick is to make the telling itself funny, and to make yourself funny. So. A theory of comedy, from a once and future comedian. Does it satisfy you?"

No response.

"Different strokes." The Joker sighs. "You're not really in my target demographic anyway."

He waits, and after a long silence—*Folks, I'm dying up here*—he hears a grunt, and heavy footsteps moving away into the darkness. With the motion comes a hint of something visible, a huge man-shaped outline. In his tectonic voice the stranger is mumbling what sounds like a poem. The Joker hears the days of the week and loses interest. Even when he read poetry, he never developed an appreciation for the monorhyme.

What he does appreciate is the opportunity to use this hulking sourpuss as a guide. Wherever he's going, it beats here. The Joker follows, careful to keep his distance. In his time as villain and Arkham resident he has developed something of a sixth sense when it comes to the presence of menace, and all those warning bells are going off. The longer he follows this muttering behemoth along a winding passage—which seems to be climbing? Let's hope so—the clearer his sense that he needs to tread very lightly, ha ha, lest he come to grief. After a while this nervousness slows him down enough that he loses all sense of the stranger, which would be fine if he weren't still in the middle of a cave somewhere between Gotham City and . . . where? Who knew?

A new start in New York might be fun, although he can't imagine that this cave goes that far, and he's long since lost his sense of direction. And let's be honest, since his chemical rebirth he finds that the only place he's really comfortable is Gotham City. Still, if he suddenly finds himself poking his head out of a manhole cover on Avenue A, he'll be a good long way from Arkham Asylum. It might be smart to stay away while he gathers his wits (and *Witze*) for a new Gotham City routine. "Start spreadin' the news . . . ," he's singing, to keep his spirits up, when he hears another sound and shuts his mouth—which is difficult for a man of his revised physiognomy, but he does it, and he's glad, because the chirps and flutterings he's hearing could only be coming from bats. Bats! *Hahahahahahaha*, it's too much, the irony's killing him, because the bats are locals here, and if they're stirring, they'll be leaving (which means night is falling, and he's been down here a *full day*!), and if he's lucky he'll be able to follow them. "Get it?" he asks nobody in particular. "The bats will lead me out so I can get the Batman! It's too perfect."

Then he shuts his mouth again and realizes that the bats are all around him, really, and they're starting to move. "I'm leavin' today . . . ," he croons, to the accompaniment of a million wings.

He loses track of time a little after that. When Jackanapes is honest with himself, he realizes that his sense of time isn't always too reliable—or what might be more to the point is that it's reliable, but just not quite in tune with everyone else's. Believe me, I know chemicals, he's thinking as he skips along another passage in the cave, bats above and around him in a storm of chirping, fluttering little rodent-smelling bodies. And chemicals can do things that you don't expect. He laughs out loud, and it seems that the bats give him a little more room after that. "So sorry, little chiropterans," he croons. "Come back, really, I'm haaaarrrrmmlesssss . . ."

Blam! He's not paying attention and walks straight into an overhanging rock. "Oh, hoho, ow, ouch, heeheehee," he can't stop himself. Is there anything better than a good pratfall? And he's taken two pretty fine ones today. When he can blink the stars out of his eyes, he's humming along to an old Perry Como song and wondering out loud where the bats all went. "Well, they must have gone somewhere," he muses. "All that guano came from somewhere."

The only thing to do is start looking. He feels along the wall, the floor, eventually the ceiling where he can reach it . . . and bingo! His hand finds a hole.

"If one can dignify such a minimal aperture with the name *hole*," he says with great high dudgeon. "Proud? Me? Too much so to crawl through? Why, thank goodness I maintained my girlish figure during my period of rest."

With that, he's up and into the hole, legs dangling in what must have been a genuinely comical fashion before he catches his heel on the same rock that dented his forehead and pushes on. There's light ahead! Real light! Worthy of a bad novel about near-death experiences, it's calm, pale, suffusing the low passage ahead of him with a positively empyrean gleam. He follows it wide-eyed and ablaze with curiosity . . .

. . . and when he sees what lies at its end, the Joker thinks he's died and gone to heaven.

The first thing he lays his eyes on is the car. Low, matte black with one-way windows, it crouches back against the far wall as if ready to spring. The Joker remembers this car, the way it appeared out of nowhere, from under the reservoir in Robinson Park, at the very moment when what he has come to think of as his Audition . . . well, he didn't get the part, as they say, but he is right now preparing for his callback. But how does it get out? He looks, and looks, and there: he sees a pair of great steel doors, on the other side of which must be, as P. T. Barnum would have put it, the Egress. Quite a stylish entrance that particular automobile must make.

Tearing his eyes away from the car, although his hands are already itching to drive it (and oh my, is there a punch line there?), he looks around. There, in a frame that looks like you could use it to pull an engine block, is a Batsuit. The Joker's stomach does a little flip. On polished stainless-steel shelving next to it he counts one two three utility belts, two pairs of boots, and a truly stupefying array of gear. Most of it he can't identify, but there are grappling hooks, the little Bat-shuriken doohickeys whose sting he can still feel along his arms and chest . . . and oh ho, what's this over there?

An elevator door.

The world expands its horizons as the Joker realizes that all he has to do to discover the identity of his nemesis is walk right up, press the button, and see where this elevator lets him off. For a moment he wishes he were a bat, or at least a passenger pigeon, so he'd have the kind of sense of direction that would survive his trip through the cave. *Where am I?* He can't stand not knowing, it's like that last piece of candy that you're just a little afraid to ask for since you know you'll love it but it might come back to haunt you. Oh, what I could do if I knew your name, he thinks. The jokes I could play, the fun we could have. We could have fun that is funny.

But no (the Joker has always loved Steve Martin). What would happen to the spice of the interaction, its supreme animosity, its superheated mano a mano quality, if he knew who Batman was . . . and could not return the favor?

"Play fair," he says to himself. "What's good for the Bat is good for the Joker."

So he will not. But oh, the knowing that the answer is right there . . . sweet longing fills him . . .

. . . and then goes away as his eyes fall on a broad worktable and a row of Lucite cubes arranged against the wall. Could it be, there on the gleaming worktable next to a hanging Batsuit? Could it be, thinks the Joker, that I am seeing, with mine own very eyes, shelved with care befitting a museum exhibit . . . my favorite corsage?

Too good to be true.

He's a kid at Christmas, a babe in toyland, a returning sailor seeing the familiar red-light district of home. Everywhere he looks, there are goodies, and every one of them belongs to Batman. The Joker's shoulders are trembling with the effort of holding in his laughter; it was quite an irony that bats should have led him out of his subterranean wilderness, yes, but to have them lead him to the sanctum sanctorum of his archfoe . . . ? Wonderful!

Whoever Batman is during the day, he's been a busy little bat. Dust hangs in the air, and large piles of rocks lie in out-of-the-way corners. Power equipment lies everywhere, and the Joker can see the beginnings of a fine laboratory hideaway beginning to emerge. He's tempted to move right in, play chemist for a while again, be the mockingbird in the Bat's nest . . . but no. The joke there would only be on Batman. Why play for those stakes when he can have his fun with not just Batman, but every unsuspecting nincompoop in Gotham City as well? An idea takes shape in his head, and he likes it very much. Very much indeed.

And yet more when the elevator door opens and a codger of maybe seventy years old, who looks like he's wearing a tuxedo under a set of gray canvas coveralls, steps out. He's talking on a cell phone, and the Joker catches just the last sentence—"Yes, well, since you've returned I'll start tidying up a bit." The codger flips the phone shut and starts doing exactly that. Well, well, the Joker thinks. Were I the deductive sort, I might begin to think that Batman is, in his quotidian life, a man of some means. Or else he hangs upside down around here somewhere and the butler and all the goodies are paid for by nefarious concerns whose names we might not wish to know.

There is a time for deduction, and a time for action. The Joker has a sudden sense that this is one of the latter sort. He springs out of the shadows, dusts himself off with all the panache of which he is capable, and says to the old bugger with his winningest smile, "My good man! I have traveled far, through the—dear me, is this *guano*?—wastes of yonder cave, and I seek your hospitality. Have you a room for the night?"

The old bugger takes it with aplomb, give him credit for that. "You *scoundrel*," he says, and pulls an actual gun from somewhere in his coveralls. A hundred of him would make one tough room, that's for sure, but there's only one, and the Joker closes the distance on him before he can get off more than a single shot.

9

July 30, 2:32 AM

In the dream, Joe Chill is sometimes Batman.

Bruce is holding his father's hand and reaching to find his mother's when the shadows begin to speak and his heart stops at the cold gleam of distant streetlights on the barrel of a gun. He has been feeling bad because he was weak back there in the theater, letting the costumes and the spectacle worm their way into the place where he keeps his fears. Now they have come out the back door of the theater and his father is walking just a little too fast for Bruce to keep up easily. He hurries, and wants to say something, and doesn't know what it would be, and in any case his mouth is stopped by shame at his weakness, and sadness at having disappointed his father. And now by the voices speaking from the shadows through the barrel of the gun. His father folds into himself, his mother sways and falls in a graceless sweep of silk and tulle, and Bruce Wayne will live the rest of his life testing his memory to see if there was a third shot meant for him.

Lucky or spared? It matters.

But not right then in the alley, when the shadows have stretched and grown and crept right up next to Bruce, and it's Batman, it's always the same living shadow with the same empty gaze, the gaze that Bruce Wayne will learn to mask but always know awaits him in the mirror . . .

. . . unless Joe Chill is Bruce Wayne, and here's where Bruce always feels like he's awake enough to know what's happening, and be horrified by it, but not stop it. Are you supposed to be able to reflect on what your dreams mean while you're dreaming them? He does. He sees his own face coalescing from the shadows and he thinks, I killed them. If I had not been afraid, we would not have been there. And after I killed them, I used them to re-create myself.

Or Batman was there all along, wanting to get out, and preyed on their memory to set himself free.

Bruce, you wanted it this way, Bruce says in the dream, and Bruce kneels between the bodies of his mother and father, and Bruce slips the watch from Thomas Wayne's wrist, and the diamond necklace from Martha Wayne's flawless throat, and Bruce fades back into the shadows, leaving Bruce there in an agony of mourning and dimly intuited rebirth.

He opens his eyes and sees shadows cast by the setting moon through his bedroom window, but he is still dreaming because the shadows on the ceiling all look like bats. The breeze through the window sets the curtains moving, and the shadows on the floor creep like blood across wet pavement, and the knocking of the water pipes comes to him as the sound of Joe Chill's boot heels echoing away into the midnight wastes of the Gotham of his childhood. Lucky or spared? In the elas-

tic space between dreaming and waking, Bruce Wayne
believes he was spared, if not by Joe Chill then by a force
larger, more impersonal. The word he prefers is *fate,* just
as he wants the forces of corruption and venality in
Gotham City to see Batman as fate. The backswing of
the karmic pendulum. He will personify the scales of
justice, the wheel of fortune, the tendency of the universe toward equilibrium . . . which means, Bruce Wayne
is thinking as his conscious mind gradually wins control, that when push comes to shove, he believes Batman
is entropy. Heat death.

But only when he is dreaming, and now Bruce really
wakes up. It's not even three in the morning; he's been
asleep for less than an hour after a second night rounding up escaped Arkham inmates, but he knows there will
be no more sleep tonight. The dreams flee into the re-
cesses of his mind as the doors of will and discipline
come booming down behind them. What persists is a
stray memory of the Gotham City Police Department filing room. When he was twenty Bruce spent an afternoon looking at the police report from his parents'
murder. Reading about the event in the spare, impersonal idiom of the report had a strangely cathartic effect
on him; he wonders, in fact, if it was not that afternoon
that broke him free of his adolescent self-pity and sent
him off on the first of his travels to the East . . . where he
traveled among men whose skill and ruthless devotion
he aspired to match . . . where he became himself.

Or where Batman became himself.

Or where Bruce Wayne became Batman.

If those three statements are anything more than semantic facets of the same single event.

Bruce sits up, feeling the burned skin on his legs

stretch. It hurts, and he allows it to hurt for precisely as long as it takes for him to decide that he will no longer allow it to hurt. His mind is on the filing room, on the photographs and the typescript reports and the paper-clipped documents detailing the later death of Joe Chill. He has worried the event, gnawed at it, built walls around it and then broken holes in the walls because he cannot stand to be without it—and in the process, perhaps, changed it? If he saw the photographs from the police report today, would they look like his memory?

And why is he thinking of the filing room? He has an intuition that his subconscious is sending him a message, and he begins circling the idea. What message might be manifesting itself this way? Something about records, the past, his past, things he has done with or for or to the police, some of Batman's activities . . .

He's not getting anywhere. It occurs to him that he hasn't seen or heard Alfred, who typically has an almost supernatural ability to appear with coffee and fruit at the exact moment Bruce is waking up. The sun has not yet risen, but Bruce often wakes before sunrise, especially when he dreams, and oddly he dreams more often and more vividly following the exhaustion of pursuit. Enfer has escaped him twice now, once with the break-away arm and then last night by simply outrunning him. Bruce is beginning to feel that Enfer is going to be one of the difficult, consuming ones. Like the Joker was.

That thought snaps him fully into wakefulness. After the Arkham fire, he's going to need to find out who escaped, and also who was still at large after last night's second dragnet. Plus there's Enfer to consider. Bruce gets up and works through the slow physical routine he uses every morning. It's part calisthenics, part tai chi, part yoga, and part just wanting to break a sweat and get his blood circulating before the day really begins. He allows himself time for this because the routine sensitizes him to the state of his body, where it's strong and where it hurts; once that picture is complete, he dresses and walks down the hall toward the computer lab he installed adjacent to Wayne Manor's old library. "Alfred?" he calls as he walks. No answer. Bruce doesn't worry about it; Alfred takes care of things, and he can't always be right there with coffee and orange juice, especially not at three in the morning. Veering away from the computer lab, Bruce goes downstairs and brews coffee himself. Like the morning physical routine, this simple set of tasks is centering. He doesn't have to do it—with the number of zeroes in the various Wayne accounts, Bruce Wayne doesn't strictly have to do anything except eat and breathe—but one of the lingering effects of his Eastern sojourn is that Bruce has learned the value of the mundane. He's particularly comforted by the mundane this morning, after last night's all-you-can-eat smorgasbord of Gotham City lunatics. Speaking (or thinking) of which, he needs to get the latest on Arkham survivors and escapees. The coffee is ready. Bruce takes the entire pot up to the computer lab.

He's sitting in front of the terminal, blowing steam off the first cup, when he has second thoughts about using the Wayne Manor network to get at the information he routinely siphons out of GCPD headquarters. There's no good reason to mistrust his security arrangements, but he does anyway. Bruce finds one of his cell phones in the pocket of his bathrobe and calls Alfred. No answer. He leaves a short message asking Alfred to meet him in the wine cellar, which is what he's decided to call the cave when someone might overhear. Alfred, practical-minded as he is, questioned this code on the grounds that at some point Bruce might really want to meet him in the wine cellar, but it hasn't happened yet, and the truth is that Bruce can't figure out any possible reason why it might. So wine cellar it is, and in any case Alfred isn't answering his phone. Bruce has a passing worry about Alfred's health—he's getting up there, and as hale as he's always seemed, age is age—but he shrugs it off. If sunrise comes and goes with no sign of Alfred, then Bruce will worry, but sunrise is three hours away. Until then, he'll sift through the communications from GCPD and see if he can't scare up Captain Gordon for a more recent Arkham update.

The elevator to the cave runs from a utility closet behind Wayne Manor's kitchen, so Bruce retraces his steps, leaves the coffeepot on the counter, and heads down. The car is big enough to drive a forklift into, and turn it around if you're a skilled driver . . . which Bruce is. He's smiling a little at the memory of telling the crew that installed the elevator that he was building a bomb shelter; it'll be one more crazy-Bruce-Wayne story circulating around Gotham City, and that's so much the better. He could probably contract out more of the work on the cave, but he's already gotten a lot of concrete poured and rock blasted. What remains is finish work, and moving in the equipment he hasn't yet bought or informally requisitioned from Lucius Fox's techno-wonderland in the basement of Wayne Enterprises. Maybe, if the Arkham situation looks like it's finally under control, he can spend the day working in the cave before heading out after Enfer tonight.

Tonight I'll get him, Bruce is thinking. Or, I should say: tonight Batman will get him.

The elevator door opens, and the hair on the back of Bruce's neck stands up. He steps out, scanning the cave, noting and cataloging everything that seems out of place. Things aren't where he left them, and the changes don't look like the sort of measured refinements Alfred tends to make. One of the things Bruce Wayne knows for certain is that Alfred would not have left a gun on the worktable next to the lathe where Bruce machines small tools such as his Batarangs. It's Alfred's gun, though.

"Alfred?"

The cave swallows his voice, and as if the sound waves have shaken something loose from the air, Bruce smells gunpowder. He walks to the gun, sniffs the muzzle, drops the clip, and counts the shells out onto the worktable. One shot fired. Reflexively he scans the cave floor for blood, and when he doesn't see any he walks in a widening circle until he's following the walls. Still he sees no blood, but he does find the shell, and at the moment when he picks it up Bruce finally realizes what it is he's been missing since he stepped out of the elevator.

The car is gone.

Back through, Bruce tells himself. Miss nothing.

He tears the cave apart, touching nothing but seeing everything, and at the end of five minutes he knows what has happened as well as if he had been there himself. Missing: the car. One Batman suit, with cape. One utility belt with full complement of tools. One set of backup files from the central terminal. Several items from his small museum of gadgets collected from adversaries.

One loyal friend.

Relocated, formerly on the body of that loyal friend and now hanging in place of the missing Batman suit: one set of coveralls.

Relocated, formerly in the museum case and now pinned to the lapel of those coveralls: the ace of spades.

Bruce plucks it free and turns it over in his fingers.

Written on the back of the ace of spades, in handwriting Bruce knows all too well, is a jovially cryptic message: *We have met the enemy, and he is us.*

Motion catches his eye, and Bruce turns to see a mouse on the floor of the cave. It runs in a narrowing spiral before finding what looks like a bread crumb. The mouse takes the crumb, stashes it in one cheek, and begins another spiral, this time widening, until it finds a second crumb. Looking past it, Bruce sees a trail of the crumbs leading toward the back of the cave and the passage he left open for the bats. All at once he understands.

10

July 30, 3:37 AM

I thought I'd driven some nice cars, the Joker is musing, but this one takes the proverbial cake. (And what would a proverbial cake look like? He imagines Moses coming down from the mountain with layer cakes in either hand . . .) What a car. Why, it stood out even in that fantabulously ritzy neighborhood where he emerged after skedaddling through the steel doors and up a concrete tunnel that led through a small cave mouth onto a dirt road. Who needs a custom Bentley when you've got the Batmobile? Heads sure did turn, at least those heads that were awake and abroad in the middle of the night, when he went tooling down those roads on the north side of the river.

   That part of town is not at all his typical haunt. Never has been. He's much more at home now, cruising north in the dying hours of night from downtown toward the little hideway he put together in the East End, lo these many moons ago before his little Arkham hiatus. It ought to still be there. No reason why it shouldn't; no one, to his knowledge, has entered that particular building on purpose in years, unless it was to indulge in a little recreational chemistry. Which, as it happens, was his own reason for installing himself there. The building at one point housed an electroplating shop and a gaggle of other businesses whose function required a number of odd and wonderfully reactive substances, large amounts of which were abandoned in the basement when said businesses closed one by one during Gotham City's most recent cycle of depression. Which, as it happens, coincided with his own transformative escapade at the Monarch Playing Card factory. Thinking about all of it makes him feel a little holistic, unified and interconnected with this great steaming mess of a city and the great steaming mess of its denizens. Some of whom are more messy and steaming than others, thanks to his unfamiliarity with the Batmobile's more specialized control mechanisms— and, well, let's not neglect to note his general depraved indifference to human life. Yow, do people get out of the way when they see this set of wheels coming around the corner. Except, *hahahaha,* the ones that don't.

"Now I know what they mean by breakneck speed," the Joker says out loud, and laughs.

He roars across the Sprang River and, suffering a belated attack of discretion, chooses the more abandoned of the East End's thoroughfares—they're all abandoned at this hour, really, but one takes one's caution where one finds it—until he arrives at the empty six-story brick building whose basement contains his once and future laboratory. A crime laboratory, really, in a much more meaningful sense than the police facilities that bear the name. He wishes he could put a sign in one of the windows advertising his services . . . well, no he doesn't, because who knew what kind of yahoos and miscreants might show up wanting ridiculous and boring concoctions to kill their lovers or burn down their shabby storefronts for their insurance? Ugh. "That's not the life for me," the Joker is singing, to the tune of some Sinatra song he can't really remember, as he rolls the Batmobile down the alley and parks it in front of the loading dock. To the left of the dock is a ground-level door that if he has any luck at all will still open when he finds the key between . . . those two bricks right there. He blows mortar dust off the key, opens the door, and does a little soft-shoe across the dark shipping floor until he gets to the garage door on the other side of the dock. He has to kick it a couple of times to loosen the rust from the track, but it opens, and in a jiffy he's got the Batmobile inside, the door locked behind it, and the Bat-cowl off his head. Whoever Batman is, he doesn't sweat, because if he did he'd drown inside that thing, is what the Joker thinks.

"I need a Bat-name," he says to the echoing space. The floor stretches unbroken across the entire footprint of the building, interrupted only by steel support beams at code-mandated intervals. You could play football in here, if you didn't mind running into an I-beam once in a while. Hm, the Joker thinks. A game.

But first he needs a Bat-name, and he needs to replenish his repertoire of standard *blagues* and *Witze*. For that he needs the lab that lies behind the bolted door at the other end of the room. Now, what has he done with that particular key? It couldn't be the same one that opens the outside door.

He sweeps the Bat-cape about himself and strikes a thoughtful pose, then just as quickly abandons it when he realizes that it isn't doing him any good. "The key, the

key, the key . . . ah." There is, if he's recalling correctly—
which is by no means certain, since the gentle ministra-
tions of the Good Doctor Crane have further scrambled
the Joker's already precariously organized memory—a
key in the fire extinguisher cabinet. If the local idiots
haven't broken in and had some kind of Neanderthal
fun with the fire extinguisher, it should still be there. Looking around, the Joker sees no evidence of intrusion during his year's absence. A stroke of good luck there. He
finds the cabinet, opens it, and removes the key. Still more
good luck.

Now to the real crux of the matter, which is that he
has a dim recollection of laying some variety of nefarious trap on the door. Exactly what variety is unclear to
him. He thinks the key will bypass it, but there's no way
to really know, is there, when one is trying to dredge up
one's past and said past is somewhat obscured by the in-
tervention of Arkham-style therapies?

He turns the key and is neither poisoned nor incinerated nor electrocuted.

Perhaps, though, the trap is sprung not by turning the
key but by opening the door. "Dear me," the Joker says.
"Horns of a dilemma."

He opens the door and once again suffers no conse-
quence beyond a disconcerting amount of dust agitated
directly into his nostrils by the portal's swinging open.
Surely he would have done better trap-wise than that.

"Well," he says. "The benefits of good planning."

Gathering the Bat-cape about him, he skips down the
stairs and turns on the light at the bottom. "Honey, I'm
home!" he sings out, and even if the various assembled
centrifuges and filtration systems and apparatuses for

catalysis don't respond out loud, he can feel the warmth of their welcome.

Home, sweet home . . . and thanks to the prank he played back in Batman's cave, he'll have some time to get things done. The Caped Crusader, as one of the papers has dubbed Batman, will surely set about rescuing his loyal footman before resuming his crimefightery.

The Joker flings the Bat-cape away and gets to work.

Three hours later he's feeling slightly better about his repertoire, and while certain of his favorite gags are given time to cool or mix or otherwise complete their preparation, he decides that it's really time to get serious about giving himself a Bat-name. Somewhere in the corner, under plastic sheeting, is a computer. The Joker fires it up and sets about learning a little something about the order Chiroptera—which, it turns out, means "hand-wing"—some of whose members were kind enough to lead him out of his subterranean post-escape travails. As it turns out, there are four families of bats native to North America: vesper, leaf-nosed, free-tailed . . . and ghost-faced. "Oh, my," he says with great delight. *Obviously* he's from the ghost-faced family, but wait. The Latin family name for ghost-faced bats is *Mormoopidae*? And the genus is *Mormoops*? He can't even say those words out loud, can't even *think* them, without . . .

He's laughing so hard that the only thing holding his guts in is this marvelous Batsuit, or maybe he should call it a Mormoopisuit, and oh God Mormoopisuit *hahaha-hahahahahahaha* . . .

Eventually he gets himself under control. Mostly. *Mormoops*. If he says it enough times, eventually it will no longer paralyze him. But right now he's still quivering, and tears are leaking from the corners of his eyes. So be it. *Mormoops,* and the Latin for the species that will include him and only him . . .

Of course. *Mormoops ioculatoris.*

He's inspired to do some research, almost, but he settles for walking down the street to get a newspaper. One of the problems with being, ahem, recognizable is that he has to dress altogether too warmly for the current weather. Not that he would trade his enhanced existence for such mundane pleasure as wearing a wife beater and shorts; quite the opposite. Still, he has pangs. All humor comes from pain. Ha.

The front page of the *Globe,* even two days after the event, is all black background and orange fire. What's this? The fires spell out HAHA.

My guardian angel, the Joker thinks. Decidedly a mixed blessing. He didn't have to advertise me quite so brazenly. I'm more than capable of announcing my own presence.

Nettled now, he takes a paper—the *Gazette* machine is empty—and returns to the hidey-hole. It seems that whoever set these fires had as his goal the liberation of little old me, he thinks with equal parts delight and suspicion. Who is he? More importantly, why is he doing this?

"I don't like it," he says, with the air of a police inspector in an old British noir. Being part of someone else's agenda is rarely part of the Joker's modus operandi. He must meet this person, this putative rescuer, and clarify the situation.

First, though, there's the matter of setting the scene. He's recovered some of his toys from Batman's cave.

Now that he's back in his laboratory, it's time to get the rest of his repertoire back up to speed. There are chemicals to synthesize, compounds to catalyze, lofty goals to realize! *Avanti!*

"Rehearsal," he says in his best pedantic tone, "is the invisible key to great performance." And he believes it. A glimmer of an idea is taking shape in his head, a tribute to Batman's worthy opposition. Imitation, after all, is the sincerest form of flattery, is it not? Oh my, he thinks. This will be good. Unless, of course, the elementary little trap he left back in the cave is too much for the Bat. If that's how it plays out, it will be too bad, but it will also have been a sign that he has overestimated his adversary, and better to know that before he gets too invested in the relationship. I am a man of limited emotional resources, the Joker thinks. Best not to invest them unwisely. If Batman can't handle this little Alfred puzzle, I'll give my heart to another.

He flings the newspaper up into the air and stands as the sheets flutter down around him, a cascade of HAHA and immolated Gotham City. Suddenly he's feeling competitive. Time to get back in the headlines, and he knows just how to do that.

But first, dear God. Now that the sun is coming up and people are on the streets, how can he not take another ride in that wonderful car?

BULL'S-EYE: *SAISON EN ENFER*
Rafael del Toro, *Gazette* Columnist

I try not to do this very often, but over the past few days the spirit has moved me to embark on actual reporting, complete with phone calls and interviews. The reason for this is that my voice-mail and email boxes are full to bursting with reports that at the Otisburg fire and the Arkham conflagration, a certain personage was observed acting in a highly suspicious manner. This person wears black, only comes out at night, and . . .

. . . no, it's not Batman. We'll get to him later.

An anonymous Bull's-Eye correspondent reports that this person "was of average height and weight, and wore what looked like a fireman's outfit [*ed. note—that's "firefighter," if you please*], only all in black. Hat, coat, big wader-style boots, the whole works." Anonymous reports seeing this person on top of the former Shulevits Tannery building across the street from the Otisburg tenement fire. Shortly after the sighting, he [*ed. note—or she . . . who says I'm not gender-neutral?*] reports seeing this faux-Bravest chased off the rooftop by another black-clad nighttime provocateur: Batman.

Other reports echo Anonymous's account. Witnesses of the 50-plus fires set in the aftermath of the Arkham inferno reported seeing a man dressed in a black full-length coat of the type worn by firefighters, with a patch on the left breast in the shape of an orange flame, as well as firefighter-style pants and boots. Reports differ on whether he was wearing a helmet, and yet more sightings of this latest addition to Gotham's abundant history of criminal lunatics describe him as wearing a bomb-disposal suit, but the flame patch is constant. A villain's got to brand himself, you know. And this one's apparently calling himself Enfer, if you can believe that, and is prone to quoting passages from the French poet Blaise Cendrars.

(Get it? Blaze? Ha. Ha. At least I'm quoting Rimbaud way back there in the title of this column; now, *there's* a Frenchman I can get behind.)

So not only do we have a loony pyromaniac on our hands, we have a loony pyromaniac on our hands who calls himself Hell and hates firemen. And not only that, but he's a Francophile. With any luck, he'll be inspired by the example of his beloved *république française*, and he'll surrender as his definitive act of villainy.

Until then, we'll rely on Batman.

God help us.

11

July 30, 6:01 AM

Bruce has followed the trail of bread crumbs for what must be miles through the cave. He's barefoot and in his pajamas, carrying only a flashlight scooped up from the broken-into locker containing his tools, and he's berating himself silently for anything that comes to mind: not sealing off that part of the cave, not knowing more about cave ecology so he can have a better idea of what else might be eating the bread crumbs, not finishing the capture of escaped Arkham inmates. Or at least he could have found out who was still missing. To have spent all of that energy chasing garden-variety lunatics when the Joker was loose again . . . unforgivable.

By force of will he changes his frame of mind. Recriminations are useless right now. After he finds Alfred, after he takes care of the Joker again (or Batman takes care of the Joker), after all of Enfer's fires are put out for good, then will come the time to assess and make the necessary changes. Right now the clock is ticking. He's kept track of the bread crumbs so far, but he's also seen more mice, and there's no way to know whether the trail will disappear before he gets to Alfred.

Also, there's no way to know what awaits him when he does find Alfred. I've never intentionally killed anyone, Bruce is thinking. Batman's never intentionally killed anyone. But that's going to change if Alfred . . .

Again he cuts off his train of thought. There are useful ifs, and there are ifs that become mental death spirals, draining valuable mental energy away from the problem at hand. Find Alfred first, Bruce thinks. Then the next move will be clear.

Focus.

Ahead, the next bread crumb, pinned in the flashlight's halogen beam. Each one is like a blaze on a forest trail. Bruce brackets it between his feet and scans until he finds the next. It crosses his mind that the Joker could be leading him not to Alfred but—to pursue the Hansel-and-Gretel metaphor—straight to the witch's oven. He turns the thought over in his mind, then switches gears and turns it over in the Joker's mind. Unlikely; Bruce's assessment of his adversary is that the Joker would much prefer Batman to find Alfred, and then experience the punch line. Whatever that's going to be.

Focus.

The next bread crumb is on a ledge, visible only when Bruce stands on tiptoe. Sloppy, he thinks. Is the Joker taller than I am? He doesn't remember it that way, but it could be so. Or this could be a subtle upping of the stakes, removing the next clue from direct linkage to the previous. Bruce files this away and hoists himself up onto the ledge. There's a small seam there, and a dead bat. He shines the flashlight into the seam and sees that it's big enough to get through, but not by much. How the Joker got Alfred through there (*if he did,* a skeptical part of Bruce's mind—Batman's mind?—chimes in, but Bruce ignores it) is an interesting question. The Joker is stronger than your average human, that much was obvious on the night of the near catastrophe at the reservoir, but Bruce isn't sure if he's strong enough to have dragged Alfred through a cave tunnel barely large enough to get through on hands and knees.

Which could mean that Alfred was conscious and proceeding under his own power, at least during this part of the abduction. Bruce gets his head and shoulders into the tube, pushing the flashlight ahead of him. It must be nearly dawn, he thinks.

A hundred yards or so later there's still no bread crumb, and Bruce is weighing his options. Go back and see if there was another crumb visible from the ledge, or assume that the next one lies at the end of this tunnel? The question answers itself when he realizes that he can't turn around. Onward, then.

A few minutes later the tunnel corkscrews up and ends in a depression in the floor of a large room. A drain, Bruce imagines, millions of years ago when the river was two hundred feet higher and I'd have had to be a fish to get this far. He wonders how far from the surface he is now; his sense of direction, challenged by the cave but still operative, pegs him a mile or so west-southwest of Wayne Manor, which would mean he is still hugging the edge of the bluffs overlooking the North Channel separating the suburbs from Gotham City proper. Either the surface or a cliff-face outlet can't be too far away, which increases the likelihood that animals from above travel in this part of the cave hunting the albino fauna native to its passages and chambers. Many of them would be happy with bread crumbs instead of eyeless crickets. Bruce shines the flashlight around, covering first the floor, then the visible surfaces of any ledges and protruding rocks, then the crevices between stalagmites.

No bread crumbs.

He goes over every square inch of the room, discovering four outlets but still no bread crumbs. He feels his heart rate increasing, and his mind once again is turning to murderous thoughts. If this is the game Gotham's villains are going to play, then perhaps Gotham City is no place for a paladin. What it needs instead might be reprisals of the sort that Carmine Falcone would understand.

And there Bruce reels himself back in. The day that I am on the same wavelength as Carmine Falcone, he thinks, is the day that I go back to being the so-called billionaire playboy full-time.

Again he plays the flashlight over every surface in the room. He discovers deposits of guano, several eyeless spiders, a number of remarkable gypsum flowers, and not a single bread crumb. Not even a footprint or drag mark that would indicate human passage, except his own barefoot trail in a chaotic swirl up and down the rugged perimeter of the room.

A test, he thinks. The Joker is upping the stakes, but he'll want the joke to pay off, so there's got to be an answer.

He's about to begin a third circuit with the flashlight when, just at the edge of audibility, a whisper: "Master Bruce."

Bruce snaps to attention and turns off the flashlight

on the off chance that the loss of vision will improve his hearing. "Alfred?"

"Light on," Alfred whispers.

Bruce's reflex is to tell Alfred to speak up, but there must be some reason for the whispering. He switches the flashlight back on, and as he does so figures out what Alfred is doing.

"Alfred," he says. "I'm going to show the light down each way out of this room. Tell me which is the right one."

Not waiting for an answer, he tracks around the perimeter one more time, pausing at the visible exits in case Alfred responds. At the third one, an esophageal passage descending from the north side of the room, he hears a faint affirmation. Bruce plunges into the passage. It's so steep that he has to go in feetfirst, and at times he's chimneying before he puts his feet on solid ground again.

"Stop," Alfred says, just as the light from Bruce's flashlight falls on him and Bruce sees the punch line.

Alfred stands in the center of the room, stripped to his underwear, an expression of exhausted dread on his face. Around his neck is strung a lei of flowers taken from the museum locker. Bruce recognizes those flowers. The Joker used them to murder a group of lawyers planning a case against one of his associates, back before the reservoir business. Motion-activated, they release a lethal dose of what *Gazette* reporters called Joker Juice. Even Alfred's whispers have provoked a small puff of vapor from the one nearest his mouth; Alfred screws his eyes shut and holds his breath while the slow circulation of the cave air gradually moves the vapor away. Bruce watches and

holds the flashlight on Alfred's face, until he is certain
that the vapor has dissipated.

"Breathe, Alfred," he says. "But quietly."

Alfred shoots Bruce a look that tells him the qualifier
wasn't necessary. Even faced with agonizing death, Alfred is master of the butler's subtle rebuke.

So here's the punch line, Bruce thinks. I can't move to
take the flowers off, and sooner or later Alfred will col-
lapse, triggering them. For a moment he's tempted to
look around for a hidden camera, although there's no
way the Joker would have had time to gather the resources during his flight from Arkham.

The question of the Joker's resourcefulness, however,
is thrown wide open by the fact that, while on the run
from every cop in Gotham City, he somehow managed
to stumble through the caves that riddle the bluffs over
(and apparently the bedrock below) the North Channel
to find the one way into the cave. There's no way it
could have been anything but an accident, but Bruce
Wayne has trained himself not to believe in accidents,
and he takes it as a lesson in his failure to anticipate
adequately all of the possible ramifications of using the
cave.

Now, though, the problem is how to get Alfred out.

"The only way I can think of to do this," Bruce says,
"is just to do it. On my signal, you hold your breath and
shut your eyes, and I'll get them off you as fast as I can."

It won't work. He knows it won't work. But he will be
damned, literally, if he is going to watch Alfred die before his eyes and not try to do something about it. Alfred
is stock-still, but Bruce can see in his eyes that he doesn't
want Bruce to take this desperate chance. All the arguments rehearse themselves in Bruce's head: Gotham needs

you, what good will it do if in trying to save Alfred you kill yourself, and so on. Behind them there lurks the question of what exactly the Joker plans to do with all the Batman regalia and gadgetry that he's stolen from the cave.

There is an awful calculus to be performed when the saving of one life might require the sacrifice of another. Bruce is performing it now and rejecting the results. If he can walk away from his oldest friend, he isn't the man he thought he was, and walking away would extinguish Batman as surely as the Joker Juice will leave Alfred cold on the cave floor with a death's-head grimace.

And would that be such an awful thing, to be free of Batman?

Revulsion, as much as resolve, spurs Bruce Wayne into a lunge across the ten feet of rugged limestone that separate him from Alfred. Several things happen at once. Alfred's face pinches shut; Bruce's right hand clamps over Alfred's nose and mouth; Bruce's body bears Alfred to the floor; the flowers begin to spew their lethal gas . . .

. . . and the cave is suddenly full of bats.

Bruce and Alfred crash to the floor as the torrent of tiny bodies washes over them. The hiss of the flowers mingles with the rustle of bat wings, which as the main bulk of the colony arrives builds to a steady roar. Bruce's eyes are burning. He wants more than anything else in the world to vomit—more than anything, that is, except to survive, and to keep Alfred alive. He can feel the Joker Juice crawling in his nostrils, burning in his tear ducts, stinging the corners of his mouth, but he will not let it in. Alfred thrashes in his grasp, and Bruce fills with slow horror as he realizes that he might in his blindness be feeling the death throes of the one man who has kept his life together. No, he thinks. I deny this. I refute it.

The bats are gone, or at least the sound of them is. Bruce realizes he has been counting in his head and reached ninety. He opens his eyes and does not die. He takes a breath and does not die.

He looks down at Alfred, seen in the oblique glow of the flashlight's beam, and realizes that although Bruce Wayne is more than capable of holding his breath for a minute and a half, Alfred is not. "Oh no," he says, and takes his hand away from Alfred's face.

Alfred does not move.

"No," Bruce says again and drops his face to Alfred's, breathing life back into him while all around him bats are fluttering out the last of their lives. He breathes and compresses Alfred's old man's chest; and breathes and does it again; and for the first time in years Bruce Wayne loses track of time.

Until Alfred's throat spasms and he sucks in a greedy breath, then coughs as if he might yet die. Bruce lifts him into a sitting position, and the worst of the coughing passes. Alfred's face is pale but mottled with dark blotches; his eyes are streaming, and when he looks up at Bruce, his lips are fighting the impulse to peel back in a poisoned rictus.

"Come on, Alfred," Bruce growls.

Alfred's eyes focus, and the grin falters. But when he tries to speak, what comes out is, "Ho ho ho."

Bruce slaps him, hard.

Alfred's head snaps around, and he sneezes. "Ho," he says again. "Ha ha."

"No," Bruce says, hauling him to his feet. Get his

blood moving, he is thinking. Flush the toxins away. "Walk with me, Alfred."

They walk together, in small circles, crushing beneath their bare feet the bodies of bats. Bruce looks down at them and sees their lips peeled back from their teeth. You saved us, he thinks. The rush of your passage cleared the Joker Juice, and you died, and we did not.

At least not yet.

"Alfred," he says. "We're going back to the cave. I need you to stay with me. Can you do that?"

"Ho ho ho," Alfred says with a terrible grin.

Of the trip back through the cave, Bruce will recall very little. The unemotional steel surface of Batman's psyche fails him and allows the agonized turbulence of Bruce Wayne to boil up and obscure the journey in a veil of fear and recrimination and—most cruelly—hope. All Bruce knows at the end is that he is back in the cave, and his body is ringing with exhaustion, and Alfred is limply staggering next to him, head down and his only sound an occasional, faint *ho ho ho*.

Bruce lays Alfred on his back on the same table where a few nights before Alfred was dressing Bruce's burns. About time I gave you something back, old friend, Bruce thinks. Long past time.

He tears open the medicine chest built into the rack of cabinets at one end of the long worktable, finding a vial of adrenaline. Either it will give Alfred a heart attack and finish what the Joker Juice started, or it will get his heart pumping and finish the job of purging the toxin from his system. Another difficult calculus, and one Bruce wishes did not have so many variables.

It does, though, and he's made his choice. He draws

the clear serum from the vial, finds a spot between Alfred's ribs just to the left of his sternum, and plunges the needle home. Alfred jerks up into a sitting position. His eyes fly open and his jaw drops. Veins bulge in his neck and forehead.

For an interminable moment Bruce lives with the knowledge that he has killed his last remaining link to his father.

Alfred breathes.

Bruce breathes.

Alfred falls back onto the table.

Bruce cradles his head. He has no words, and Alfred's eyes are wide and unfocused. Bruce can feel Alfred's pulse fluttering unevenly in his neck. After a while he lets Alfred's head sink back to the table and says, "Alfred. If you're dead, tell me now so I can stop hoping."

A ghost of a smile deepens the wrinkles at the corners of Alfred's mouth. A real smile.

"Despite," he manages to say, "your best efforts, Master Bruce."

July 30, 11:57 AM

Enfer is coming out of Finnigan's at about noon, having indulged in a couple of Zesti Bombs and as a result feeling pretty good about the universe and his place in it, when he sees Batman's car come screaming around the corner and, without even slowing, crush a young woman and her dog. The shock of this event reverberates within Enfer the way great shocks always do: time slows to a crawl, and he becomes intensely, even painfully, sensitive to every detail of his surroundings. He smells caramel corn from a street vendor. He hears the screams of pedestrians rising and falling like the sirens that will soon be coming. He feels the roar of the engine and can almost feel the vibrations of the car's tires as they come out of their skid and find their purchase on the asphalt of Cowan Street, and together with the restrained growl of the monorail just then passing overhead the sounds and vibrations momentarily make Enfer feel as if he's an engine, too. He wants to rev up, get started, finish the plan that Jonathan Crane conceived but could not imagine in its true dimensions.

Drunk, he thinks. When did that happen?

As the car passes him, he sees that the passenger-side window is down a crack, and there's laughter from within. Realization dawns, and when he glimpses the grinning figure behind the wheel Enfer runs aground on a mental reef of sheer amazement. He can't quite decide whether he's hallucinating or he's really observing the Joker in full Batman regalia mowing down pedestrians in downtown Gotham City. That's big-time, he thinks admiringly. He's suddenly recharged, newly resolute in his ambition to make his mark on Gotham City—not that he hasn't already, in the literal sense of the city blocks that are freshly burned out as a result of his previous enterprises, but the truth is that setting a fire all by itself is, let's face it, kind of ordinary. He's got scale, that's for sure, and the HAHA gag was brilliant if he does say so himself . . . but the Joker has upped the stakes.

We've got to get together, Enfer thinks. He wants the Joker to know what he's done. A scheme like the Arkham breakout deserves a little acclaim.

The Batmobile disappears around a corner. The dog walker lies unmoving in the crosswalk. Her dog is feebly scratching at the pavement with its front paws, trying to get up. At first there is a hush, the taut silence of a hundred people unwilling to believe what they've just seen. A crowd gathers around the woman, and all of a sudden there are screams, people tell each other to call an ambulance, they go running off in all directions. Others come to see what all the fuss is about. What I need to do, Enfer thinks, is smoke Batman out now, while he doesn't have all his toys. Mano a mano, just me and him. We'll find out if he's so tough when he doesn't have the gadgets to hide behind.

At the same time, he also thinks that he just might be able to kill two birds with one stone. What if he can draw both of them, the real and fake Batmen? The way to do it would be to convince each of them that the other will be there, and that can't be that hard, can it?

Except it won't work if anyone else saw who was really driving the car.

"Did you see that?" he screams at the top of his lungs. "Batman just ran over that girl. And her dog!"

Near him is a young woman, looking puzzled, her head swiveling back and forth between the battered body in the street and the direction the Batmobile went. "I thought . . . ," she begins.

"Batman!" Enfer yells again. He grabs the person nearest him. "That son of a bitch! I saw him right through the window! He ran that girl down with the window open!"

And he keeps right on saying it, to anyone who will listen and most of those who won't, until the police arrive two minutes later and he can tell them all about it. His insistence sends a current through the crowd, and pretty soon they're ready to lynch Batman on sight. An old woman, her market basket in the crook of an elbow, berates the cops in language more befitting, well, a fire-fighter. Up and down the street children cry baffled tears and groups of young men mutter darkly about what they'll do if they ever catch Batman unawares in their neighborhood. Perfect, Enfer thinks. Before he walks away down the street, he's talked to five cops and three reporters—one of them the hot *Globe* reporter who seems to get a lot of the Batman stories—and he really regrets having to duck away from the photographers and insist that his name not be used. Even in the middle of performance euphoria, you've got to play things smart.

Plus it's time to get back to the hidey-hole, flesh out the details. The Joker set the bar high, Enfer is thinking. But he's not the only one who can make a plan work.

The first thing he does after locking the door behind him is remove the prosthetic arm. It's an ordinary piece of plastic and metal, and the straps chafe his neck. He's done much better work himself, but wearing a more or less off-the-rack arm when he's in public during the day makes him feel like he's invisible. He tosses the arm on a swaybacked couch he rescued from an abandoned plastic surgery practice around the corner, and as he wanders around his lair Enfer considers what he's seen today. The Joker is big-league, that's for sure. To actually get into Batman's sanctum sanctorum and make off with the car and a suit . . .

"Set the bar high," he says out loud, and goes to the locker where he keeps his working arms. They're different from the standard prosthesis he wears as part of his mundane camouflage, each designed for a specific purpose. He's got another one like the little bomb he surprised Batman with the other night; he's got a couple that are built around a pump-and-nozzle system that can be primed with a number of different flammable substances; he's got one that's specifically designed to let him handle superheated substances. Next to them hang a number of prototypes and partial designs, including the Creeper. That's the one he's really dying to try out.

His arm is sore today, the phantom pain worse than it's been since right after he lost the physical arm. *I'm the man who doesn't have a past,* Enfer quotes to himself. —*Only my stump hurts.*— The poet's words get his feet back on the ground. Rubbing the stump even though he knows it doesn't help, Enfer bounces on the balls of his feet, so electrified by ambition that he's not sure how to start realizing it—but ambition's gotten him into trouble before. Slow down, he tells himself. He's looking at his fire helmet.

His fire helmet.

Once I could walk the streets without a fake arm and a fake self, he thinks, and *snap*—every time he has that thought, he's gone into himself, and this time is no different.

He's six years old, at his grandparents' cabin far away in Vermont. It's just before sunrise and he's sitting on the hearth rug, a blanket around his shoulders and the fireplace poker in his hands. It's heavy, but he stirs it through the coals of last night's fire until the glow brightens on the underside of the log he's already put in. He leans forward and blows, long and steady, eyes unblinking, until with a soft *whoosh* the log blooms with yellow flame.

He's nine, building a toy skyscraper from a bucket full of plastic girders that snap together. A vision comes into his head and he rearranges one of the skyscraper's towers, but he can't get the angle right; none of the girders is exactly the right length. He goes to the kitchen drawer and finds a book of matches.

His mistake is to hold the girder at an angle while he melts one end down. The molten plastic runs down the length of the girder and sears his pinkie finger. The pain is so encompassing and unlike anything else he can ever remember feeling that it breaks through a barrier in his mind.

He's thirteen and furious at having broken one of the forward gun turrets off a plastic model of the battleship *Bismarck*. His parents are gone. He takes the model out into the garage and sets it on his father's tool bench. There are three gas cans lined up on the bottom shelf of one of the steel storage units against one wall. He picks the one marked BAD, because his father doesn't keep good track of how much is in it, and he pours slowly through a hole in the *Bismarck*'s deck until there's half an inch or so of gasoline sloshing in the gray hull. But he's getting ahead of himself; he goes back into the house, finds a pack of firecrackers, and with care works one loose from the long fuse that ties all of them together. With that single Black Cat and a book of matches—he always has a book of matches now—he returns to the garage.

The city keeps saying they're going to pave the road that runs past his house, but they keep not doing it, and last night's rain has filled one of the bigger potholes with maybe eight inches of water. He sets the *Bismarck* afloat in the puddle and works the firecracker about halfway down through the hole left when he broke the gun turret off. He strikes a match, waits for it to settle into a steady burn, and lights the fuse.

Boom, another wall in his mind comes down in a black-threaded ball of fire and a clicking shower of gray plastic fragments.

*   *   *

He's twenty-seven and utterly drunk on the smell of paint thinner. Patience, he tells himself. It's his first time trying a time-delay device. Three, two, one . . . there it is: a glow from behind a stack of pallets up against the side of a lumberyard warehouse. He checks his watch and congratulates himself. Right on time. Starting his car, he heads down to the station, hoping he'll get there before the first call comes in.

He's thirty-two and craning to see the fire across the street, but it's hard to move his neck that way because Batman is kneeling on the small of his back. *No,* he's trying to say. *There's someone in there.* This is the one where he took the step he's been trying not to take. Anyone can set a fire, and anyone in the fire department can set a fire and then be part of the company that responds to it. According to what he's read—and he's read quite a bit on the topic—torching an inhabited building is the inevitable next step, the one that lets the arsonist play hero.

Enfer (he wasn't calling himself that yet, but that's the way he remembers it now) doesn't shy from that term, *arsonist.* It's as good a description as any. And he doesn't shy from the descriptions of people like him as disturbed or sociopathic or pathologically self-aggrandizing; that's a certain perspective that he understands, although of course he doesn't share it. He's different, that's for sure.

Right now all he wants is to get this black-caped nutcase off his back so he can get in there and pull the night watchman out, and maybe the homeless guy who beds down under the back stairs, if he's there. He starts to say something, and Batman raps him on the back of the head. "Talk later," the hero says, and Enfer's arms are twisted behind him. He feels the bite of thin handcuffs.

Then a wail from across the street, and just like that the weight is gone from his back. He rolls onto his side and sees Batman looking at him with disgust etched in the lines around his mouth. "You'd better hope I get there in time," Batman says and is gone.

He's thirty-three and laying in a complicated series of charges in an open-air chemical storage facility known only to international arms dealers and close observers of satellite images. The scrubby near-desert of North Africa stretches away in every direction, reminding him of Arizona. Just after he joined the fire department, he went to a series of training exercises in Arizona, part of some kind of interdepartmental exchange. It's a place he wouldn't mind visiting again, but those plans will have to wait because he can't go to the United States under his own name anymore. It's been six months since he split on his court date back in Gotham City, having taken his particular combination of interest and expertise to a group of discreet individuals who thought he might be an asset to them. Intensive training in demolitions and incendiaries followed, and now he earns an excellent (and tax-free) salary making things go boom. It's a good life. Definitely worth being run out of the fire department and humiliated, although he's not lying to himself; if he ever gets a chance to put his new skills to work on the GCFD, he's going to. Nothing wrong with holding a grudge.

This particular job concerns large amounts of unstable and toxic substances left behind after the assassination of one of those erratic geniuses who finds a home in

the arms trade. Enfer doesn't much care about the local
politics involved, and he doesn't have any clear idea of
what he's blowing up. He lays the charges, shaping them
so their force will be directed inward. No sense blasting
the stuff all over the landscape so it can poison local
tribesmen for the next hundred years. To make sure he
gets all of it, he seeds smaller charges in the center of the
depot and times them to go off a tenth of a second after
the perimeter detonations. That ought to do it, he
thinks. Sweating in his blast suit, he sets the last of the
slave switches keyed to the master he's got back in
the jeep about five hundred yards away. He glances over
his shoulder at it and sees one of his local liaison party
leaning in the passenger's door. They're always stealing
his cigarettes.

Except this time they're not. He has the flash of in-
sight, and the flash of fear, and then the perimeter
charges go off and the blast wave crushes him down into
an infinitely dense plasma. He goes blind and feels his
eardrums blow out. He can't breathe. He can smell,
though, and the acrid smell of vaporizing chemicals
burns its way down into his lungs. A similar burning
spreads across his skin, and down inside him; if he could
move he'd look down at his suit, but he already knows
it's failed him.

A tenth of a second later the central charges follow,
and the one closest to him takes his right arm off just
below the shoulder. He's on the ground, and either he's
opened his eyes or his vision has come back; whichever
it is, he's seeing colors above him that he never knew ex-
isted, and he's got a taste in his mouth unlike anything
he can name. He's on fire, can see the flames playing
about his body, dipping into and out of the holes in the

suit. He sneezes and breathes fire. The overpressure is
starting to lessen, and lying on his back he watches the
superheated swirl of vapor and smoke and fire. His ears
are screaming now, and he screams with them, and fire
comes out of his mouth.

That still happens once in a while, when his metabo-
lism really gets revved up. His sweat isn't what you
would call highly flammable, but it does burn. While he
was recovering, in a tent hospital financed by his employer and staffed by people who wore burnooses and
spoke French, once in a while a change in the weather
would fill his bedding with static, and when he rolled
over tiny bursts of fire like solar flares arced out from his
body. Sometimes when he snaps his fingers, the action
strikes sparks. Because of this, he hasn't owned a car in
some time, not because the eruptions harm him but because the cars get wrecked. Also, living in Gotham City
doesn't require a car, and let's face it, he spent the first
part of his most recent Gotham residency under the care
of Dr. Jonathan Crane.

For this he blames his former employers, who sent
him to Crane for what they termed "reassimilation
therapy," by which he assumes they meant they wanted
Crane to tinker with his head until he could pass for
normal in regular society again. They might easily have
just gotten rid of him, but clearly they think his transmogrification might be of some future use, so they
stowed him away in Arkham Asylum while they figured
out what to do.

At least he got a free arm out of it. And when Crane
heard a little more about Enfer's situation, he guided his
patient in the direction of a certain poet, "as a way for

you to form a healthy identification with a survivor of a similar situation." Then he suggested that they might collaborate on a decisive effort to rid Gotham City of its nocturnal paladin.

"Only if I can even the score with the fire department, too," Enfer said. By then he had adopted his new name, learned some French, used some of his remaining salary and some of Arkham's outdated home-economics equipment to outfit himself, and begun tinkering with some of the incendiary experiments that have paid off so handsomely during the last few days.

The doctor agreed, and that was that. (At least that's what Jonathan Crane thought; Enfer had good parenting and was taught not to gloat, but in this case he can't help it.)

All of this in eighteen months, give or take. Enfer imagines addressing Batman: *When I was a hero and wore a badge, you were nobody. Wheel of fortune goes 'round and 'round.*

And I am on the way up.

JOKE'S ON US AGAIN
ARKHAM ARSONIST IN CAHOOTS
WITH CLOWN PRINCE OF CRIME
Rafael del Toro, Special to the *Gazette*

Tuesday's fire at Arkham Asylum, the first of many across the city, not only killed dozens of inmates and burned the venerable structure to the ground but may also have been part of an ingenious plot to free the facility's most notorious resident: the Joker.

More than 50 separate fires were set across the midsection of Gotham City on Tuesday night, from the off-ramps of the Trigate Bridge to the Dillon Avenue Bridge. It was the worst act of arson in the city's history, and the second series of fires—after the initial blazes that leveled Arkham Asylum and sprang its population to roam our streets—appears to have been designed to send a message to Gotham City authorities.

The message, seen in the pictures at left: HAHA.

GCPD assistant spokesdrone Ashlyn Giles declined to comment on the pictures beyond a calming reassurance that "the GCPD is examining all aspects and possibilities related to this terrible act."

A terrible act indeed. One hundred seventeen people are now known to have died, with the toll sure to rise whenever Arkham Asylum director Jonathan Crane can be bothered to issue his list of inmate fatalities and those still missing . . . i.e., those still creeping around your backyards. What's the holdup, Doc?

Through spokeswoman Angela Rodriquez, Crane issued a statement that "extensive damage to Arkham has drastically hindered efforts to identify remains and reconstruct records."

By which they mean: we don't know who was here, we don't know who's still under the wreckage, and we don't know who's still on the loose.

By which they also mean: we do know who we've got back again, but if we tell you, you'll get all worried about the names we didn't list, so for your own good we're keeping you in the dark.

You will be shocked, Dear Reader, to learn that this shifty approach has won Crane no fans among local residents. "He needs to keep people informed," said Adrian Wingard, whose condo on the northeast corner of Robinson Park forms the lower left foot of the first A in the picture above. . . .

13

July 30, 2:48 PM

Once, Jim Gordon thought he had dealt with the oiliest of Gotham City's unelected officialdom, but two days of suffering through Jonathan Crane's evasions have convinced him otherwise. Never has he seen a public official blessed with Crane's combination of unctuous courtesy and total commitment to the lie as a way of life. Gordon's objective is simple enough. He needs—has needed, for nearly forty-eight hours now—a list of the known fatalities from the Arkham fire, so he can run it against the list of Arkham inmates. Inmate population minus fatalities minus those caught by the GCPD and Batman equals number of deranged wackos still at large, and that number is one Gordon badly needs because the horrified epiphany he experienced in the helicopter the other night won't leave him alone. There's no record of the Joker having been caught, so if he's not dead he's on the loose, and Gordon has a strong suspicion that if the Joker weren't on the loose, Crane wouldn't be nearly so cagey about his facts and figures.

Third time's the charm, he tells himself without believing it. He's pulling through the gates of Arkham Asylum, which are open since all of the known survivors are temporarily housed on a military base fifty miles upriver. The building itself is a ruin, not just your ordinary burned hulk but torched so completely and evenly that Gordon wonders just how much time this Enfer character had to wander around inside setting his fires. That thought leads him back to the question of an inside job, which was never far from his mind in any case, and makes him even more eager to get things sorted out with Crane.

The good doctor, it turns out, is just emerging from the wreckage with a box full of charred and still-wet personal items. He's media-savvy enough to be wearing a hard hat that makes him look to the credulous like someone inclined to roll up his sleeves and get to the bottom of things, but Gordon knows this to be the exact opposite of the truth.

He waits until the doctor is less than five feet away before saying, "Anything in there I should know about?"

Crane looks at him and adopts an expression of self-righteous distaste. "Absolutely not," he says.

"You sure?"

"Certain. And I'm also certain you know what a personal as well as professional tragedy this is for me. I have dedicated my life to the welfare of these unfortunates, and to have lost so many . . . let me put it this way: your emphasis on figures, on body counts, nauseates me."

"Well, Doc," Gordon says, "your bobbing and weaving is starting to upset my stomach a little, too. If you're all that dedicated, I'm sure you've been able to do some basic arithmetic and run a quick database check to see who's still missing."

"A number of the missing are no doubt still buried in that . . . charnel house," Crane says, and now he's looking over Gordon's shoulder. Gordon doesn't have to turn around to know there's a camera crew there; even without his doggedness, the local media is looking for a scapegoat and tempted to make it Crane. "I have answered your questions in the most forthright and complete manner possible given the circumstances. Please direct your questions to Angela in the future."

Angela being Crane's assistant and spokeswoman Angela Rodriquez, who stands at a distance observing the interaction between Gordon and her boss. Gordon makes a mental note to work her over a little; everyone who works at Arkham can't be as corrupt as Crane.

Gordon beckons Crane closer. Suspicious, Crane takes a step toward him. Gordon leans in close, and in a whisper he's pretty sure even the directional mikes won't catch, he says, "Not a bad performance, but it doesn't go with the hard hat. Most of the simpletons in your audience will prefer words of fewer syllables."

He winks. Crane stares at him, and Gordon, for perhaps the thousandth time in his life, knows what it is to be touching distance from a man who would kill him if he could.

"I'll serve a warrant if I have to," he says. "There's got to be one honest judge left in this town. You want me to go find him, or can we proceed on a more cooperative basis from here on out?"

"Get your warrant," Crane says. Now there's a real light of instability in his eyes. Gordon, behind his immediate anger and disgust—behind even his cop's thick

skin when it comes to the sufferings of criminals as a result of their crimes—feels a sudden pang of sympathy for
Arkham inmates. He's looking into the face of a crazy
man. Another thing to ask Angela Rodriquez about.

"Guess I'll do that," he says. "You know where to
find me if you change your mind."

On his way back to the car, he's thinking that at least
he parked close to the gate. Saves him a bit of a walk.

Before going back to the station, he stops by his
house. James Junior is full of two-year-old vim, and Barbara has the look she always gets around lunchtime:
combine the famous World War Two photograph of the
thousand-yard stare with a portrait of the contemporary
urban housewife slightly stoned on the possibility that
she will survive to another naptime, and you'd have it
exactly. Gordon stays longer than he should, because
after the near failure of their marriage while Barbara
was pregnant, he's exceedingly sensitive to the need to
make the kind of little gesture that is usually only noticed when it doesn't happen. When he gets back to
headquarters he can tell right away that something has
happened while he was gone, and that it has to do with
him. There's the odd tension in the air that everyone
feels when a practical joke is about to be sprung. Even
the victim always feels it, Gordon thinks, but he's the
victim because he doesn't know what it's about even at
the end. That's the feeling he has as he walks into his office, find his coffee mug, and goes to pour himself a cup
and cogitate over how else he can tighten the screws on
Jonathan Crane.

The way he's got it figured, someone with an intimate
knowledge of the asylum set the fires. That requires a

certain kind of leisurely access available only to someone whose presence Crane had signed off on—which in turn makes Crane a likable candidate for accessory.

So why would Crane be in on a plot to torch his own little kingdom?

And where does the Joker fit in?

It's obvious that whoever burned Arkham did it to spring the Joker. Gordon figured that out the minute he saw the HAHA, and if this Enfer guy is the firebug (he's obviously *a* firebug, but Gordon is trying to maintain enough objectivity to entertain the possibility that he might be working independently of whoever burned the asylum), then he went in there with the intent to spring the Joker, and he went in with the knowledge of Jonathan Crane.

Which, unfortunately, does not necessarily mean that Crane knew Enfer was going to burn Arkham. If it did, Gordon would have the doctor under a lightbulb downstairs right now. The problem is, he has to acknowledge the possibility that Enfer, whoever that is, could be a confidant of Crane's for other reasons and have generated the Joker caper on his own. It's unlikely, that's for damn sure, but he'd be a lousy cop if he didn't consider it.

Okay, he thinks. I considered it, and it's bullshit. There's no way someone could have pulled that off without Crane knowing about it.

A new angle presents itself. Gordon wonders if he can bring Crane in for questioning related to the fire itself. Crane probably has good lawyers, but he's also smart enough to know that one informal conversation could save him a lot of trouble later. He might, however, also be smart enough to know that Gordon has minimal capital to expend on something like a speculative interrogation of one of Gotham's more prominent medical officials.

"Crane's probably tapped right into the sixth floor," Gordon grumbles into the coffee mug. He wonders if Commissioner Piskura, up on the sixth floor, has his office bugged. It's not impossible, but considering it makes Gordon feel unpleasantly paranoid. He's not the kind of cop who needs to feel like everyone's out to get him. There are enough of those around Gotham City.

He also wonders if it's true. Jobs like Crane's are part of the Gotham patronage structure, but Gotham is a city of many patrons. Piskura? Falcone? Mayor Hill? The three of them more or less have the city divided up, but there are lesser players who might have sought approval for a specific act of nepotism, cronyism, whateverism. Gordon thinks he might drop by a couple of bars tonight. Over on the edge of Old Gotham, in an area called the Cauldron, there's a place he knows where a couple of the city's more ethically challenged doctors like to bend an elbow when they aren't removing bullets from, or injecting pharmaceuticals into, local hardcases. Should have thought of this earlier, he chides himself. They'll have an opinion about Crane, that's for sure. Whether they'll give it to me is another story, but I've been a damn fool not to get over there sooner.

Then he settles down and cuts himself a break. It's only been forty-eight hours since the fire broke out. Not even that, really. Maybe forty.

Someone's knocking on his office door. He looks up to see Sergeant Grimaldi stick his head in. "Hey," Grimaldi says. "Did you hear about your bloodsucking buddy?"

Gordon doesn't bite on the insult, and he doesn't say anything about Grimaldi's insubordination. "Hear what?"

"He ran over a jogger and her dog today. Hit-and-run in broad daylight, right in front of Finnigan's." Grimaldi spreads his hands wide and makes a farting noise with his tongue. "Real mess, from what I heard. Might do to be careful who you take to the dance next time."

Gordon doesn't believe him. He has no idea why this conversation is taking place, since it's ridiculous enough that it doesn't even bother him.

"Go away," he says.

Grimaldi does, and when Gordon runs through his phone messages and email he sees one of particular interest. It's from a dead-drop address, but it got through the department's spam filters one way or another, and it consists of a single sentence: *The joke was almost on me.*

It takes a minute, but Gordon puts it together. Batman knows the Joker's out, and from the sound of it he's already had some kind of contact. Suddenly Grimaldi's visit makes more sense. What if someone is spreading rumors about Batman? Something like a hit-and-run would be the perfect way to corrode Batman's reputation.

But even that is secondary right now, since this confirmation of the Joker's escape instantly reshuffles Gordon's priorities for the immediate future. He's going to have to get in touch with Batman, he's going to have to pull the old files on the Joker and see what light they might shed on his future actions, and he's going to have to turn up the heat on Jonathan Crane. The last one, at least, will be enjoyable.

His phone rings. It's Commissioner Piskura. "Gordon."

"Yes sir."

"This is one of those times when I admire your enthusiasm but regret your methods."

"I'm not sure I follow."

"Jonathan Crane very much wishes that he could proceed with his recovery and information gathering without your interference."

"With all due respect, Commissioner," Gordon says, wondering exactly how much respect is actually due a man like Piskura, "the people of Gotham City need to know which Arkham inmates are still on the loose. And if the people don't need to know yet, the police sure do. If the Joker or one of the other Hall of Fame wackos is loose, the uniforms need to know about it."

"The uniforms need to know what you tell them," Piskura says. "And you need to know what I tell you, which in this specific case is that you are to wait a reasonable length of time for Doctor Crane to compile his report."

"What should I take *reasonable* to mean?"

"Doctor Crane is a reasonable man, Captain."

"I see." And what I see is that the back-channel phone calls happened even faster than I figured, Gordon is thinking.

"I hope you do. Also, I hope that you won't find it necessary to reiterate your mention of a specific inmate."

That does it. "You can trust me to act in the city's best interests, Commissioner," Gordon says, and hangs up. It feels good, but he knows it'll just end up with him getting another letter in his personnel file . . . if not another little welcoming committee like the one led by Detective Flass, back when Gordon was new to Gotham City.

I handled that one, Gordon thinks. And if it happens again, I'll handle it again.

He doesn't have much time to enjoy this feeling of resolve, though, because right then his office door flies open and Detective Ruben Cuellar stalks in. He's furious, and Gordon wonders why. Ruben is one of his few friends on the force.

"Jim." Ruben drops a copy of the *Gazette* on Gordon's desk.

EXTRA!: BAT AND RUN
Gillian O'Connor, *Gotham Globe*

In full view of horrified lunchtime pedestrians on Cowan Street today, Gotham City vigilante crimefighter Batman struck and killed a woman walking her dog before leaving the scene, in the words of one witness, "like a bat out of hell." Merilee St. Pierre, 27, was pronounced dead at the scene. Her dog, a terrier mix called Chanel, was euthanized shortly after by Gotham City Animal Control.

Ms. St. Pierre, a junior analyst at Firebird Securities, was walking with her dog when Batman, behind the wheel of his custom car widely known as the Batmobile, came around the corner from Bjornsson and struck her near the center of the street. Witnesses agreed that she had the pedestrian light, and that she was in the crosswalk at the time of impact.

Gotham City police, whose relationship with Batman has been difficult since the hero's appearance on the scene two years ago, immediately put an investigative team together, said department spokeswoman Erin McNamara. "The team will be examining forensic evidence from the scene in an effort to winnow out clues that might lead us to Batman's identity," she said.

Commissioner Eric Piskura vowed that the department's uneasy truce with Batman was permanently over. "I've never approved of vigilantism, and I've never approved of Batman's methods, but the truth is he occasionally did some good. Now he's demonstrating the same disregard for human life as any other common criminal, and like any other common criminal we're going to put him out of business."

At the scene of the accident, few witnesses would step up to defend the Caped Crusader. One who would was Anthony Stevenson, a 22-year-old unemployed electrical contractor who, when asked whether Batman might have had a good reason for what he did, replied, "Sure, he might've. How do we know he wasn't off doing something else that was going to save 10 other people's lives?"

Stevenson's words provoked a sharp exchange with other witnesses, and police had to step in and separate the agitated parties.

St. Pierre's family declined comment, releasing a statement through a family friend that said only, "Our deepest wish is that our privacy be respected in this time of grief."

What effect this incomprehensible act might have on the state of crime in Gotham City is difficult to judge. Batman is widely credited with causing the two-year-long drop in violent crime seen within city limits, but his detractors consider him a wild card. A number of those detractors were lunching at Finnigan's Tavern, which caters to police and city emergency workers. A Gotham City police officer who wished to remain anonymous said he was speaking for many of his fellow uniforms when he said, "The average cop on the street doesn't consider Batman a friend, that's for sure. This city will be better off when he's put away, especially after this. Leave police work to the police."

14

July 30, 7:08 PM

I did that, Enfer thinks. Me.

He's looking at twenty-five copies of the front page of the *Globe*, and another twenty-five of the *Gazette*, taped in long rows on the walls of his hideaway. HAHAHA-HAHAHAHAHAHAHAHA, on and on and on, fiery letters as far as the eye can see. Not a bad calling card. The tenement fire in Otisburg was a dry run, a tentative step. Arkham and HAHA, now, those were epic. The poet wrote about his failures, blaming himself for not being able to "take it all the way." Enfer learned from this, he believes. He's taking it all the way, he's going to be Gotham's great poet of fire and fear. If he isn't already, he thinks, allowing himself a moment of hubris. Whether or not he ever does anything else, he will be remembered for Arkham and HAHA.

He is going to do something else, however. More than one thing, as a matter of fact. Enfer has learned a great deal about self-awareness during the past years. He knows that setting fires is wrong by commonly accepted ethical standards; he knows that revenge is equally frowned upon, except when the state apparatus gets involved. Also, he knows that his burgeoning obsessions with Batman, not to mention the Joker, mark him as psychologically nonstandard.

He remembers hearing on numerous occasions that if you worry that you're crazy, you aren't crazy—that, in other words, crazy people don't know they're crazy. What I am, Enfer thinks, is walking proof of just how wrong that old adage is. I not only know I'm Crazy, whatever that means, I can tell you the exact nature of my Mental Illness. In this I am unlike your average wacko. Also, I have skills not available to the average wacko, and it could be that my skill set somewhat overlaps the Joker's. He's a chemical enthusiast, that's for sure. All the gases and poisons and sprays and whatnot— not just anyone could do that.

Put that together with what I know, Enfer is thinking, and we could make some serious hay together.

Part of the hideaway—the most important part, where he does his work—is done up to replicate a stanza from the poet's work. *A newspaper is strewn across my table.* Check: lots of newspapers, in fact; Enfer has put together a sizable gallery of photographs from his activities current and past. *I work in my empty room, behind a cloudy mirror . . .* This one is true only by happenstance; part of the hideaway used to be some kind of department store, and the smooth paneling of the walls on the floor above is interrupted every twenty feet or so by one-way glass. When he discovered this place, seeing that, and hearing it resonate with the poet's lines in his head, made Enfer believe in destiny. . . . *Bare feet on the*

red tiles, and play with balloons and a little toy trumpet.
He's laid red tiles around his workbenches, and he's got
balloons filled with various gases. The little toy trumpet
he had to go out and get, but it hangs in a place of honor
over one of his compressors.

I'm working on THE END OF THE WORLD.

That one goes without saying.

Well, maybe not the end of the world. The end of
Gotham City for sure, though. The end of this place he
has left and come back to after a desert transfiguration,
this place where *on shore it's a dungheap / Where two
or three skyscrapers are growing . . .*

He realizes he's teetering on the edge of a poet-fugue.
There's no time for that now. He needs to be putting
together a follow-up spectacle, he needs to be talking to the Joker, and he needs to be laying the rest
of the groundwork for the Batman project. Dr. Crane
might forgive and forget if Batman is taken care of;
after all, he's going to get plenty of grant money to rebuild Arkham, and he'll be able to siphon enough of it
into his own pockets that he can have his own little research arm, somewhere down in the basements, where
no light penetrates and the only sounds are the drip of
condensation and the soft, soft murmer of the Crane-
voice.

Abruptly Enfer's nose is full of the smell of rubbing al-
cohol, and he's about to vomit. He holds it in until the
sense memories have receded. When he's got himself together again, he thinks that he might make it a habit to
practice the chemistry of combustion on whichever facility Dr. Jonathan Crane occupies. For the rest of the
doctor's natural life. A new vendetta follows close on

the heels of this idea. First Batman, Enfer thinks. Then, Doctor Crane, I think we might yet have a score to settle.

He's grinding his teeth, and his mouth is full of smoke.

15

July 30, 8:14 PM

What with his incarceration and all, the Joker hasn't
seen Bud and Lou in nearly a year, and they weren't that
easy to track down. He made some calls to associates,
who weren't necessarily glad to hear from him, and
eventually got a message to Bud and Lou at the Queen
of Hearts strip club in the East End. Now they're sitting
around playing cutthroat pinochle in the hidey-hole,
just like the old days. Ah, the old days. It feels good to
be getting back in touch with old friends. The Joker remembers when Bud and Lou were resentful of their new
names, although he has forgotten what their real names
are. His memory is tricky like that.

"So, fellows, trusty sidekicks," he says while figuring
his meld. "What have we been up to this last year?"

"Oh, you know," Bud says. "Little of this, little of
that. No steady gigs."

"We was working with Falcone for a couple months,"
Lou chimes in. "That didn't, ah . . ."

"Wasn't mutually beneficial, I suppose," the Joker
says.

"No, not a bit," Lou agrees.

"Paid okay, but Falcone lacks imagination, is the truth, you know?" Bud says.

The Joker does know. "What did he have you doing?"

"Well, we ain't supposed to talk about it," Bud says.

"Of course not," the Joker says. "So what did he have you doing?"

There is a short silence. "Mostly driving," Lou says. "We do have one more thing lined up with him."

"Is that right? When?"

"Not sure. Soon, Carmine said. Sorry, boss. But that was the only way we could get out of, what do you call it . . ."

"Future obligations," Bud finishes, with a sour expression. "Plus, we have to use our own truck."

"I understand, boys," the Joker says. "So. Driving what?"

Bud and Lou study their cards.

"Boys, comrades in arms, fellows, why the reticence? You're not worried about what will happen, are you? You're with me again now. Carmine Falcone not only lacks imagination but also suffers from a positively debilitating desire to avoid confrontation with people like me. He is a superstitious and cowardly nincompoop. Now spit it out."

"Well," says Bud, "we was doing some environmental disposal."

The Joker adopts a look of confusion. "Is this a euphemism for circumventing the regulations meant to keep our air and water clean for future generations? Or do I detect a more sinister connotation?"

"Actually, kind of both," says Lou.

"Well. Let's try another angle. This waste you were disposing of. Was it at one time ambulatory? Sentient? Did it yearn to breathe free?"

"Might have," says Bud.

"Not all of it," says Lou.

"Nope, not all of it," Bud agrees. "Sometimes it was just chemicals and such. Other times it was—"

"Organic compounds?" the Joker suggests.

"Once in a while, yeah," Lou says.

"I don't have to worry about some of Commissioner Piskura's boys showing up here because they followed you, do I?"

Bud and Lou fall all over themselves to discount this possibility. "We're clean, boss," Lou says. "Falcone's got enough juice with Piskura that we don't got to worry."

"And you know this how?"

"He told us so," Bud says.

It is with great effort that the Joker minimizes his sarcasm. "Right. Well, then. Tell me more about your chemical disposal. Did everything end up in the bay, or is some of it still on terra firma?"

"*Terra firma* means 'dry land,' " Lou informs Bud.

"Oh," Bud says. "Yeah, actually some of it's not too far from here."

The Joker grins. Oh yes, it's good to be in touch with old friends.

"Boys," he says. "You need a truck for your Falcone Finale anyway, right? And we need a truck here. Great. Get me one and meet back here in an hour, okay? In the meantime, I might just take another ride in this wonderful car."

* * *

It turns out to be more like two hours before the boys return, but when the Joker sees the mother lode of chemical goodies stashed in the bottom floor of what used to be a small-appliance factory in the East End, he's willing to forgive the tardiness. You've got your perchlorates, your radionuclides, your various dioxins and PCBs, your pesticides and solvents . . . and lo and behold, ladies and gentlemen, is that . . . could it be? . . . it could! Polybrominated diphenyl ethers!

"We heard Mr. Falcone was planning to torch this place pretty soon," Bud says. The Joker doesn't hear him right away because he's too busy doing a hornpipe around the PBDE drums and singing a jaunty little ditty about aromatic hydrocarbons:

"Polybrominated diphenyl ethers
You make me feel divine
Polybrominated diphenyl ethers
I cannot wait to refi-i-ne you
Into some fire-retardant novelties
You wonderful, wonderful PBDEs
Oh, don't disappoint me, let's catalyze, please
Polybrominated diphenyl ethers!"

His henchmen are looking at him like he's crazy, which he is, and which also it's good to remind them of once in a while. "Torch it?" the Joker says.

"That's the word we got," Lou says.

"Well, here's the new word. Boys," the Joker says, "all of it goes on the truck and into the hidey-hole. But take special care with this stuff right here. I've got to make some new flame-retardant Joker Juice."

While Bud and Lou load the truck, the Joker paces and thinks. Part of this is just for show, since Bud and Lou get restless if they don't see him pacing and thinking and occasionally bursting out in fits of uproarious laughter. So he does that, too. His brain, though, is as focused as a grandmaster plotting the endgame.

Bud and Lou make a run back to the hidey-hole with the first load of chemical wonderfulness. While they're gone, the Joker paces and thinks while he ad-libs new verses for his ode to aromatic hydrocarbons. The PBDEs are a happy find because he's got a little Jokerly intuition that Enfer's intentions might not all be on the up-and-up. Nobody does that kind of favor without expecting something in return.

Noise from the back part of the building catches the Joker's attention. He tiptoes with great panache across the expanse of dusty concrete, among heaps and pyramids of rusting drums and splintering crates. Oh, for an audience; but rehearsal is solitary, and key to a great performance. One must always be mindful of this, he tells himself.

He distinguishes several male voices and one female, the latter obviously distressed. Typical of the neighborhood this time of night. Bo-ring, he thinks at first . . . but then! An idea! While he's busy throwing the people of Gotham the proverbial (there's that word again) curveball where Batman is concerned, he might just be able to put a new spin on his own reputation. What fun!

A fire door on the south side of the building stands open, and just inside it a young woman is in what might delicately be termed distress. She's obviously been waylaid on her way home from work, her white shirt and black pants a dead giveaway that she waits tables at some local joint with pretensions of respectability—like maybe the Queen of Hearts, which isn't far away. Surrounding her are five punks straight out of East End Central Casting.

"Unhand that maid!" the Joker calls out as one of the punks grabs her arm. All five of them turn to look at him. The expressions on their faces crack him up.

"Damn," one of them says. "It's the Joker."

He glides up to them. "It is," he agrees. "And I'm thinking that you lads need a lesson in the proper execution of a joke. I can see that you're having some fun here with . . . I'm sorry, miss. What's your name?"

There is a silence. The punks look expectantly at their prey.

"Dear girl," the Joker prompts. "Your name?"

"Kathy," the waitress says.

The Joker looks out the fire door, seeing a slice of the street: shuttered storefronts, abandoned cars, the occasional dim glow of light from behind a door that must lead to an unlicensed bar or something equally sordid. He feels an upwelling of glee. On his right pinkie finger is a false nail, in the perfect shade of green, and perfectly doctored with his finest elixir. He has had it made for other purposes, but the true measure of a tool's usefulness is flexibility, is it not? Time for a little show.

"Kathy," he says. "What on earth is an honest girl like you doing in a place like this?"

She doesn't answer.

"Fellows," the Joker says. "What is she doing here?"

"Looking for trouble," one of them sniggers.

"That she is!" agrees the Joker. "And it appears that she's found it!"

The punks all laugh. Kathy the waitress appears to be receding within herself. Her eyes are vacant, and her lips move slightly as if she's constantly about to say something but doesn't know what it might be.

The Joker spreads his arms and says, "I've been thinking about Shakespeare today. All the world's a stage, and we're all players, and we're going to stage a little drama. You," he says to the first punk who recognized him. "How about you get over next to our Kathy and, hm, get one of your hands in her hair. Perfect; wait. Let me fix this one thing."

A little scratch from the nail and the punk stiffens, his face stretching into a beautiful grimace. "Grand!" the Joker says. He takes a step away from Kathy and taps his chin thoughtfully. "Now for the rest of you . . ."

They almost get away. But the Joker is not just quick of wit, oh no, he is quick quick quick with the flick flick flick of his nail, and in a jiffy he has arranged a wonderful tableau, at the center of which stands dear Kathy, so very lucky. Around her he has arranged the five stiffening reprobates in attitudes of adoration. Two of them kneel, one raises his arms in supplication; two more fight each other for the right to touch her hand.

"Why so quiet, Kathy my love?" the Joker croons.

Kathy does not answer.

"Why, you're not afraid I'm going to indulge my baser impulses, are you?" The Joker draws himself up in mock indignation. "Goodness, no! I am your guardian angel."

Kathy's eyes are wide, her mouth a little open. She is

breathing slow and shallow, and her pulse is like a rabbit's. Gently, the Joker draws the nail along the line of her jaw. "Think of me sometimes, won't you?" he asks. "Dear catatonic Kathy, please think of me when you remember this day."

16

July 30, 10:18 PM

Since early afternoon, when the doctor came and went after pronouncing Alfred overworked and underappreciated but basically sound given his advancing years, Bruce has sat in his study trying to ask himself some questions whose answers he is certain he won't want to hear. He's unfamiliar with being indecisive, doesn't like feeling that way, and is more than a little disturbed that he's sitting in his study telling himself he shouldn't be sitting in his study. Get up, he tells himself, and he does, but instead of doing what needs to be done—which is, in order: going downstairs and putting together a new set of gear; calling Lucius Fox to set up a private consultation to replace certain items that now only exist in the Wayne Enterprises research wing; and setting about the reclamation of his gear, not to mention his reputation—he stands there, making lists instead of taking action.

Then there's the matter of settling the Joker problem. Permanently.

Every rule has an exception, Bruce thinks. The Joker is mine. He doesn't like the direction this train of thought leads him in, but before he can make good decisions he needs to figure out exactly what he's thinking. The problem is that he's thinking about the Joker as a way of avoiding a genuine confrontation with the set of issues raised by Alfred's abduction.

So: strip away the irrelevant and the illusory.

Night has fallen. It's time to be moving. He walks down the hall, down the stairs, through the kitchen, feeling the familiarity of Wayne Manor like a mild sedative. Alfred is sleeping upstairs. He seemed fine when Bruce got him back into the house, but no man in history has had a stiffer upper lip than Alfred Pennyworth, and thinking about this stoicism has Bruce wondering just how often he has taken Alfred's reliable, wise constancy for granted. That question in turn leads Bruce to the uncomfortable knowledge that the circumstances of his birth have let him take a great deal for granted—including the *Wanderjahre* that taught him so much in the dojos and mountain citadels of the Himalayas. The truth is that Gotham City is rife with orphans, and that Bruce Wayne's pain is far from unique. What *does* make his circumstance unique, the inherited wealth of Wayne Enterprises, also set him on the course he has taken; a poorer version of Bruce Wayne might well have grown up more like Joe Chill than Bruce would like to admit.

Admit it, then. Admit it and go down the elevator that Wayne money bought into the subterranean laboratory that Wayne money bought and make sure that nothing like this ever happens to Alfred again. That's what Bruce is thinking as he taps the elevator button, and he focuses on the thought, holds it in front of him like a diamond that he's examining for flaws. He finds none. It does nobody any good for Bruce Wayne to feel guilty about his wealth; it might do a great number of people a great deal of harm for Bruce Wayne to let guilt interfere with his ability to make a difference in the safety and morale of Gotham City. He has taken Alfred for granted, there's no denying it. He acknowledges this, owns it, vows never to repeat it . . . and already the elevator door is opening onto the work-in-progress, the laboratory that will be his retreat, his nerve center, his library and garage and proving ground.

He gets to work.

First he retrofits a spare suit, incorporating some of the changes he made in the latest redesign. He's jury-rigging, but it'll have to work until he can get in touch with Lucius Fox, and that will have to wait until Bruce is comfortable that when the time comes for him to leave the cave tonight he will be outfitted as well as he can be. Where the new suit has layered-in carbon micro-fiber armor, he's settling for old-fashioned Kevlar; the cape he'll be using stiffens only along a series of spines, which gives a truer bat-wing effect but isn't nearly as flexible and multipurpose as the smart fabric that makes up the new one.

The one the Joker has.

Bruce redoubles his efforts. Using an old utility belt, sent into semi-retirement because three of the compart-ments are perforated by buckshot holes, he compiles an arsenal of obsolete Batman gear. He's still missing the bat-shaped shuriken, and the Joker has gotten away with all of his smoke canisters. The first problem is solved by firing up the lathe and machining a new batch of throwing stars (throwing bats, Bruce supposes, but he can't think of them that way); the second, by improvis-ing with the tiny gas cylinders that power his grappling

hooks. He likes the grapple design and has seen no reason to improve on it recently, which is good since it means
he's more or less by accident acquired a large surplus of
the cylinders. Drained of their pressurized propellant,
they are fairly easily refilled with good old-fashioned
sugar plus saltpeter for the smoke, plus a little flash
powder to ignite the mixture and a friction-ignition fuse
built into the cap. It's not high-tech, but it'll work. It'll
work better when Bruce has some potassium perman-
ganate to stir into the flash powder, but that's a question
for another day. Tonight the important thing is to get
back out onto the streets, and to banish self-questioning
by the tried-and-true method of pure action. He's ready.
Even if the marathon manhunt following the Arkham
fire hadn't gotten his juices flowing, the insult of the
Joker finding and defiling his home would have put him
on the warpath. And that's not even considering Alfred.

His one stroke of luck during the past twenty-four
hours has been the Joker's choice to spare the lab facilities and electronic equipment. While he works, Bruce
has been listening to the Gotham City PD radio bands;
when he hears that there have been sightings of a "Batman" on the daylight streets of Gotham, he isn't surprised. When he hears that this "Batman" has killed a
pedestrian—and right across from Finnigan's, maybe
the most self-identified cop bar in all of Gotham City—
he is surprised. Also charged with an electric fury born
of pride in the transformation he has wrought in himself, as well as sadness at the murder of an innocent. He
channels it all into renewed determination. Now he is
fighting for the family of Merilee St. Pierre. He always
was, in the same abstract kind of way that he has always
fought for the kids who were like him save for the ab-

sence of a family fortune; now all of it is becoming more real. There are faces in Gotham City, real individuals that need to be saved and if not saved, remembered. Avenged. One of them is Merilee St. Pierre. He needs to keep their faces in front of him, lest he slip into the easy trap of fighting solely for ideals. I do fight for ideals, Bruce acknowledges. But I also fight for people.

And one of those people, he thinks, is himself.

So now that the GCPD is looking for Batman, his job has become that much more complicated. The men in blue have always—even the ones not so corrupt and/or cynical that they view him as an active enemy—viewed Batman with some ambivalence, and now that Merilee St. Pierre is dead the average Gotham City cop is going to be that much more likely to view Batman as just one more of the costumed crazies who make his life more difficult than it really needs to be. I won't be surprised, Bruce thinks, if some of them just start taking shots at me on sight. That's the department culture, after all; three years ago the GCPD turned the Robinson Park demonstrations, which involved a bunch of artists yammering about rent control, into a mini Tiananmen Square. It's not even news anymore when one of them kills a kid fleeing down a random street with a pocketful of shoplifted candy.

Well, Bruce takes that back. It is starting to be news again, and at least part of that is because of him. Because of Batman. If he has done nothing else, he has made casual murder newsworthy again, even when the victim isn't particularly wealthy or promising or beautiful. All of which, apparently, Merilee St. Pierre was, which makes him that much more determined to expunge this blot on his record.

He puts part of his mind to work on the problem of finding both the Joker and this Enfer character, and the rest he dedicates to finishing up a viable second-tier set of Batman gear. Without the car, there's the problem of getting from Wayne Manor to the parts of Gotham City where his quarry roams. Bruce dresses slowly, feeling Batman gradually engulf his psyche the way the suit and cape encase his body. When he is done, he clips a light to the seam where the cape fastens to the body of the costume. If the Joker could get from Gotham City to here through the caves, then Batman can reverse that path.

Bruce leaves himself behind and disappears into the caves beyond the cave.

ROGUE
A JITTERY GOTHAM CITY
LOOKS ASKANCE AT ITS DARK KNIGHT
Vicki Vale, *Gotham Gazette*

The family of Merilee St. Pierre wants justice. It's a poor substitute for having their vivacious 27-year-old daughter back, but a maniac on Cowan Street made sure that Merilee is gone for good.

The maniac's name?

No one knows, but everyone calls him the Batman.

"I rooted for Batman as hard as everyone, you know, for cleaning the city up," says Merilee's grieving fiancé, Brian Sylvester. "But now, if he can do this . . ."

Merilee St. Pierre was jogging with her dog Chanel across Cowan the day before yesterday. She had the green light, not just on the street but in life. A new job as a junior analyst at Firebird Securities, a new engagement ring from her high school sweetheart Sylvester, and by all accounts a new perspective on life after a rocky period following the death of her beloved brother Justin.

All of that changed yesterday when the armored car widely known as the Batmobile came around the corner, ran her down, and burned rubber away from the scene as if the driver hadn't even noticed.

"If he can do this," Brian Sylvester goes on, "then he wasn't who I thought he was."

That sentiment echoes through the minds of many Gothamites, especially in the wake of the apparent rescue of an East End woman from a gang of would-be attackers . . . by the Joker. Kathy Watts, 29, has given no public statement since a resident of the neighborhood noticed suspicious activity in the abandoned factory where Watts was subsequently found. She was taken to East End Receiving Hospital for treatment.

Five bodies were recovered at the scene, each bearing the telltale rictus and pallid skin of poisoning with what is popularly known as Joker Juice. "It's a real puzzle," admits Gotham City police spokeswoman Erin McNamara. "We're not accustomed to the Joker acting in the public interest."

McNamara cautioned, however, that all of the facts in the case are not yet clear. "As we all know," she said at a press conference this morning, "things are rarely as they seem where the Joker is concerned."

Watts's mother, Emilia Fonseca, begs to differ. "I don't care what he's done in the past," she said by phone from her daughter's hospital bedside. "He saved my baby. He's all right in my book."

These recent uncharacteristic actions by two of Gotham City's most famous (or perhaps infamous) outlaws have sown uncertainty among a populace that, whatever other problems it might have had, has always been able to count on Batman . . . and, in a different way, on the Joker.

"When you know who the bad guys are, that's one thing. But this, what are you supposed to do?" asks Brian Sylvester.

The same question is being asked all over a jittery Gotham City today.

17

July 31, 9:30 AM

Gordon understands that Gotham City fire chief Ed Coover has problems. He even understands why Chief Coover has focused most of his anger on the GCPD for failing to catch Enfer, who continues to set booby traps for firefighters all over the city. What he doesn't understand is why Chief Coover was sent to him. The paranoid part of his mind—which has gotten stronger during his tenure in the GCPD—wonders if someone sent Coover his way because they're hoping that Gordon will say something about Batman, who after this Merilee St. Pierre debacle is squarely back in the sights of the GCPD rank and file. Could be they're setting me up, Gordon thinks as he waits for Chief Coover to get his corn-fed bulk settled in Gordon's office. Could be they just need me to let slip that I talk to Batman, and Internal Affairs will ring me up on conduct unbecoming.

Could be I stopped caring about that problem a long time ago, except insofar as it gets in the way of my ability to do my job.

"Meaning no disrespect, Captain," Chief Coover says,

"but I'm a bit puzzled that a meeting of this significance is taking place without any higher-ranking police department personnel."

Meaning he's annoyed at being foisted off on a captain, or at least pretending to be annoyed. Gordon finds it difficult to proceed because he doesn't know yet which game he's supposed to be playing.

"I've lost more than a dozen firefighters," Chief Coover goes on. "What is your department doing about it?"

"I'm not in a position to speak for the department," Gordon begins.

Coover cuts him off. "That is exactly the position you are in. This meeting has put you there, and I expect to leave this meeting with some kind of firm plan to deal with this menace."

The first part of the game becomes apparent to Gordon. "Chief Coover," he says, "the police department extends its sympathies for your loss. We're doing everything we can to track down this Enfer. I'm sure I don't need to remind you that he's killed five cops?"

"I'm not interested in scorekeeping, Captain."

Except for when the score is in your favor, Gordon thinks. It's also true that all five of the cops Enfer has torched so far were dirty, and deep down inside part of him is glad they're gone; not glad they're dead, but glad they're not tainting his badge by association anymore. "I mention it only to point out that we have as much reason to want Enfer off the streets as you do, and that goal will be realized that much sooner if we cooperate instead of laying the groundwork for assessing blame later. Can we agree on that?"

Coover leans back in his chair. Gordon can't decide

whether the fire chief is making a show of consideration, or whether he really has something to say and is figuring out how to proceed. "I'm listening," Coover says, after some time.

"Good. Me, too. So we have a problem, which is that there is a serial arsonist with access to sophisticated explosive and incendiary devices. He apparently has a grudge against firefighters, which has led some of our investigators to wonder if he either was a member of the department at one time or tried to join and was rejected. It might help if we could talk about any internal problems you've had with your people setting fires."

There. He's said it. The phenomenon isn't that uncommon. Both firefighters and arsonists like to spend time around fires, and the number of documented cases of firefighters setting fires—either to look heroic when they rescue people, or for less obvious reasons—is higher than any fire department wants to admit. Gordon is also fairly certain that it happens more than is reported. He can easily imagine a department quietly cashiering a member found to have been doing this, or even just suspected of it. He's already looked through the GCPD database of arson cases and has people running them down, but he doesn't expect to learn anything from them except that Gotham City has an extra allotment of firebugs just like it has more of every other kind of deviant.

While Gordon has been lost in his thoughts, Coover has been pinning him with a stare meant to convey the impression that Gordon has overstepped some line of propriety. "I don't like your implication, Captain Gordon," Coover says.

"I don't like the implication, either, Chief. Enfer clearly has a grudge against your department, though, and the scenario I outlined is the most likely reason for that, whether either of us likes it or not. If we're going to cooperate, that will start with sharing information."

Still frowning, Coover says, "I'll see what I can come up with. But I'm telling you ahead of time, I think you're barking up the wrong tree. What we really need to worry about isn't psychology, or profiling, or whatever your brain trust calls it. Gotham City needs your department to do its job and catch this maniac."

"True enough," Gordon says. "Since we're on the topic, I think I was told that you had some ideas about how to do this."

This is the part of the conversation that he's looking forward to the least. The last thing in the world Gordon needs is advice about police work from a political hack like Ed Coover, but he knows he's going to get it, so he might as well get it over with.

Coover leans forward. "What you should do—what we should do—is trap the son of a bitch like he's been trapping us."

What a revelation, Gordon thinks. "Okay," he says, keeping derision out of his voice. "How?"

Warming to the topic, Coover leans his elbows on Gordon's desk. He's been thinking about this for a while, Gordon thinks. Or else—adds the paranoid part of his mind—someone told him to pitch the idea.

"What if we get someone to set fires, and we publicize that there's a copycat?" Coover says. "This guy's obviously some kind of egomaniac. That'll bring him right out of the woodwork."

"It might," Gordon says, although he's not sure how it would be obvious that Enfer was out of the woodwork. What might he do differently? Maybe he'd redirect some of his attention away from firefighters and toward the copycat.

That still doesn't address the problem of why Enfer sprang the Joker from Arkham, though. Gordon doesn't want to bring that part of the equation up with Coover, but in truth it's the one that has him worried more than anything else. He had a quiet conversation with Angela Rodriquez about it—one of those conversations that yielded no immediate result beyond an initial cracking of loyalty on Rodriquez's part. Gordon saw it happen and backed off right away. He has a feeling he got to her, and now he'll have to see how it pays off.

"And then you can nail him," Coover says vehemently, bringing Gordon back to the present. "If there's this sudden series of copycat fires, he'll start hanging around incognito to watch them. Sooner or later, he'll give himself away, and then you can take him out."

Something about the last phrase leaves Gordon with no doubt about what Coover would really like to see happen to Enfer. Sometimes he wonders why anyone in Gotham City even pretends to care about the rule of law. As far as the proposal is concerned, he's already wondering how they can keep it away from the reporters, who are all over the Enfer story—although some of them are distracted by Merilee St. Pierre.

Just like that, it comes together. If I get Batman involved, Gordon thinks, this might just work. And God knows Batman could use a little PR boost right now. Whatever the truth is about the St. Pierre killing—and Gordon can't for the life of him believe that Batman would casually mow down a pedestrian—it has utterly ruined Batman's image. This is a problem not just for Batman but for Gotham

City as a whole, since the city had just started to believe in him, believe that someone was looking out for them.

"I'll look into this, Chief Coover," Gordon says, and stands. They shake hands.

"I'll be hearing from you soon," Coover says. When Gordon doesn't answer, the fire chief walks out of Gordon's office without shutting the door.

Gordon sits back at his desk and shuffles through files without looking at them, just to give his hands something to do. He wants a cigarette and sublimates the craving into a momentary storm of desk cleaning. When that passes, he sits again. Will it work? They'll need to identify buildings they can safely burn, and anytime a building burns, firefighters are in danger. Coover is taking a big risk with his own people, but it might be the right thing to do if it reels Enfer in without the deaths of any more firefighters. Or cops.

What it means is that he has to get in touch with Batman, which is even more risky now than it was before Merilee St. Pierre. Still, Gordon doesn't see what else he can do. He opens his desk drawer and peels a piece of paper off the underside of the desktop. Over by the university there's a wired coffee shop whose owner owes Gordon a favor because Gordon once got an assistant DA to take it easy on the owner's kid when the kid was up on an iffy possession with intent; he can send a message anonymously there.

He hopes Batman will answer soon, but he's also dreading the answer, because in Gordon's worst nightmares the answer will include a confession about Merilee St. Pierre, and that would mean that the next time Gordon saw Batman they would no longer be tacit allies. I don't want to live in a Gotham City where Batman is just another criminal, Gordon thinks. Even if it was a mistake, Merilee St. Pierre is dead. Someone has to answer for that.

If that someone is Batman, so be it. But that'll be the last arrest he ever makes in this town.

CRANE BLAMES JOKER FOR ARKHAM BLAZE
Gillian O'Connor, *Gotham Globe*

Arkham Asylum director Dr. Jonathan Crane, under increasing public pressure due to his delayed response to questions about which Arkham inmates survived Tuesday's fire, today claimed to have "conclusive proof" that the Joker was "directly responsible" for the conflagration. Crane also suggested that the Joker had a hand in the devastating sequence of fires that swept through Gotham City after the Arkham fire. Despite this, Crane would not rule out the possibility that the Joker died in the fire, possibly after setting in motion a plan that included external assistance.

Accompanied by his lawyer, Kyle Whisler, Crane expressed sympathy for the families of those killed in the fires and said he and his staff were doing "everything humanly possible to expedite the release of information about losses at our institution."

Speculation about responsibility for the fires has been widespread but inconclusive. Numerous reports of a suspicious figure in a modified firefighter's uniform have sparked concern that a new villain has appeared in Gotham City, especially in the wake of the deaths of more than a dozen firefighters during the past week. Other city officials have pointed to the arrangement of the post-Arkham fires, which spelled out a large HAHA across the city's midsection, as clear evidence that the Joker was involved.

Crane refused to address these questions directly, saying only that he and his staff were "processing important information" in consultation with Gotham City police and fire investigators.

If the Joker was indeed responsible for these fires, said Ben Ridley of the Trigate Citizens Alliance, his organization would be vindicated in its long-term concerns regarding security at the institution. "If the Joker can plan to burn down half the city from his cell, what's the point of him being in the cell in the first place?" Ridley asked Crane at today's press conference.

Crane refused to answer the question, and Gotham City police escorted Ridley from the room after he refused to leave on his own.

GCPD spokesmen refused to comment on Dr. Crane's statements. Captain James Gordon has publicly blasted Crane in recent days for not releasing information sooner. Today, however, department spokeswoman Erin McNamara remained silent on both Gordon, whose outspoken nature has been a source of embarrassment to the department before, and Crane's actions.

McNamara also refused to elaborate on reports that as many as a dozen of Arkham's inmates may still be at large. . . .

18

July 31, 6:35 PM

Okay, so I'm moody, Enfer thinks. It's only natural.

Everyone wants credit for what they've done, or blame. Enfer isn't any different. He spent weeks planning the Arkham job and the fiery joke that followed, and goddammit, he wants everyone to know he did it. About a dozen times today he's come close to picking up the phone and telling someone at the *Globe* or the *Gazette* that the Joker had nothing to do with any of it.

So who did, he imagines the reporter—who in this scenario is always Vicki Vale—on the other end of the phone line saying.

Me. Me. I did it. Me.

And who are you?

You can call me Enfer.

Then he would quote one of the poet's beautiful lines: *The city trembles. Cries and smoke and flames . . .*

Of course he can't do that. But seriously. Crane claiming that the Joker is responsible? He must be just trying to get a rise out of me, Enfer thinks.

Nuance has never been Enfer's strong suit. He is too

easily drawn into internal death spirals of confusion and paradox when he tries to figure out why other people do what they do. Often it's more than he can handle to figure out why *he* does what he does, which is why he has been happy this last year. Know thyself, and all that. It's taken a lot of energy and discipline for him to understand himself and adhere to that understanding. Now, with Crane playing some kind of game, and the Joker not reciprocating, Enfer is confused, and confusion makes him want to burn.

Soon enough. He's got a plan for his Annunciation that will make HAHA look like the striking of a match. The Arkham fire has made this easier because the at-large inmates are occupying the police; also, because he's nailed a few of his former brothers, more police manpower is drained away to increased patrols around Gotham City fire stations. This is a mixed blessing for his big plan, since he needs to get at fire stations to make it work, but Enfer is nothing if not innovative. Once the shipment arrives (if it ever arrives; high on Enfer's list of things he'd like to torch is a particular shipping company owned by a particular Gotham City mobster), he'll find a way. First, though, he needs to clarify his thinking.

One thing he doesn't get is why Crane hasn't thrown him to the wolves yet. Crane knows who set the fires, and Enfer knows that the doctor isn't happy about Enfer's departure from the plan they put together. He would have expected Crane to do everything but give the GCPD all of his former addresses. Instead, not a word.

He still wants something from me, Enfer thinks.

What could that thing be? If Crane still wants Enfer to take care of Batman, that's no problem. On that topic they have no disagreement.

Another thing that's started to bug him is the fact that he hasn't gotten any kind of message from the Joker. If someone had done for me what I did for him, Enfer thinks, I would definitely get in touch. It's just common courtesy.

Could it be that the Joker *wants* people to think he did it? The ingratitude of that would be amazing, but Enfer has to suppose it's possible. Not everyone has the kind of manners they should. Also, it's possible that he's gotten a signal and missed it, but Enfer doesn't think that's likely; after all, he wrote his greeting across half a mile of Gotham City, and it seems like the Joker would respond in kind.

People need to start being a lot less goddamn mysterious about their agendas, Enfer thinks. Clarity of thought and expression, that's what makes for good communications, good human relations.

There must be some way to send a bulletproof message that will leave no doubt as to both sender and intended recipient. Enfer ponders this while he rewires one of the prostheses that isn't spraying correctly. By the time he has that done, he's hungry, and he also has a bit of an idea. He considers it and finds it good. It's witty, which the Joker will appreciate, and it's also decisive. There will be no way in the world to misinterpret it. If the Joker doesn't respond, his intentions will be clear. That would be sad, but Enfer's been sad before. He can handle it.

With any luck, he won't have to. His mother always

said he had a temper, and truth be told the last two years have done nothing to improve it. If the Joker turns out to be the kind of person who won't reciprocate when he has been done a rather large favor, Enfer is afraid he will be very angry for quite some time. It would be nice to avoid that, and he hopes his next set of signals will accomplish that goal.

So what he needs now is a fistful of Cherry Bombs, and maybe a couple of other toys. He looks out the single window and sees that it's dusk. The streetlights are on, and the sky is clear. Even if it were about to rain, he would still head out, but the summer drought is making his work that much more pleasurable. In another hour or so he'll be able to get down to business.

His first target—or, the way he's thinking of it, the first word of the greeting card he's sending the Joker—is Arty McGee's World of Novelties. It's a student institution, having occupied a four-story brick building a block east of the Gotham University campus since 1911. At various times during its history Arty McGee's has maintained sidelines in office supplies, university-themed T-shirts, and whatever else struck the most recent McGee proprietor as worth taking a flier on. In recent years they've discovered first the catalog business and then the world of online commerce, so now it's all novelties. You want fake dogshit, handshake buzzers, whoopee cushions . . . you'll find them there. You'll also find coffin-shaped boxes containing candies shaped like all of the various parts of the human body, rubber animals of every description, various items that burn or smoke or leap or jump or stink. Enfer has loved the place since he was a kid, but this is the time to make a statement. He can't let sentimentality enter into this particular equation.

Besides, he's not really that kid anymore.

He comes in the back door and goes down through a door marked EMPLOYEES ONLY. McGee's basement is stuffed to bursting with cardboard and, he assumes, flammable plastics. One little spark down here is all it will take, really, but Enfer isn't in the mood to let things take their natural course. He sets a timer on a Cherry Bomb, giving it ten minutes. On his way back up the stairs, he bumps into a multiply tattooed and pierced employee. The interaction is almost without incident, but after Enfer says, "Sorry, took a wrong turn," the employee eyeballs his costume and gets a look on her face. He doesn't bother trying to talk his way out of it; he punches her hard right on the hinge of the jaw and she goes down without a sound, bouncing off the wall right into his arms. He tosses her into a fireman's carry and leaves her leaning against the back door.

On the first floor he leaves a Cherry Bomb in an empty slot in a display of books about magic tricks. That one's set for eight minutes. On the second floor he tries on a dunce cap, then leaves a Cherry Bomb in it: six minutes. On the third floor he just rolls one under a counter piled high with T-shirts: four minutes. On the fourth floor he excuses himself when he sees that he's looking at offices. Most of McGee's management and white-collar staff has gone home, so he finds an unlocked office and sets his last Cherry Bomb in an ashtray bearing a sentimental Christ and the words JESUS HATES IT WHEN YOU SMOKE.

He's out the door seven minutes after he walked in.

When the first Cherry Bomb goes off, he's three blocks away, headed down a side street toward Robinson Park. By the time the last one goes off, he's just gotten to the trail that encircles the reservoir. He climbs a little rise overlooking the Finger River and uses the vantage point to observe his handiwork. The view isn't ideal, but Arty McGee's is burning like a signal flare, that much is obvious.

One down, three to go.

From the front, the Laughing Monkey looks like it's barely big enough to fit a wooden Indian, but Enfer knows from previous visits that the width of the storefront conceals an interior space that goes on for what seems like miles. This being Chinatown, everything is open all the time, and Enfer takes the direct approach. He walks in with an armed Cherry Bomb and throws it directly through the one-way glass panel at the back of the store. For a moment, through the curtain of falling glass, he sees the pop-eyed expression on the store employee watching for shoplifters. Then he's gone back out the door, counting backward from thirty until he hears the muffled thump of the Cherry Bomb going off.

Two down, two to go.

Chinatown's other novelty store, Glory Laugh, specializes in costumes as well, so Enfer doesn't draw a second look from anyone inside. Not with the eye-catching assortment of live-action role-playing aficionados, drag queens, and the occasional beleaguered community theater costume designer already cramming the floor space. To stay unobtrusive, he looks at a few costumes, thinking he'd like to incorporate something from the poet in his garb. If only poets were more distinctive dressers; you couldn't make an identity from a beret and a carelessly held hand-rolled cigarette.

Enfer wonders if the fires at McGee's and the Monkey have gotten GCPD thinking they should have a look at the city's other purveyors of gags. Probably not; Gotham City's Finest do not appear to be a bunch of deep thinkers. Anyway, he's not going to worry about it. He can take care of them if they do show up.

In his pocket is a Cherry Bomb set for thirty minutes. He rolls it around in his palm, thinking he'd really like a symbolic place to put this one. Not that anyone will ever notice, but it will make him feel better, more fully realized, to have done it. So he looks around, and when he sees the pair of clown shoes sticking out from under a low shelf he thinks, Perfect.

That's the kind of little grace note that makes the difference, he's telling himself as he heads down Corvallis Street to the monorail station. This next part of the evening will be the most fun by far.

Three down, one to go.

At about the time Glory Laugh is bound for glory, Enfer is stepping off the monorail at the Diamond District station, maybe two hundred yards from his next stop: the WayneTowne Mall. The ground floor of Wayne Enterprises was redone and expanded last year as part of an urban-revitalization project—funded of course by Bruce Wayne, or one of his trusts or charities or whatever—and now the WayneTowne Mall covers what was once a windswept and lifeless expanse of concrete. It's been a good thing for the city. Enfer is wearing socks he bought there. He paid too much for them, but he remembers thinking that was okay because it was worth it once in a while just to feel glitzy for a few minutes. Like the poet, he has an appreciation for fine things.

Ah, the poet. The monorail has put lines into his head: *The train had slowed down / And in the perpetual screeching of wheels I heard / The insane sobbing and screaming / Of an eternal liturgy . . .*

Fire. The voice of fire, the eternal liturgy sung by the universe to its maker. In his excitement Enfer's heart has started to pound, and he can smell himself. If he snapped his fingers right now, he'd get little blossoms of flame. He's tempted, but there's business to do.

One of the stores in WayneTowne is a national novelty chain called Diamond Dooley's. It's actually bigger than Arty McGee's, but what it gains in size it more than trades back in atmosphere. Diamond Dooley's appears to have been designed on the principle that the more a novelty store looks like a surgical ward, the more novel the novelties will look. Enfer is going to need to do some fairly aggressive seeding here if he wants to get any kind of result.

As he walks in the front door, an announcement over the store intercom states that Diamond Dooley's will be closing in fifteen minutes. Plenty of time, Enfer thinks. He's got eight more Cherry Bombs.

"Costume party," he says to a teenager stocking shelves. "Where can I find a rubber ax?"

"Believe we might have some in aisle seven," the kid says without making a move to escort Enfer, who walks off in search of aisle seven feeling aggrieved by the lack of customer service at these national chains. "With all of the medieval stuff," the kid calls after him.

Enfer's mood shift has something to do with not being able to watch his handiwork at the other sites. He sure would have liked to see Arty McGee's go up, and he'll be surprised if the Laughing Monkey fire doesn't leave the whole block in ashes. And this job won't be as spectacular as either. Too many streetlights, building lights, neon signs, animated billboards, and all kinds of other electronic eye pollution. How the hell do people stand this?

The fun's gone out of the errand, just like that. Enfer moves into professional mode, distributes the eight Cherry Bombs with emotionless efficiency, and gets the hell out. If the Joker doesn't get that message, then either the Joker isn't nearly as smart as Enfer has given him credit for or the Joker is utterly lacking in social skills. Neither possibility gives Enfer any joy. He sublimates his foul mood by molding a little bit of what he likes to call Go-Stuf around each of the Cherry Bombs before positioning them. That'll give his traitorous former brothers in the FD something to occupy their time.

He gets to the front of the store and realizes someone is talking to him. "Didn't find the ax?" It's the kid he saw on the way in.

"Never mind," he starts to say, but in a fit of helpfulness the kid says, "Hang on a sec," and jogs off to aisle 7. He's back ninety seconds later with, sure enough, a four-foot ax with a black plastic handle and silver-and-red blade and pick.

So this is the kind of night it's going to be, Enfer thinks. You can't even trust surly adolescents to stay surly. What that might portend for the Joker's reaction to Enfer's outreach, he doesn't know, but he's got a feeling it isn't good. He thanks the kid, pays for the ax, and is getting back on the monorail to make the northern swing toward Old Gotham when the Cherry Bombs start to spray Go-Stuf all over the interior of Diamond Dooley's.

BAT-TERY WITH A MOTOR VEHICLE
Gillian O'Connor, *Gotham Globe*

After 48 hours of hit-and-run crashes involving the Bat-mobile, Gotham City authorities today stepped up patrols on the city's main thoroughfares and began installing traffic-light cameras in an effort to record the comings and goings of Gotham City's newest serial traffic offender. Three people have been killed and six injured in five separate incidents in-volving the Batmobile since the hit-and-run death of Merilee St. Pierre, whose funeral yesterday attracted hundreds of mourners including Mayor Horatio Hill and police commis-sioner Eric Piskura.

"Batman is clearly now more of a menace to the public safety than he ever was a benefit to the public order," the mayor declared at a post-funeral press conference. "These deaths are ample evidence that the vigilante mentality knows no loyalty to the rule of law and knows no value except the pursuit of the next vendetta. Citizens of Gotham City, I en-treat you: if you know anything about Batman's where-abouts, or about his identity under the mask and cape, we have set up an anonymous tip line. Please use it."

One result of Batman's vehicular depredations is in-creased ridership on the city's monorail and bus systems. Commissioner of Public Transportation Felix Dyk said mass-transit use is up nearly 25 percent, although he specu-lated that part of the increase was due to traffic tie-ups caused by the numerous police roadblocks and other security measures.

"I don't mean to be flip," he said, "but the harder it is for people to get where they need to go, the more likely they are to use public transportation and the less likely they are to be in the path of the Batmobile."

Rumors have circulated that city hall is considering a proposal to position rocket batteries on some city buildings, but officials vehemently denied any such plan, pointing out that it would require federal approval. . . .

19

August 1, 12:01 AM

"Well, I have *got* to do something about this, don't I?" the Joker is saying to Batman as he watches half a block of Corvallis Street burn. "I don't get down to China-town much anymore, but when I was a boy I spent many a fond afternoon at Glory Laugh, and now this upstart firebug has gone and carbonized it. Enfer. Puh-leeze. Why not just name yourself H-E-double-hockey-sticks, as me sainted mother used to say?"

He looks over his shoulder. Batman is watching the fire, too, but the Joker isn't dumb enough to think that the Caped Crusader isn't also keeping an eye on him. Waiting, not to put too fine a point on it, for him to make a mistake, at which point Batman will pounce like a mongoose.

The Joker, in his borrowed Bat-regalia, is sitting on the edge of a rooftop down the block from the now for-mer location of Glory Laugh. His feet dangle over sixty or seventy feet of sooty Gotham City air, below which is the gum- and scum-stained sidewalk of Corvallis Street. Batman could rear back and kick the Joker right off the edge of the roof, which action would result in a great deal of force being applied to fragile parts of the Joker's body, possibly inducing death. But he won't, because of Wally Gilroy.

"I mean, really," the Joker goes on. "What's with the patina, the veneer, the filigree, of Continental respectability? This is America, isn't it? I should think we'd have no patience with this kind of faux-Europhile posing. What's your take?"

Batman is silent.

"Oh, don't just hold it all in. You're so repressed. Talk, palaver, converse! You'll feel so much better. I always do. And please, let's not let the little fact of Wally Gilroy here interfere with the free play of your emotions. You did tell me that Gilroy was your last name, right, Wally?"

The seven-year-old boy sitting in the Joker's lap nods. His feet, like the Joker's, dangle in space.

"Hand me the boy, and you get a free pass tonight," Batman says.

The Joker smiles. Well, he's almost always smiling, but this one is genuinely sentimental. "You mean it, don't you? You really would feel duty-bound to adhere to your promise if I handed this boy over. It's beautiful. I'm glad the whole world isn't like that, but it's wonderful that you are. Admirable. But no, I believe Wally Gilroy and I will continue our snuggle. And you and I will continue our talk. Where were we? Ah. This Enfer person. What can he be up to? The HAHA was a nice gesture, sure, but was the point of springing me out of Arkham so he could then destroy all of my favorite places? Some favor."

Silence falls. The Joker has talked himself out for the

moment, and he's also distracted by the chaotic beauty of the street scene below. Flashing lights, arcs of water, billowing clouds of smoke and steam . . .

"It's not really that hard to understand why he would find this so captivating," he says. "Not just the fire, but everything that comes with it. What a show!"

"People died in there," Batman says.

"I know," the Joker sighs. "And poor you, sitting here talking to me when you could have been rescuing them. It must have been difficult. But Wally Gilroy is worth it. Aren't you, Wally?"

Wally doesn't say anything. The Joker gives him a little poke with the long green fake fingernail he put to such theatrical and fulfilling use in the old warehouse. He hasn't even had to tell Wally—or Batman—that the tip of the fingernail is, shall we say, doctored. In this instance his reputation has preceded him. Wally gasps at the touch of the fingernail.

"Aren't you worth it, Wally?" the Joker prompts.

"Yes." Wally's voice is barely audible.

"See, Wally thinks he's worth it," the Joker tells Batman. "The lives of children are precious, don't you think? Certainly more so than the lives of adults grubbing out a dead-end existence in a place like this. Wally's got potential. Not much of that down there. So you've done the right thing, my worthy adversary. Don't lose sleep over that."

Batman is silent.

"You know," the Joker says, "it's not too much to ask that you participate in the conversation."

Batman is silent.

"Fine," the Joker says. "Maybe a change of subject is called for. Say! That's some car you have. I sure have enjoyed cruising around." He lifts the cape and lets it drop. "Nice suit, too. Oh, and is your butler all right?"

"Yes."

"Glad to hear it."

"I'm sure you are."

"It's true. The joke works either way, but I sort of took a shine to that old geezer. Do you know, he actually shot at me? Missed, of course, but you have to admire the gumption. But back to the car. How are you getting around these days?"

"Enjoy the car while you have it," Batman says. "It won't be for too much longer. Same goes for the suit."

"Ah, there's the Dark Knight," the Joker says with delight. He claps his hands, and Wally flinches at the sound. "I want you to know that the thing with the dog walker was an accident."

"Her name was Merilee St. Pierre," Batman says.

"Okay. The thing with Merilee St. Pierre was an accident. A happy accident, though. I was inspired to do it again, and again, and again. Never gets old."

One of the engines on Corvallis Street turns its lights off and growls away in a belch of unburned diesel smoke. Apparently things are winding down. Police cars, marked and unmarked, have arrived. "Oh boy, forensics time," the Joker says. "Wally, do you like forensics?"

"Yes," Wally whispers.

"Good boy. I like forensics, too. And Batman is a positive maniac for forensics. I saw that in his laboratory. He's got a very nice laboratory in a cave. That's where bats live, in caves. Except the ones who live in barns or trees or abandoned warehouses or freeway underpasses. But mostly caves. Isn't that right, Wally?"

"Yes," Wally whispers again.

"Do you want to be a fireman when you grow up, Wally?"

"No," Wally says.

"What do you want to be?"

"I want to be a baseball player."

The Joker applauds. "A noble aspiration!" he exclaims. "The world needs more baseball players. Do you know who Batman is?"

Wally looks over at Batman. "Yes."

"Did you hear that he ran over a woman in the street, and then just drove away?"

"Yes."

The Joker thinks that Batman must be about ready to jump out of his skin. It's a delicious feeling, to have the paladin of Gotham City on pins and needles . . . and it's only going to get better. It's a beautiful thing when a plan comes together. He leans close and speaks just loud enough for Batman to hear. "I'll tell you a little secret. Batman didn't run over that woman."

He waits for Wally to say something. It takes a while for Wally to figure out that he's expected to respond, but a little prod from the fingernail loosens his tongue. "Okay," Wally says.

"You know who did run over that woman?" the Joker asks. "I bet you don't. But I'll tell you. I did."

"Okay," Wally says.

"Batman is a good guy. I'm a bad guy."

"Okay," Wally says.

"Glad we could get that straightened out."

Keeping an eye on Batman, the Joker stands up. He's got one arm wrapped around Wally Gilroy. With the other he flips the cape out of the way and mimes firing a gun at Batman. "I'll have a little chat with our upstart firebug."

"Beautified with our feathers?" Batman says. "A bit ironic for you to complain about that."

"Oh my, he has read deeply in the literature of the Renaissance, has our Batman," the Joker says with admiration that is only half mocking. "Would that make me Shakespeare? You do catch all of the subtleties. Well. To pursue the comparison: consider that I might just have a tiger's heart wrapped in a player's hide. *Hahaha.* Wally, you're out past your bedtime. I think you should probably go on home. How does that sound?"

Wally is too busy clutching the Joker's forearm with both of his hands to answer.

"Look at the poor little tyke. He's too sleepy to talk. Off to beddy-bye, Wally Gilroy."

The Joker says this with a wink at Batman, and as he shakes Wally loose and lets him fall from the rooftop, Batman is already tensing to spring. The Joker bounces back, away from the edge of the roof and diagonally away from the path of Batman's lunge. He watches with clinical admiration as Batman goes headfirst off the roof, simultaneously flicking a line out to catch Wally and with his other hand firing some kind of grapnel into the wall of the building. "Bravo!" he calls when Batman has caught the boy and landed against the wall, with young Master Gilroy hanging a couple of stories above Corvallis Street. People are already gathering below.

And now is the time to, as they say, make good my escape, the Joker thinks. He bows to the assembled crowd and then hightails it out of there.

* * *

There's a home-security specialty shop on the edge of Burnley—one of the areas of Gotham least likely to need the shop's services, but people don't always want the things that they need, now, do they?—and the Joker collects a little box to disguise his voice, as well as several other things that strike his fancy. The store is just closing when he walks in, but the Joker could, as they say, sell ice to Eskimos, and even were it not for his irresistible charm the shop's proprietor is hardly in any shape to complain by the time the Joker walks whistling back out of the store and begins the long meander back toward the East End.

One of the things he loves about Gotham City is the way that at night he can walk just about anywhere and not draw a second glance. During the day he draws somewhat more attention, but when the sky over Gotham is sodium-arc pink instead of smog-choked taupe the Joker is just another citizen.

Ha. Hardly. But that appears to be what most of the genuine regular citizens think. No one leaps back in alarm, no one reaches for a cell phone or goes dashing into the nearest liquor store to commandeer the pay phone from the patient legions of drug dealers and bookies waiting in line. It's almost insulting.

Speaking of phone calls, the Joker has one to make. That sooty interloper Enfer has stepped far outside the bounds of villainous propriety, and he's due a comeuppance. One possibility would be to arrange a meeting, since it's obvious that Enfer wants to meet—"and who wouldn't want to meet me?" the Joker says out loud— and that their failure to connect has angered him. But really, burning novelty shops? It's petulant, the action of an arrested psyche interested purely in attention. Plus it's insulting. Plus plus, it's made the Joker deeply furious. He can't remember the last time he was this angry. Even having Batman land on him like a ton of black-clad bricks, just when he was on the verge of turning the reservoir into a gelid, poisonous mass, hadn't made him angry the way this has.

But!

All humor is sublimated anger, isn't it?

Goes without saying, he answers himself. So this means it's all just funnier, and I'm just funnier when I'm angry, and Enfer is about to get the laff riot of his soon-to-be-extinguished life.

First, though, I'm going to have a little more fun with Batman.

There's a pay phone that, for as long as the Joker has been in Gotham City, has allowed free outgoing calls. It's at the northern end of the monorail bridge over the Sprang River, tucked away against one of the bridge footings. The phone's origin is a mystery, and its continued existence even more inexplicable, and perhaps this is why the Joker loves it so. "Hello, phone," he croons as he walks up to it. "Such a long separation we've endured. But absence makes the transistors grow fonder, does it not? Pray tell, do you contain anything so outdated as a transistor? I'll wager you might. These newer phones, with their digital displays and their electronic processors . . . phooey. I love you, your weathered black plastic, your rotary dial, your obsolete technology." He holds up a quarter in one hand. "Would you like one? I know you don't ask for them, but you don't have to keep secrets from me. And I can spare it." Pantomiming the act of listening, the Joker nods. "Yes. Yes, I thought so. Very well, then, you shall have it. And no, I won't hear of any reciprocation."

He drops a quarter into the slot, lifts the handset, and holds the voice-disguising thingamabob against his lower lip. It's all just for fun; there's no way, really, that anyone who answers this particular line is going to recognize his voice. He is famous for other qualities, although secretly the Joker admires his own voice and never hears enough of it.

"Hel-lo, Chief," he purrs when the other party picks up. "I understand you're having a little trouble with a local hooligan? Someone with a grudge against those who would keep our city safe and uncombusted?"

He waits through the expected litany of demands.

"Chief, Chief, Chief. Chiefy, surely you can't expect me to answer all those questions. Such terrible danger that would put me in. I tell you, though—by the way, I hope you're recording this, since you'll want to run it through all of your favored methods of analysis before sending it on to others who will need to hear it. Are you?"

More demands.

"My, oh, my," the Joker says. "That sort of language might be offensive to certain of the parties who will soon need to be in on our little secret. Are you recording this call or not? Never mind. I'm sure you are. Let's get down to brass tacks, then. The heart of the matter, the crux of the problem. In short, let's stop pussyfooting around the bush, shall we? Enfer has a retreat, a safe haven, a homey little nest right here in Gotham City. Would you like to know where, or is it your preference that he continue his reign of terror?"

A long pause. Then the Joker hears what he wants to hear.

"Of course I don't want anything in return. This is civic duty. I could do no less for our fair city. But you'll want to act fast, Chiefy. I don't know how long you can count on our little firebug to stay put." The Joker pauses dramatically. "There's a charming little bungalow on Grant Street. You'll know it by the front window blinds; for some reason, he always keeps one up and one down . . . where can you contact me? Don't be ridiculous. You can't. If you miss this golden opportunity, I probably won't ever contact you again. Probably you have enough time. So consult with your masters and get going, hear? Ta ta."

Then he calls Bud and Lou. "Boys, have you prepared the setting for our little masquerade? What? What do you mean, someone was there?" The Joker pinches the bridge of his nose. "Lou, Lou, Lulu, repeat to me the address of the house you are in. Yes, now. Of course I'll wait; nothing in the world would please me more."

He waits. Lou returns and reads him an address, after which there is more pinching of the nose, together with rueful shaking of the head. "Lou, I thought you were the smart one. The street was Grant, not Sherman. I'm afraid you've got the wrong Civil War general. We want the noble drunk, not the leveler of cities . . . you did what? Well. Much as I'd love to drop by and gussy things up, you're on your own. Make it look like a robbery. And get over to Grant Street. Now now now. Who knows how long it will take these public-servant types to do anything? It could be an hour, could be a week. Maybe you'll run into them on the way . . . no, I'm kidding, Lou, darling, would I want that to happen to you?"

Hanging up, the Joker bursts into song, a little bit of doggerel for his old sidekick Lou.

"In a pig's eye I'd want Lou in the pokey
In a pig's ear I'd want him riding Old Smokey
In a pig's mouth I'd want him writing in trochees
But the truth
The saa-a-aad truth
Is that life is long, and sidekicks short
And Lou will have to do
To hold the fort . . ."

Then he's off to the next thing, which is a change of clothes and a technical rehearsal at their new location. It's going to be a grand show, the Joker is thinking. He hopes simply *everyone* turns out to see it.

COMEDY OF ENFERS?

Vicki Vale, *Gotham Gazette*

His black firefighter's regalia more recognizable now, neophyte Gotham super-arsonist Enfer set four blazes last night, killing at least 17 people and destroying the city's four largest novelty stores. In a three-hour period, Arty McGee's, the Laughing Monkey, Glory Laugh, and Diamond Dooley's were all burned out.

The founder of Arty McGee's, neighborhood institution Arthur Zagajewski, was among the fatalities. Witnesses said he died after reentering the burning building to make sure all of his employees had made it safely out.

Finger-pointing has already begun between local business owners and the Gotham City Fire Department, with merchants—particularly in Chinatown— accusing firefighters of reacting slowly because of Enfer's known taste for booby traps. GCFD chief Coover angrily denied any such failure of nerve, declaring that "every member of this department knows that it's a dangerous job. Enfer has made it more dangerous, but our job is to fight fires, and we have done it as professionally and with as much dedication as any fire department in the country."

That may not be the only dispute in play, says Dr. Lindsay Kaplan of Gotham University, a specialist in abnormal psychology and the psychopathology of master criminals.

"Just as the HAHA was a fairly clear signal that Enfer either was working with the Joker or wanted Gotham City to believe he was," she said, "last night's fires are a shot across the Joker's bow, if you will."

Kaplan speculated that this sudden outburst, so unlike Enfer's previous acts of arson, could be read as an indication that relations between Enfer and the Joker have soured, although she qualified that theory by noting that no one is quite sure what sort of relations the two villains had previously.

"If you made me guess, though," she concluded, "I would think that Enfer is trying to erase the Joker's presence in the city by striking at symbolic targets associated with him."

August 1, 10:46 AM

It was one of his father's favorite proverbs: *Lie down with dogs, get up with fleas*. This morning Bruce is feeling as if all the times Thomas Wayne said those words, he was somehow looking ahead to exactly this moment, when his son would walk through Wayne Manor feeling tainted and powerless and estranged from the man he had once imagined it possible to become.

I saved Wally Gilroy, Bruce tells himself. And I didn't kill Merilee St. Pierre.

So why do I feel exactly the way polemical yahoos like Duane Trask want me to feel?

The answer, of course, is that he's still berating himself: first, for not having anticipated that the Joker would be covering himself somehow; second, for not having a plan in place to surmount whatever obstacle the Joker would present; and third, for speaking civilly to him. For God's sake, he joked about Shakespeare with a murderous lunatic who was about to throw a child off a building.

Lie down with dogs, get up with fleas.

Am I becoming compromised by prolonged contact with the unhinged? Is this some kind of variant Stockholm syndrome? How long before I am completely curdled by surrounding myself with the worst of humanity?

How long before I become what much of Gotham City assumes I already am?

The isolation gets to him sometimes. Not the maintenance of the Batman secret, but the simple isolation that is part of the territory when you're a billionaire by accident, and everyone in the world wants something from you. And I would want something from me, Bruce thinks, if I didn't already have it.

He finds Alfred in the kitchen. "So tell me about the thing this afternoon."

"Your presence is requested at the Van Gelder Foundation's neighborhood garden initiative," Alfred recites. "And Miss Phoebe Lemieux is very eager to accompany you. Very eager."

He follows Bruce to the elevator and down into the cave. Eventually Bruce gives in and asks the question. "Who is Phoebe Lemieux?"

Bruce looks around the cave while Alfred tells him all about Phoebe Lemieux's extensive and impeccable social contacts, her family's long involvement in both government and philanthropy, her own achievements at Vassar and the Sorbonne, her current work with nongovernmental organizations promoting public health, and a laundry list of other fascinating characteristics . . . during all of which Bruce is mentally cataloging the things he still needs to do in the cave. "She sounds like quite a girl," he says, because Alfred will expect him to say something.

"She does indeed," Alfred says. "Although I harbor

no illusions that any of her sterling credentials interest you."

"Sure they interest me." Maybe a gate of some kind back there, Bruce is thinking. So the bats can still get out, but not wandering psychotics. And I really need a clean room.

"Obviously," Alfred says.

Despite the humid ninety-degree weather, the neighborhood garden party isn't as bad as it might have been. The hors d'oeuvres are tasty; Phoebe Lemieux is charming and gorgeous enough that if he hadn't already decided she was going to be the latest victim of Bruce Wayne's legendary fickleness, he would be tempted to ask her on a real date. That's one of the costs of being Batman. Bruce doesn't like it, and he likes it even less as he gets a little older and starts to realize that at some point the state of being alone acquires enough inertia that it maintains itself permanently. Part of his mind splits off and indulges a fine daydream about a house by the sea, with the voices of children wafting in through the open window, and a woman . . . she has Phoebe Lemieux's face. Meanwhile he's smiling and chatting and shaking hands, promising to follow up on this or that, suggesting that people get in touch with his people. He's probably committed more than half a million dollars of Wayne Foundation money by the time everyone has munched through the sandwich platters and gathered in the Fifty-fifth Street neighborhood garden to hear Marvin Van Gelder give his speech about the way neighborhood gardens connect children to their world and Gotham City residents to their neighbors. Agreed, Bruce thinks. Community gardens are great. He smiles at Phoebe when Van Gelder tosses off a metaphor about healthy children being the real harvest of community gardens. She smiles back.

When the speech is over they mingle some more, sit down to a fine dinner, clink glasses, listen to another speech; then it's back out to the garden, just after sunset now, some of the heat starting to leak out of the air as a breeze comes in off the bay. There are journalists everywhere, and various social hangers-on, people who will never contribute to causes like this but who like to be photographed at the events. Speaking of dogs and fleas . . .

At some point a rustle moves through the crowd; the faces of the assembled apostles of neighborhood empowerment undergo a change. They're shocked, saddened, confused, regretful.

Bruce listens, but he's distracted and can't piece together the conversation. Something to do with the Gotham City Police Department, it sounds like, which probably means another brutality brouhaha. Just another day of superlative public service in Gotham City.

"Oh my God," Phoebe says.

"What's that?" Bruce says.

She looks up at him, then back in the direction of the conversation she's overhearing. "I just heard someone over there say that the police shot Batman today."

Twenty minutes later Bruce has pleaded a prior commitment and made a seemingly endless series of hasty good-byes. He's sitting in the limousine, Alfred outside the passenger door waiting for Phoebe to finish her rounds of air-kisses and promises to get in touch, while

Bruce runs through the different news channels on the television in the back.

Channel 9 has jittery aerial footage of a thick knot of emergency and police vehicles surrounding a house in Otisburg. It's a neighborhood of small—and, to varying degrees, decrepit—bungalows gradually giving way to new condominium developments that spill over from the Hill and up from Burnley. Not one of the places Bruce would have pegged as likely operational territory for the Joker. The voice-over from 9's reporter at the scene sounds slightly hysterical as he shouts over the sound of the rotors: ". . . during a raid on the suspected hideout of the infamous arsonist who calls himself Enfer. Police will not confirm this, but witnesses at the scene say that Batman made his escape down the alley you can see across the top of your screen. Forensics teams are on the scene . . ."

To Channel 11. More aerial footage, then a quick cut back to a reporter on the street, his face strobed by blue and red. "Three Gotham City police officers are confirmed dead, and a fourth is clinging to life as we speak . . ."

I didn't kill Merilee St. Pierre, Bruce is thinking. And I didn't kill those cops.

I might, though—just might—kill the Joker.

There comes a time when all the principles in the world have to yield to the immediate imperative to protect yourself and those you love. Bruce has a feeling that Batman is nearing that point. He will fight it, as he was taught to fight it, but for the first time since he put on the cape and cowl serious doubts gnaw at him. He's heard the arguments before and dismissed them: what good does it do to play by the rules when you're the only one? You can't win that way.

Yes, I can, he's always answered before. And if I can't, then I'll lose and still be able to look at myself in the mirror. Someone has to do things right. Someone has to believe in doing what's right and be an example of doing what's right.

That's what he's always said before, but the same original question ricochets through his mind now, and it's no longer so easily dismissed.

Over to Channel 34. ". . . one of the more interesting things about this event is the possibility that DNA testing of blood samples from the scene may actually solve the long-running mystery of just who this Batman person is. Now, I haven't been able to confirm this, but if Gotham City police are not taking samples of the blood from the scene, this would be the first murder investigation in the modern history of the city not to include that kind of sampling . . ."

Now, that will be interesting, Bruce thinks. Whoever the Joker was before he was the Joker, he might well have left a DNA sample in a database somewhere. If the testing yields any results, everyone in Gotham City is going to think that they've discovered a truth, when in fact that truth is unknowable. *I* don't even know who Batman is. All the same, the testing—if he can get hold of the results—might go a long way toward helping Batman track down the Joker. Bruce makes a mental note to see who at Wayne Enterprises he needed to contact.

The satellite news networks are primarily interested in new evidence of financial shenanigans in international charity endeavors. Bruce comes back to the local stations and settles on Channel 6, which has always hated Batman. Their lead woman-on-the-scene reporter, Adrienne Arnow, is just now turning away from what looks like an interview with one of the uniformed cops on the scene. The uniforms were prohibited from talking to the press, so Bruce isn't sure what might be going on there, but Adrienne Arnow sure looks happy about what she has heard.

"The officer who fired on Batman made a positive identification," Arnow says, smiling her talking-head smile. "Gotham police say they have no doubt that Batman was there, that he attacked them, and that they were able to wound him before he got away. A full-scale manhunt is under way as we speak to find Batman and bring him in. It's a little ironic, since it was just a few days ago that Gotham City police relied on Batman's help to sweep up the dozens of escapees from the Arkham Asylum fire. Now it appears that they should have put the cuffs on him, too."

Voice-over from the studio anchor: "What are Gotham police and city officials saying about this? Merilee St. Pierre was one thing. A terrible thing, to be sure, but this is killing cops. Is there any sense among city officials or police that they should be somehow giving Batman the benefit of the doubt?"

Adrienne Arnow's smile broadens to the point that Bruce momentarily thinks she must have gotten a dose of Joker Juice. "None. None whatsoever. Everyone I've talked to says that this was bound to happen, that sooner or later Batman's operating outside the law would come home to roost. And most of them are furious—furious—that they weren't allowed to take action against him sooner."

"Bullshit," Bruce says.

"So you must really be a big Batman fan," Phoebe says.

Bruce hasn't even noticed her getting into the car. He gives her his billionaire-playboy smile. "I admire the guy, it's true," he says.

Her face clouds over. "Even after he ran that woman over?"

"Well, if he really did, that's different," Bruce says. "But I have a feeling there's more to the story."

"Right," Phoebe says. "Sure. She was probably part of an underworld syndicate. Honestly, Bruce."

"That isn't what I meant," Bruce said. He's already lost interest in the conversation. Now he won't have to invent an excuse not to see her again. If she's part of the crowd rallying under the banner of Merilee St. Pierre, she won't want anything to do with him anyway. "All I'm saying is that nobody has heard Batman's side of the story yet."

Ain't that the truth, he's thinking as he says it. In more ways than one.

TAKING THEM TO TRASK
Duane Trask, *Globe* Columnist

Hey, Batman, make up your mind. Are you the depraved wacko who ran over Merilee St. Pierre, or the selfless hero who jumped off a building to save a little boy named Walter Gilroy?

Gotham City wants to know. We want to know whether you're the hero we thought you were at first, or the criminal the St. Pierre family thinks you are, or the hero Mr. and Mrs. Gilroy think you are this morning.

You can't tell us, can you? Because you probably don't know yourself.

And this is the problem with these heroes and villains, folks. They aren't like you and me, and when we expect them to be, people get hurt. Batman might not even feel bad that he ran over Merilee St. Pierre; he might look at her as necessary collateral damage in his private war on our collective behalf. And from his perspective, knowing what he knows about the nighttime denizens of our not-so-fair city, he might be right.

But that doesn't make Merilee St. Pierre any less dead, or her family any less distraught.

I'm starting to come around to the notion that it's not just the villains—your Joker and Two-Face and Enfer and whoever else—that are Gotham City's real affliction. It's the heroes, too. The truth is, anyone who lives in Gotham City and makes decisions that affect the citizens of Gotham City should be making those decisions on grounds that the citizens themselves might use.

If a cop ran over Merilee St. Pierre trying to catch a bank robber, we'd be all set to lynch him. It wouldn't work, because as we all know cops in this town have the kind of prosecutorial immunity that you used to have to be pope to enjoy . . . but we'd have the impulse. And the reason we'd have that impulse is that we'd feel that the cop should have known better than to endanger an innocent life in an effort to put a crook in jail.

We can't be sure that we should hold Batman to that same standard, though. Why not?

Because we can't be sure he's human. We can't be sure he thinks like us, understands the world like us, has feelings like we do.

So what does it all mean? What am I saying?

I'm saying I want all of them gone. The costumed villains, the superbrainiac maniacs, the mysterious heroes who fly by night . . . all of them.

Gone.

Gotham City for its ordinary, human citizens. We can solve our own problems. We don't always, but we can. We're capable of it.

And we never will as long as we think we have them around to do it for us.

So hey, Batman. Forget what I said about making up your mind. Why don't you just do us all a favor and disappear?

21

August 1, 7:48 PM

There's a half-moon low over the ocean, and high cirrus clouds just losing their last tinge of sunset pink. In a more affluent neighborhood, or in a city with functioning public services, streetlights would be coming on. Here, only one is struggling to life down the block, and it's too feeble and far away to make any difference. Gordon sits in the unmarked van across the street from the house. It's a brick bungalow with two curtained windows facing the street. Probably two bedrooms and a partial basement, with a small porch on the front covered by an aluminum awning. There's a bird feeder, some empty flowerpots, a lone beer can on the porch stairs. A driveway on the side leads to a garage that doesn't look anywhere near big enough to shelter a car. Gordon's got a strange itch in the back of his mind, the veteran cop's natural cynicism about the anonymous tipster. Sometimes they pay off; more often their purported tips turn out to be grandiose fantasies or outright lies told in the interest of some petty personal vendetta. He doesn't like the way this one feels, and he particularly doesn't like the way Coover brought it to him so soon after their previous conversation. Police work is never that cut-and-dried.

It seems airtight, though, starting with the description of the window blinds. The van carries a portable chemistry lab, complete with sampling apparatus, and through sniffing the local air it's found both flame-retardant chemicals and common accelerants in concentrations wildly above normal, in a plume extending downwind from the address the tipster gave.

Intercoms are crackling as the teams get into place. The SWAT boys are coming in the back, there are snipers pretending to nap in cars at both ends of the block, and a van of uniforms in riot gear waits around the corner. In the lab van Gordon sits in the passenger's seat. The driver, two techs, and two uniforms—Vasquez and Tyler, both men he trusts—wait in the cargo area. "Status," Gordon says into his mike.

"Sixty seconds," says Vince Ferragammo, the SWAT leader.

Gordon hears the creak of upholstery as the two snipers wake up and settle into a firing position. "Ready north . . . ready south . . ."

"Say when," comes the voice of the van driver.

"SWAT, update when you're in place," Gordon says. A pause. "We're there."

"You guys good to go?" Gordon says over his shoulder.

"Say when, Captain," the driver answers.

Gordon draws his gun, checks the load, and shrugs into a vest. He takes a deep breath, and exhales his uncertainty.

"Okay," he says. "When."

*   *   *

The back door of the house disintegrates with a *bang* audible all over the neighborhood. "Police!" the SWAT team members are screaming as they spread through the house. The riot van squeals around the corner and disgorges its cargo. Uniforms take up positions behind parked cars, and Gordon can almost feel the reptile calm of the snipers as they sight through the house's living room windows. He's out the van door and crouched behind an ancient Buick sitting on flat tires in front of the house.

Flash-bang grenades go off, lighting the windows with the flat white glare of the big percussion charges that always punctuate the end of a fireworks show. One of the windows cracks and falls in, the sound lost in the continued shouting of the SWAT team inside.

Then there is a moment of silence.

"SWAT, talk to me," Gordon says.

"Bad tip, Captain," comes Ferragammo's disgusted voice. "We've cleared the place. There's nobody here."

"What do you see in the way of chemicals? Any drums, boxes, processing stuff?"

"Hell, I don't know. Nobody's lived here in forever, you can tell that. There's crap everywhere. Some of it might be chemicals."

"Okay," Gordon says. "I'm going to bring in the techs and see what we've got."

"Roger that, Captain. We'll open the front door."

Gordon stands up from behind the Buick and looks over his shoulder. The two techs were listening on the intercom and are already out the back door with cases of lab equipment. "Let's get a line all around the place," Gordon says to the uniforms who were in the lab van. "Close the street, too. Anyone comes by, doesn't matter if they live here or not, ask them who they are and send them around the block."

They work smoothly. Gordon has picked this team because he trusts them, because they stand out from the disaffected and cynical GCPD like pearls in a gumball machine. In two minutes the techs are inside, the uniforms have strung a provisional line, and the scene is as secure as it can get with more than a dozen people—however professional—stomping all over it. Gordon walks up the sidewalk, routinely scanning the cracks for any little thing, cigarette butt, ticket stub, anything that might be useful. He gets lost doing this. Sometimes he thinks he could spend his life looking for tiny bits of significance scattered across a background of Gotham City concrete.

That's when everything goes wrong. Gordon doesn't register the screaming from inside right away—it gets mixed up with the echoes in his short-term memory of the SWAT team's yelling as they barged in—and even the gunfire doesn't snap him out of his reverie right away. He's just looking up when the somersaulting body of one of the SWAT guys hurtles through the window and crashes down into a stringy hydrangea bush in front of the porch. Floodlights from the department vehicles snap on and find the front of the house, catching a shadow just disappearing from the window.

The snipers have night-vision equipment. Why didn't they fire? Gordon wonders, but he doesn't have time to think about it any further because the front door splinters off its hinges and another SWAT cop lands flat on his back on the porch before skidding and flopping down the stairs. Gordon is up, gun out, shouting something useless along the lines of *come out with your hands up,* which he's never actually said but which always runs through his mind exactly like that when things get hot. The other front window shatters as a black-clad body comes to rest on the sill. One of the uniforms on the street opens up, putting three or four holes through the front door. Gordon screams a *holdyourfire* into the mike—who knows how many of the SWAT guys and techs are still in there?—and Batman comes out of the house with the limp body of a fourth SWAT cop held up in front of him.

"Lay him down, slow, and step away!" Gordon shouts. He takes a step closer and assumes a firing position. "Batman. Do it!"

Batman never speaks. He holds up one arm as if displaying the toothy (bat-wingy?) flaps on the gloves, and then he slashes the flaps across the cop's face.

Automatically Gordon's mind narrows itself to a single, near-instantaneous calculation: can I hit him without hitting the cop?

He can. He's practiced enough, God knows. He's dropped terrorists and kidnappers and hostage takers of every description, mostly in simulations but more than once in real life. His finger tightens on the trigger. *Where are the goddamn snipers?*

Batman lets the bleeding cop fall. He's smiling, and a great pain of betrayal washes through Gordon.

He bites down on it and says, calm and clear as he can manage, "Hands up. Last warning."

Batman puts his hands up. Gordon notices that one of them holds a small silver device. Batman casually flips it over his shoulder. The *thunk* of it hitting the wood floor inside is followed by a *pop* and a hungry glow from just inside the living room. There are still cops in there, and all Gordon has ever known about right and wrong collides inside his mind. You were the last thing I could believe in, he thinks. Even when I could not believe in myself, there was you.

And now this.

He pulls the trigger four times. Two of the slugs hit the cape, billowing it out as if a sudden wind has come up. One strikes sparks from the utility belt. One sends a spray of blood arcing away from Batman's right side.

Spun off balance by the two sudden jerks on his cape and the impact on his ribs, Batman windmills backward. Gordon fires again and misses; then again, missing again as Batman gets his feet under him and vaults over the porch railing onto the driveway that runs alongside the house. By the time Gordon gets around the corner, Batman is vanishing past the garage into the alley behind the house. There's no catching him now, Gordon thinks. And I don't think I hit him bad enough to slow him down for long.

It's uncharacteristically bad shooting on his part, but Gordon doesn't want to look too closely at why that might be so. Dark, moving target, surprise . . . still, he should have done better. He *has* done better in every range exercise and simulation GCPD has to offer.

Department policy is that when you shoot, you shoot to kill. I did, Gordon thinks. The one that hit the belt was an inch off, the one that got him maybe six inches from lethal. Hell, the two through the cape didn't miss by much, either.

He can't think about it. He's got four uniforms down that he knows of, and what the hell happened to the snipers? Either of them had easy shots, and he didn't hear them. The gunfire has already brought the sound of sirens. Gordon goes from one downed officer to the next. Three are dead, and the fourth—the one just going down when Gordon shot Batman—is barely hanging on. His face is slashed and his uniform gleams blackly in the flickering streetlight.

When I shot Batman, Gordon thinks.

A shout comes from the parked car where the sniper on the south was set up. "Captain! Man down!"

Gordon turns to see the uniform who called opening the car door, and the sniper slumping headfirst out to hit the pavement with a meaty *thud*. He doesn't even have to look the other way to know he'll find the same thing in the other car.

I shot Batman.

Outside the line a van pulls up, and a satellite antenna extends from its roof. The TV people are already here. Gordon's got six down and more than a dozen eyewitnesses—cop eyewitnesses—saying Batman killed them.

It is the worst moment of his life.

BODIES FOUND IN SHERMAN STREET BUNGALOW
FAMILY OF FIVE BRUTALLY SLAIN
IN APPARENT ROBBERY
Gillian O'Connor, *Gotham Globe*

The Northside neighborhood reeling from the shock of last night's Grant Street firefight that claimed the lives of at least six police officers suffered another blow yesterday when a Sherman Street family was found murdered.

Bradford Shanley, his wife Aralynn, and their three children—Trevor, Veronica, and Stacy—were discovered late yesterday evening when a neighbor went to their house after hearing the family dog barking for several hours.

Police at the scene were heard speculating that robbery was the motive for the slayings, but GCPD spokeswoman Erin McNamara said the department would have no official comment until information from the processing of the scene was complete. "At this time, we can confirm that the five members of the Shanley family were found dead, and that we suspect foul play," she told the *Globe*. "Speculation as to motive is premature and irresponsible at this point."

Rampant speculation has nonetheless proliferated regarding possible involvement by Batman, who is accused of setting up the Grant Street ambush and who in recent days has killed a number of pedestrian and motorists on downtown streets. McNamara refused to address the possibility that Batman was involved in the murders.

"When we have a suspect and can comment on this case without compromising the investigation, we will," she said without mentioning Batman by name.

Neighborhood activists, however, were quick to denounce this latest evidence of what appears to be Batman turning against the city he was previously believed to be protecting. The police tip line set up to field calls regarding the Batmobile has been swamped with calls, and McNamara said the department was pursuing "a significant number" of leads. . . .

22

August 1, 8:38 PM

The Joker reels through the back door of the hidey-hole and stumbles into the parked Batmobile before falling to the floor. His head is buzzing, and if he were the sort of man who worried about things, he'd be a little worried that his feet feel like they belong to someone else. Also that his mouth is dry, and there's a strange blurring in his peripheral vision. "This getting shot is for the birds," he slurs, and adds the slurring to the list of things he would be worried about if, et cetera, et cetera. There's a lot of blood making the inside of the Batsuit sticky, and the Joker cackles himself nearly to unconsciousness imagining taking the suit to a dry cleaner's. Then he shakes his head, struggles to his feet, and spots the Luigi's Produce truck. In his blood-deprived and bullet-perforated state, it takes him longer than it should to connect this observation to a possible course of action, but connect it he does.

"Boys!" he calls out. "A little help here!"

Bud and Lou appear from upstairs, where they've

been doing God knows what. "Say, boss," Lou says. "You don't look so good."

"That's for sure," Bud says.

"Like the Batman getup, though," Lou says. "I meant to tell you that before. I mean, not so good now what with the holes, but still good. Where'd you get it, anyway?"

"Long story," the Joker says. "Tell you later. Right now I need you to go find Doc Fleming. You remember where his office is?"

"Sure do," Bud says. "Carmine uses him all the time."

The Joker files this away under the heading One More Thing That Changed When I Went to Arkham, subheading That I'm Going to Change Back Immediately If Not Sooner. "Fine, boys," he says. "Get a tarp over the car. Then go. If he's not at his office, find out where he is and bring him here now. Are we on the same page? Fabulous. Go."

They go, and the Joker finds his way to a ratty yellow couch in what was once the break room adjacent to the shop floor. Apart from suffering blood loss and structural damage to the right side of his torso, he's peevish about the way that all this medical treatment and so forth is going to affect the timing of his next big gag. "I ain't got time to bleed," he growls, forgetting where he's heard that line before, but it cracks him up. Laughing hurts, though, and he makes himself stop. It's the hardest thing he's ever done, but he does it.

Think positive, he tells himself. That was a pretty good gag today, other than the whole bullet-wound thing. Fine punch lines delivered to a number of Gotham City's finest, and a very fine one delivered to the Caped Crusader himself. Oh, what a state he must be in!

"What a lucky ducky I am," the Joker murmurs, think-ing of his spelunking odyssey. That train of thought leads him, in a meandering and not at all efficient way, to the conclusion that he should shuck the Batsuit before Doc Fleming arrives. That sort of joke is best kept secret as long as possible.

While he wrestles out of the suit, the Joker considers that it's been a pretty good week. He's not only turned Batman into a Gotham Bad Guy, but he's given the poor Dark Knight a witness who is perfectly unreliable by virtue of being seven years old! Ha! And by saving poor Katatonic Kathy, he's planted a little seed of uncertainty in the public mind about the proclivities of that Big Bad Bogeyman, the Joker.

I would burst into song if I wasn't bleeding so much, the Joker thinks. He's a remarkably resilient person, if he does say so himself, but he's never been shot before. Bullets take it right out of you, literally and figuratively. Looking on the bright side, he speculates that he would quite likely be in much worse shape had he not under-gone his remarkable transmogrification at Monarch. This is a pleasant thought, and he indulges it for a while, letting himself drift until he is prodded back into aware-ness by the indelicate attentions of Doc Fleming.

"Unhand me," the Joker says.

"Settle down, Joker," Doc Fleming says. He's tapping a syringe.

"And what might that be?" the Joker inquires.

"Leave it to the professionals," Doc Fleming says, which strikes the Joker as highly comical given Doc Fleming's, ahem, entanglements with the state medical board. The syringe is already in his arm, though, and laughing becomes much more difficult. For a raconteur such as myself, the Joker thinks distantly, sedation is deeply embarrassing. Doc Fleming is digging at him, or more precisely in him, and after a protracted period of invading the Joker's rib cage he holds up a flattened piece of metal. "Looks like it skidded around along the back of your ribs for a while," he says. "I found it right up against the spine. You could see it under the skin back there. You're one lucky Joker."

"Just what I was saying before you got here," the Joker says, or thinks he says. What with all of the pharmaceuticals Doc Fleming has injected, the boundary between thought and action is fairly indistinct.

"Nothing's broken, really," Doc Fleming goes on, "although there's a chip out of the fourth rib where the bullet went in. I can't find it without doing a lot more exploration. You want me to?"

"Heavens, no," the Joker says, and this time he's sure that his mouth actually made the words because Doc Fleming nods and says, "Well, then, I'll stitch you up and be on my way."

"Capital," the Joker says, and then he's nodding off to the soothing rhythm of stitch and pull, stitch and pull . . .

He wakes up to silence and the feeling that if he does not immediately eat an entire steer he will have to resort to cannibalism. Also, and paradoxically, he feels much stronger than before, no doubt as a result of having his structural integrity restored. What a resilient creature is man, the Joker thinks, or whatever variant on man I might be. "Boys!" he sings out. "I hunger!"

Once again Bud and Lou appear from wherever they were upstairs. "Us, too," Lou says.

"Then let's eat," the Joker says. "Go forth. Procure takeout. Make sure you get far too much."

The boys embark on their errand, and the Joker sits up. He pokes at the hole in his side and is delighted to find that it doesn't hurt much. Thank you, Monarch Playing Card holding lagoon, he thinks. Such a delightful chemical soup, so unexpectedly strengthening and transformative! He dresses and feels stronger yet once he is presentable again. But an army, as the saying has it, travels on its stomach, and he won't be fully up to speed until he is nourished again.

While he waits, the Joker considers how best to finish off the Grand Batman Impostor gag. Various possibilities have occurred to him. Assassination of a prominent city official? Too ambivalent; much of Gotham City would rejoice at the demise of any bureaucrat the Joker might select. A broad assault on the public health, in the vein of the oh-so-nearly-completed reservoir caper? Attractive, but not exactly Batman's idiom, which would be fine except the Joker finds himself wanting the final act of his masque to incorporate some particular Bat-quality. Permanent replacement of the real Batman? Also attractive, but tricky. Part of the fun of being the Joker is having Batman around, and what a disappointment it would be if in the act of finalizing this wonderful joke the Joker also disposed of his villainous raison d'être.

Hm. The French phrase, so apt and concise, also puts Enfer front and center in the Joker's mind. I'll just bet, he thinks, that there's a way to accomplish all my primary goals: disposal of the firebug, torment of Batman, aggrandization of self.

Inspiration strikes! What if Batman is *killed* today?

(Or yesterday . . . ? The Joker has no clear idea of how long he was in Happy Sedative Land.) What if evidence of his body could be displayed, making any appearance by the genuine article appear false?

"Egad," the Joker says. "You clever, clever Joker."

He considers a number of possibilities, humming a little ditty to distract himself from the apocalyptic vacancy in his belly. By the time Bud and Lou have returned, staggering under the weight of enough food to feed a battalion of giants, a plan has taken shape in the Joker's mind. They've also brought copies of the *Globe* and the *Gazette,* which the Joker peruses while he eats, taking particular note of a particular leak from inside Arkham Asylum. Oh, how he eats, and when he is done he says, "Boys. I have a plan. But first there's a little housekeeping to take care of."

LIST OF LIBERATED LOONIES LEAKED
Vicki Vale, Special to the *Gazette*

An anonymous source within the secretive bureaucracy of Arkham Asylum has leaked an internal memo that includes a list of currently missing inmates.

Headlining the list, as most Gotham City residents had expected, is the Clown Prince of Crime himself: the Joker. There are 21 other names, of lesser criminals and ordinary mental defectives. [The list in full is reproduced at right.]

In another twist, the memo is dated four days ago, casting serious doubt on Crane's evasive responses in recent days to questions about which inmates might have escaped. At press time, Crane had not responded to numerous requests for comment. Asylum spokeswoman Angela Rodriquez also declined comment.

Gotham City Police Department spokeswoman Erin McNamara declined to comment on the possibility that Crane could be held civilly or criminally liable for failure to release the list in a timely fashion. "We will be looking into the situation," she said, "but our primary focus at this time is capturing the Joker, as well as Enfer and the other escaped inmates."

Ben Ridley, city council candidate for the Trigate neighborhood, blasted this revelation as "the latest in a series of unconscionable failures on Doctor Crane's part to keep the citizens of this neighborhood, and Gotham City as a whole, safe and informed." Ridley called for Crane's resignation, and for a full audit of Crane's term as Arkham director.

Such an audit would have to be authorized by the mayor's office, and neither Mayor Hill nor his staff responded to requests for comment. . . .

August 2, 9:34 AM

Enfer's temperament does not predispose him to the sort of cold fury he is feeling right now. He's hot through and through, more prone to violent rages and impulsive actions that at times he later regrets. This feeling, this almost inert, absolute-zero rage, is new to him. He kind of likes it.

The shipment has arrived, but he is currently taking no pleasure from it. The radio is on a local talk station, the television is playing a nonstop news broadcast, and the computer is pulling down every bit of news and video it can find on the Grant Street debacle. From the chaos Enfer has extracted a few useful bits of information: the police were tipped off that he was at this house, large quantities of incendiary and accelerant chemicals were found, and Batman killed at least six police officers before fleeing after being shot and wounded. Unlike anyone else in Gotham City, Enfer is able to flesh out this puzzling factual skeleton with his observation of the killing of Merilee St. Pierre, with the result that he is in possession of a complete picture of the situation.

The Joker has said all that needs to be said. The rules of the game are now clear.

It could be that I bear some of the blame for things having come to this, Enfer thinks. The novelty-shop escapade was bound to strike a nerve. Perhaps I should have been more subtle.

Although, to be fair, it's also possible that he was giving the Joker too much credit at the outset. Hero worship is fine as far as it goes, but the moment when heroes take off their socks and reveal feet of clay can be instructive. In this case Enfer concludes that the distance between himself and the Joker is not so large as he had previously thought. He left clues for the Joker to follow; the Joker did not follow them; ergo, the clues were too smart or the Joker not smart enough. Either way, Enfer's understanding of himself is altered by recent events.

His imagined conversation with the Joker takes on a new twist. *I thought you were the mastermind,* he will say. *The villain* par excellence. *Now I see that I'm on your level. You have nothing to teach me.*

I don't want to learn from you.

I can stand on my own.

All of this also casts a new light on the Crane/Batman situation. If I can so easily best the Joker, Enfer thinks, how much more slippery and formidable can Batman be?

He is feeling powerful and confident. Perhaps it is not so much that he has overestimated the Joker, but that he has underestimated himself.

What a satisfying thought that is! Very well, he thinks. I will no longer sell myself short. I will no longer seek allegiance with my more established counterparts. From now on I will know that I am capable of taking it all the way.

And from now on, the Joker is my enemy.

Perhaps it was always going to happen this way. Enfer feels a slight sadness for the loss of his illusions, but clarity is better than occlusion. Now he knows what he can do, and now is the time to do it.

Twenty-four packing crates crowd the shop floor, each stenciled with the logo of Vari-Tek Industries. He wishes he had more, but outfitting even this many is going to stretch his efficiency if he wants to stick to the timeline he's planned for his Annunciation. He attaches one of the prostheses he had made for muscle work and pries the tops from the crates, one after another. Even with the machine assist, he's sweating by the time that's done, and by the time he's got all the crawlers unpacked he's ready for a break. Over a sandwich Enfer wonders how concerned he should be about covering the tracks of his purchase. Working through Falcone is a good start as far as eliminating the standard paper trail that would normally accompany a transaction involving ninety-six robots, but even with that small reassurance he's considering whether he should take steps to erase witnesses. The drivers, for example; the one who ran the pallet jack in and out of the truck trailer barely said a word the whole time, but the other one yammered incessantly about how glad he was to be done with Falcone and back working for "the boss," whoever that is. Logorrhea makes Enfer nervous; that second driver didn't have any way of knowing how intently Enfer might be listening, or whom he might be tempted to pass information along to.

Opportunity presents itself: I can remove that particular problem, or potential problem, Enfer thinks. He remembers the logo on the side of the truck and trailer, and he remembers the how's-my-driving number on the trailer door, and he remembers a little tidbit from the catalog listing: the crawlers can be programmed to look for patterns of numbers.

Aha. Sandwich forgotten, Enfer tears open the smaller box containing one of the crawlers. For a moment he's overcome by the pure pleasure of technology. It's a beautiful thing, this Vari-Tek Krawlor. Eight stainless-steel legs fold around a torso/command module about the size of an obese beagle, on the underside of which is a small cargo space and a series of hooks for the attachment of peripherals. The whole apparatus weighs in at a little more than two hundred pounds, and it has a battery life of more than eight hours.

Thank you, Doctor Crane, Enfer thinks. This is almost enough for me to forgive you . . . almost. With ninety-six of these critters, he can do anything. Or at least get anything started.

With one, he can take care of the driver problem. It won't be as much fun as a fire, but the weather forecast is calling for rain, so he'll have to sublimate that urge for a day or two.

He installs the control software and boots up Krawlor One. When it unfolds its legs and stands at techno-arachnid attention, Enfer is as blissful as he can remember being when he isn't about to start a fire. Wait'll you see this, Joker, he thinks. Your hand buzzers and squirty carnations are trifles. When these little guys are overrunning Gotham City, you're going to wish you hadn't been quite so dismissive and ungrateful.

BULL'S-EYE
Rafael del Toro, *Gotham Gazette*

No one should have been surprised when billionaire play-boy Bruce Wayne ducked hastily out of Marvin Van Gelder's garden party two days ago. Nor should it come as a shock that dear Brucie ducked into the back of his limo with the ravishing Phoebe Lemieux for what must have been one intense conversation, since the limo sat idling for nearly 20 minutes before pulling away for parts unknown.

The word is—and oh, how I hate to traffic in the sordid trade of celebrity gossip—that dear Brucie took a powder at the exact moment when the news of Batman's shooting hit this leafy gathering of Gotham's hoitiest and toitiest.

Dear Reader, the only thing I hate worse than trafficking in gossip is midwifing unfounded speculation, but am I the only one who finds it odd that this scion of Gotham's mightiest corporation should have had such an emotional reaction to news of the downfall of Gotham's most talked-about nocturnal paladin?

What a gag it would be if Bruce Wayne was Batman. I almost wish that Brucie hadn't clearly been at the Van Gelder soirée when Batman took the bullet, so I could speculate irresponsibly along those lines. But can anyone seriously imagine pampered celebutante-predator and boozehound Bruce Wayne going toe-to-toe with the most fearsome baddies our city can gestate?

In a word: puh-leeze.

What's interesting here is a subtler question: is Wayne Enterprises bankrolling the Caped Crusader?

Wouldn't be the first time a local corporate honcho decided that Gotham's Finest weren't up to the task. Or, forget Gotham City: does anyone remember the railroad barons and the Pinkertons? Or Henry Ford's Special Service?

What if Batman is—was, now, since presumably even Bruce Wayne isn't so immune to public outrage that he could keep doing it given current circumstances—just the latest rung in the evolutionary ladder from hired squads of strikebreaking goons to private supersoldiers, accountable to no one but their paymasters?

I'm just saying. . . .

24

August 2, 1:10 PM

Bruce has cleared the pure-research wing of Wayne Enterprises for the afternoon, sending everyone except Lucius Fox home on the pretext of an executive session on security and industrial espionage. "So what's new, Lucius?" he asks once they have the place to themselves.

Lucius pauses before answering, and Bruce knows that in his engineer's mind Lucius is assessing the utility of hashing out the question of why Bruce takes such a personal yet unexplained interest in the bleeding edge of Wayne Enterprises research. A veteran of internal Wayne politics, Lucius knows the value of ignorance, but Bruce knows it must kill him to not ask certain questions. A number of times since Bruce has donned the cape, Lucius has been on the point of . . . well, Bruce isn't sure what. Asking the Question straight out? Offering a more explicit alliance in the form of a tailored research program? That would be useful, but Bruce has deliberately not started such a program on the principle that he doesn't want Wayne Enterprises associated with Batman. It sure would be nice to put his money to work more directly, though, instead of coming into Lucius's subterranean fiefdom every so often and cherry-picking what might be of use.

The closest he's ever come to having the Conversation with Lucius was right at the beginning, when he first started helping himself to the products of the man's genius. Lucius had some questions about his intended use for these products, and Bruce almost told him. He could certainly use the support, besides the emotional relief of letting someone other than Alfred in on the secret. It's not a good idea, though. He knows this, and has resisted the impulse, but Lucius is no fool. Bruce knows that if he's in here asking about various technologies that he's already taken home, it won't take Lucius long to put this information together with the spate of Bad Batman stories. Not only does Bruce not want to push Lucius into uncomfortable territory vis-à-vis the Batman identity, he most definitely does not want to look like an idiot in front of a man he respects as much as Lucius Fox. And there's no question in his mind that he would look like an idiot if he admitted to Lucius that the Joker stumbled into the cave and made off with irreplaceable gear.

So they speak to each other in carefully crafted generalities, and although the indirection is necessary, Bruce hates it. There are times, and this is one of them, when he feels as if he needs an inner circle of older and wiser confidants. Batman is too much sometimes, and the task Bruce has set himself seems impossible sometimes—and of course hanging over all of this is the specter of what nearly happened to Alfred. *I'm only one man*, Bruce thinks. *I can't see everything, but I have to see everything because if I do not, people close to me will die.*

His solution to this problem, at least so far, has been to allow no one to be close to him.

Lucius is talking about some of his new lines of research, and while he talks he pauses at the end of each thumbnail sketch, eyeballing Bruce for cues about whether this is something they should pursue further or take in a particular direction. Bruce nods in a halfhearted chief-executive kind of way, absorbing Lucius's introductions to innovations in wireless security, miniaturization, and related technologies. He doesn't care about any of it, because none of it looks like it will help him—today—with his Joker problem, and right now he doesn't have the luxury of thinking long-term.

"What about this?" Bruce asks, indicating a small black something-or-other that looks vaguely like a hand giving a thumbs-up.

"Sensor," Lucius says. "We're exploring safety applications, security uses, all kinds of different avenues. What it does is, you program it to react to particular compounds. Let's say you're in a petroleum refinery, and you want to know if there's a leak of bad gas. You set it to look for particular sulfur compounds, and if it finds them it sends out an alert to a central monitoring station."

Bruce picks the sensor up. It weighs about the same as a full mug of coffee. "Is this the only one?"

"There are several," Lucius says. "But they're not exactly the same. We're still nailing down some design tweaks."

"Can you get me, say, a hundred of these in the next couple of days?"

Lucius smiles and shakes his head. "Well, I don't know. We've got the molds, and . . ." He considers. "Believe we might be able to make that work."

"Excellent," Bruce says. "What's the new thing in body armor? And by the way, that car I took home. You said there was another prototype of that model, right? But we never used it?"

"I might have said that," Lucius allows.

"Okay, how about you drop that off at the house this afternoon?"

"Can do."

They're walking toward the firing range at the far end of the research wing. When they get there, Lucius picks up what looks like a sweatshirt from a table and hangs it from a pair of clips attached to a motorized track in the ceiling. "Sorry we don't have any silhouettes of Rafael del Toro," he says with a grin before flipping a switch to send the shirt down to the far end of the range, maybe thirty yards away. Bruce watches the shirt sway; it moves like some kind of fleece. When he looks back at Lucius it's just in time to see him raise a pistol and squeeze off three shots, spaced two seconds apart. At the first shot Bruce turns back to the shirt. It kicks off to one side, and then snaps stiff before the next two shots arrive. The second shot kicks the shirt right up to the ceiling, which it impacts with a sharp *smack;* the third misses.

"Sure wish you'd given me a chance to cover my ears," Bruce says.

"I can't hear you," Lucius answers with a wink. "You see what happened down there?"

"I saw something," Bruce says. "Looked to me like the shirt reacted to the first impact by stiffening up."

He winds the target hanger back to where they're standing. The shirt is intact, and as Bruce touches it he can feel the fibers relaxing. By the time he takes it off the clips, it's just a shirt again.

"Not bad," he says. "But it's also not much help if the first one kills you."

Lucius gives him a pitying look. "You see a hole? If I shot you while you were wearing that, you'd have a hell of an internal contusion, but no penetration. Also, it's not designed to stand on its own. The idea is, you put it under hard protection, and the shock wave of the first impact stiffens it up so you're in better shape come the next. It actually uses the energy of the impact to drive the smart-fabric reaction. And we've designed the shirt with some flex at elbow and shoulder, but not too much. You'll feel like a kid in a snowsuit, basically."

Bruce is turning the shirt over in his hands. "Okay," he says. "Got one in my size? And maybe a ski mask and some long johns, too?"

Lucius is looking at him.

Bruce looks right back. "And by the way, are these fireproof?"

"Fire-resistant, I'd say," Lucius says. "Not much in the world is actually fireproof against the right kind of fire."

A long moment passes. Each man looks the other in the eye, on the verge of saying something that would change both of them forever.

"I'll keep that in mind, Lucius," Bruce says at last. "Thanks."

DNA TESTS CONFIRM BATMAN NOT HUMAN?
RESULTS RAISE ETHICAL, LEGAL QUESTIONS
Gillian O'Connor, *Gotham Globe*

The *Globe* has learned that DNA testing on the blood of Batman, wounded in a firefight with Gotham City police two days ago, has returned results that are, in the words of the report, "characterized by markers not commonly found in the human genome."

Sources in the Gotham City biotechnology lab tasked with analyzing blood samples left behind by a wounded Batman after the Grant Street shootout in which six police officers died have confirmed to the *Globe* that the DNA in the samples bears markers that "sharply differentiate these samples from the normal human genetic code."

Calls to the GCPD were not returned, but the department issued a strongly worded statement criticizing the leak of the results.

Gotham University bioethics professor Molly Chancey says that, if confirmed, these results will cause a new kind of uncertainty about the actions of figures such as Batman. Whatever the truth of recent accusations against Batman, she says, "he's already an outsider, and if people start to believe he's somehow different from ordinary humans, that's going to make it even more difficult for citizens to trust him.

"Things like Joker Juice, or Enfer's incendiary devices, confirm our stereotype of the Gotham City villain as a sort of overachieving sociopathic hobbyist," adds Dr. Chancey. "If it becomes clear that the case is somewhat different, that at least part of these villains' power comes from the fact that they're physically or mentally different, we're going to have to consider a whole new way of thinking about them."

Embattled Arkham Asylum director Jonathan Crane agrees. "The criminal mastermind, or archvillain, typically suffers from a complex of psychological problems having to do with differences, both perceived and real, from the run of the human mill," he says. Crane denied any connection between the leak of the DNA results and the recent leak of internal memos from his office, which some commentators have suggested could be part of a deliberate attempt to smear Batman and direct attention away from Crane's own problems.

"My entire focus right now is on getting Arkham Asylum running again so we can begin serving the people of this city who need our help," Crane said in a prepared statement yesterday.

Officials refused to comment on the leak and said they were still in the process of preparing their report.

Documents obtained by the *Globe,* however, include a full draft report in which a number of differences between the samples and standard groups of human genetic markers are enumerated. Among these are DNA strings related to physical strength, eyesight, and immune-system response. How these differences might be manifested in the subject—more specifically, in the man (?) who calls himself Batman—is uncertain. . . .

25

August 2, 4:06 PM

Of all the times for the department to start paying attention to rules like paid leave after a shooting . . .

Gordon has been sitting around the house feeling
trapped and at the same time joyful at the extra hours
he's getting to spend with James Junior. His boy is a
monkey, climbing everything in the house that offers the
slightest hand- or foothold—except unlike a monkey,
Junior tends to fall a lot, with the result that whenever
Gordon takes him to the grocery store, every woman
they pass eyes him with deep suspicion. At first it worried him, but now he's been a dad for long enough that
he just accepts this as part of the game. Two-year-old
boys are constantly testing the strength of their skulls,
and the fathers of those boys are constantly getting sidelong glances from women in grocery stores. Such is the
way of the world.

It is also, perhaps, the way of the world to be on paid
leave—and thus unable to act, investigate, prevent de-
partmental malfeasance, and so forth—while Batman is
killing the Arkham employee suspected of leaking the

list of escapees. Gordon has agonized over whether he should contact Batman. He's still got that address taped inside his desk, and he could wander over to one of the student cafés, and . . . what? Ask for an explanation?

Hey, goddammit, people believed in you. I believed in you. Even after Merilee St. Pierre. Right up until the moment I saw you on that front porch, I believed in you.

Which would solve, exactly, nothing.

Still, he wants to do it, because Gordon deep down inside is an incurable romantic, if not an optimist. He doesn't always believe that people will do what's right, but he always believes that they can, and he's always just a little hurt when they don't live up to the same standard he sets for himself. If that's self-serving, so be it. That's the way he feels, and the way he feels about Batman is simply this: he wants to hear an excuse he can believe.

Junior is wrestling with a giant stuffed crocodile while his father stares out the window at a cluster of seagulls that have somehow gotten a crab all the way to the sidewalk in front of his house, where they are with great fanfare dismembering it. *I want to believe,* Gordon thinks. *And all there is in Gotham City to believe in is me, Barbara, Junior . . . and Batman. I can't believe in the badge, I can't believe in the gun.*

And I can't believe I'm still gullible enough to be uncertain about Batman after what I saw the other day.

On top of that, the DNA-test leak splashing itself all over the *Globe* today is going to demonize Batman even more. Gotham City, Gordon is coming to realize, doesn't like ambiguity. The city seems to tolerate incompetence, corruption, and downright evil, but when it comes to uncertainty, hardened and cynical Gothamites start acting like a condo association dealing with a pink flamingo in someone's yard. Batman was always an ambiguous figure, operating outside the rules to maintain the rules, and now that he has done . . . the things he's apparently done . . . the city is like a *Star Trek* computer imploding after one of James T. Kirk's logic puzzles. If Batman isn't human, the ambiguity deepens: is he responsible in the same way a regular human would be? Should we have known all along? How many other mutants/freaks/ augmented humans are among us, and *what do they have in store for us?*

The cop in him thinks it's just a testing anomaly being blown out of proportion to sell papers to the credulous and gullible. But at the same time he sympathizes with the impulse to believe, or at least to know what to believe in. I spilled that blood, Gordon thinks, and I still suffer the same problem. I believe; I don't believe; I don't believe I can still believe; I believe I can't stop believing.

As if all of that weren't enough, there's the news that's just now coming out over the cop bands (which Gordon pirates at home, thanks to a little technical advice from persons who shall remain anonymous): a certain Angela Rodriquez, until recently employed as Jonathan Crane's spokeswoman and assistant, was just hours ago found in her home with her throat cut by a bat-shaped piece of steel. Gordon doesn't even want to think about which way and how far the papers are going to run with that, and it doesn't take a genius to see that the murder will be seen as retaliation for the leak of Arkham memos. Angela Rodriquez will be deemed guilty of the leak whether she did it or not, simply because she's dead and can't defend herself anymore.

It's all too much to fight. Merilee St. Pierre . . . Grant Street . . . Angela Rodriquez . . .

Evidence is evidence. Fifty or more eyewitnesses saw Batman's car mow down a woman walking her dog. Twenty cops saw Batman torch the Grant Street house and kill at least four uniforms. And unless there's a rogue machinist with a grudge against Batman, the murder weapon in the Rodriquez case is pretty compelling.

And yet.

Break it down, Gordon thinks. If there's one thing he knows about himself, it's that he's a good cop, and good cops aren't dumb. He knew there was something hinky about the Grant Street tip from the beginning, and he went along with it against his better judgment . . . and, let's face it, because he was going to take the kind of internal heat even he couldn't handle if he called the operation off.

That's a shame for another day, though. Right now he needs to think. He needs to think hard, and think well, and tease out why exactly he can't quite bring himself to believe what is obviously true.

Question one: why the hell would Batman take revenge on Angela Rodriquez for leaking the Arkham list?

"Daddy!" Junior sings out.

"Hey, kiddo." Gordon squats next to his crocodile-riding boy, feeling his knees pop. "You ride that crockle-gator to the moon yet?"

Junior's eyes light up. The moon! "Story, Daddy," he says, dismounting from the crocodile in such a hurry that he catches his foot on its snout and pitches headfirst into the radiator under the living room window.

"Oh, buddy," Gordon says, scooping up his son and looking out the window. Rain begins to fall as the seagulls finish their meal and Junior cries and his brain divides itself into the part that's parenting a child and the part that's still, and will always be, digging deeper into the strange puzzle that is Batman. The leak doesn't hurt Batman. The leak hurts Crane, and possibly the Joker, and there's a connection there that he hasn't quite figured out. Did Crane know Enfer was springing the Joker? Is Crane after Batman for some reason?

You're telling yourself a story, Gordon thinks. Evidence is evidence, and you saw Batman at Grant Street.

Let that be. There's something in there that doesn't fit, and it's not going to be shaken loose by hard thinking. One of the things that Gordon has learned about himself is that he does his best thinking when he's not thinking. So instead of telling himself a story, he rocks his son back and forth in front of the window, and when Junior's tears begin to dry Gordon opens his mouth and says the first thing that comes into his head.

"Once," he begins, "there was a crocodile that could fly . . ."

BAT-REPRISAL?
RODRIQUEZ MURDER RAISES QUESTIONS ABOUT BATMAN, JOKER

Vicki Vale, *Gotham Gazette*

The killing of Angela Rodriquez is the latest in a series of brutal crimes that have shaken Gotham City not just because of their savagery, but because their perpetrator, it appears, is the one figure most trusted (until recently) by the Gotham man-on-the-street. GCPD investigators aren't saying much publicly, but it's clear from their actions that they believe Batman to be responsible for the Rodriquez murder, the hit-and-run killing of Merilee St. Pierre, and the killing of six Gotham police officers during a fiery confrontation on Grant Street three days ago.

In addition, the Rodriquez murder raises disturbing questions about the connection, if any, between Batman and the Arkham Asylum fire that more and more appears as if it was set for the specific purpose of breaking the Joker out of his more or less permanent committal. It was widely speculated that Rodriquez was responsible for leaking the internal list of missing inmates to media outlets, which sparked renewed debate over asylum director Jonathan Crane's failure to protect the public interest.

Crane is currently on leave from his post as asylum director.

Neither Gotham City police nor city hall would comment on the possibility that Batman and the Joker are working together. Local citizen groups weren't so shy, however. "If true, this development would bode ill for the future of Gotham City," said Christian Andrews of the Frankenstein Coalition, an association of neighborhood and interest groups banding together to pass genetic-screening and anti-metahuman laws. "As Batman's adversary, the Joker nearly poisoned the entire city. Imagine how much damage they could do if they're now working in concert."

Gotham University professor Lindsay Kaplan, who has studied the dynamics of the relationship between heroes and villains, says that it's not unheard of for such an alliance to occur. "Typically, these kinds of partnerships are short-term, and entered into because of a common enemy. Once that enemy is disposed of, the two parties go back to their previous adversarial relationship."

Kaplan wouldn't speculate as to what Batman and the Joker might consider a common enemy. "It is unusual to have more than one prominent villain operating in the city in a high-profile way," she says, referring to Enfer's recent arrival on the Gotham master-criminal radar.

Pressed on the point, Kaplan did allow for the possibility that the Joker, out of jealousy, might be turning his attentions toward Enfer, and that he might have made some kind of overture toward Batman along those lines. "I wouldn't want to say that's likely, particularly because it would be such a radical departure from what we have understood of Batman's character until now," Kaplan cautions. "But it's true that Batman's recent actions have opened up quite a bit of uncertainty about his real nature."

In any case, what was once unthinkable has now become a question on the lips of many Gothamites: has Gotham City's extrajudicial guardian angel joined forces with the Clown Prince of Crime?

The city waits anxiously to discover whether one of its worst nightmares is about to come true.

26

August 2, 7:19 PM

The Krawlors take an infuriatingly long time to charge up, and Enfer has to be careful about how much energy he siphons from the Gotham City grid, so he can't even use all of the amperage available in the charging pack. Waiting is driving him crazy, and he's been hyperconscious of the fact that he hasn't burned anything lately, so he pockets a few little toys and goes out into the rain looking for a way to release his tension. It only takes an hour to find a likely target: a flophouse right on the edge between the squalor of the East End and the rapidly gentrifying area near the marina. He fires it up, making sure that the fire will get into the walls right away, which in a building of this age and construction will mean it'll go up like a Roman candle even in the wet weather. Then, just to keep the responding engines on their toes, he scatters a bunch of Cherry Bombs on the roof. They'll make quite a scene when the roof team goes up to ventilate the building.

A smile on his face, he watches the response, concealing his sense of pride and vengeful satisfaction when the

Cherry Bombs go off and the two guys on the roof disappear as if by magic. Won't be reading about the Joker
in the paper tomorrow, he thinks.

On the way back to the hideout, he stops in a quiet
bar for a drink and a phone call to his erstwhile care-
giver and clandestine employer, who isn't happy to hear
from him.

"Wasn't a very good idea to hang the Joker out to dry
like that, was it, Jonathan?" he says. "Now he's going to
have it in for you even more than he did before."

"Are you trying to threaten me?" Crane asks.

"I'm just saying, if you can't keep your mouth shut,
then perhaps give credit where credit is due."

"I see. Well, that little strain of megalomania needs to
be removed from your personality. The next time we
have a professional interaction, I'll see to it."

"Are you trying to threaten me?" Enfer asks. His tone
is mocking, but all of a sudden he feels like his gut is full
of cold water.

"I'm saying if you can't keep your allegiances where
they belong, then I might not find the same use for you
as last time."

Enfer finishes his drink. "The Batman part of the plan
is still operational, Doctor Crane; I freelanced on the
Joker issue, frankly, because that was a better way to
draw Batman out than what you proposed. And besides,
you'll get a new facility out of it, won't you? As for the
question of allegiances, well, as my mother would have
said: you knew it was a snake when you picked it up."

"Indeed," Crane says, and hangs up.

When Enfer gets back and dries off, the first Krawlor
is, at last, fully charged. He unplugs it, spends a few
minutes giving it a set of instructions, and steps aside as

it zips out the door. The pattern of its legs hitting the floor reminds him of a tap-dance show he saw once, and the result of this recollection is that Enfer has a wretched musical theater score in his head for the next half an hour. There should be a great musical about fire, he thinks. He's not the man to write it, but if the Annunciation goes according to plan, he might be able to commission such a work from one of Gotham's leading playwrights. He'll do it, too; one of the things about reaching the top of your profession is that it gives you more time to explore and experience the arts. He thinks that's important.

One of the things Enfer didn't know about the Krawlors is that they pipe their video input back to the server that controls them. This won't be so important when he's unleashing dozens of them at a time, since he won't be able to pay attention to that many different streams at once, but right now it's extremely useful. It's also a lot of fun and reminds him of the first time he ran a remote demolition with an old Brokk AB. The Krawlor is quicker on its feet than the Brokk, probably because it doesn't have to be as careful, and the feed is of much higher quality. He doesn't even tell it where to go, although he did give it a set of parameters roughly encompassing possible routes between the Port Adams waterfront, where Carmine Falcone gets most of his seagoing freight, and the East End.

The Krawlor has a built-in default search tool that tracks how much of its delineated area has been covered, and in what pattern. Enfer watches a graphic display of this on one of his monitors, and on another he's enjoying the direct video feed. Right now the Krawlor is clinging to one of the pilings on the Aparo Expressway Bridge across Miller Harbor, so most of what Enfer sees is graffiti and bird's nests. The Krawlor moves north, creeping up onto the outside of the bridge railing and scuttling along at a pretty good clip. Enfer hopes he's never in the position of having to outrun one of them; he's fast, but no human is that fast.

It pauses to watch the traffic go by and wait for a pattern match. Enfer has set its target patterns to include the word *Luigi* and the alphanumeric string JT87EC991, which is the license plate on the trailer that dropped the Krawlors. All kinds of complications are possible—Carmine might have retired the trailer, it might have been redeployed to legitimate freight and be on its way to Oklahoma, and so on, and so forth—but there's nothing he can do about any of them, or about the fact that the rain might screw up its pattern-recognition software. He does know that there's no produce place in Gotham City called Luigi's, at least not one that advertises in the phone book or online.

While the Krawlor is observing traffic, it gets much less responsive to his remote commands. There's only so much processing capacity in its tiny brain, and Enfer makes a mildly annoyed note of this while he waits for it to respond to his command that it abandon the search until it gets to a less conspicuous vantage point.

Then it flashes a message: PATTERN MATCH.

"Yowza," Enfer says. He claps his hands, sending a little puff of smoke spiraling up into the air over his bank of computers.

An image capture appears on one of his monitors. There's the truck, heading north over the bridge. In his excitement, Enfer taps the wrong command on the touchscreen and the Krawlor drops a Cherry Bomb off the bridge before he can redirect it. Then it leaps into action and scuttles along the guardrail to the other end of the bridge, and then along the shoulder all the way across the Upper East Side to the Sprang Bridge, where it catches up. The truck is waiting on the off-ramp to an access road that curls around to feed into Dillon Avenue. Enfer orders the Krawlor to skulk under the trailer and hang on until the truck gets to its destination.

For the next twenty minutes or so his view consists of a wet, rusty undercarriage and periodic survey sweeps of slices of cars visible between the trailer floor and the street. He notes that a large number of Gotham City taxicabs are riding on underinflated tires.

Just when he's getting bored, the truck slows down with a great roar of engine braking—the neighbors must love whoever's driving this rig—and stops, to back around the corner of a building and up to a dock. Hm, Enfer thinks. Parking, or making a delivery? Either way he's interested to see who's on the other side of the door. If it's Carmine, then he can have some fun with the Krawlor and cover his tracks.

As it turns out, what's on the other side of the door isn't Carmine Falcone. The truth is so much better that Enfer can hardly believe he's about to get to do what he's about to get to do. He toggles voice command on and says to the Krawlor, "Get inside. Target priority list is as follows: truck, chemical drums, Batmobile, Joker."

He wants to see the look on the Joker's face.

TAKING THEM TO TRASK

Duane Trask, *Gotham Globe*

It's about three months too soon for city council races to be heating up (to the extent that they ever really heat up in a town as politically apathetic as this one), but this election season is shaping up to be anything but typical. Roused by the political fallout from last week's fires and the controversy surrounding Arkham Asylum director Dr. Jonathan Crane's handling of sensitive information in the aftermath, a number of neighborhood and community organizations are fielding candidates in a challenge to the entrenched incumbents currently dominating the council.

Another group of candidacies was announced in the days following the revelation (first reported in the *Globe*) that Batman either has undergone heavy genetic modification or is some kind of superhuman. This news has jump-started an acrimonious citywide debate over the role of Batman in the civic life of Gotham City. Is he necessary to counteract the criminal masterminds who have historically plagued our city, as Batman's defenders argue? Or does his presence encourage city officials to rely on him and therefore fail to hold themselves accountable?

Otisville graphic designer Ben Ridley, head of the neighborhood advocacy group Trigate Citizens Alliance, is a vocal proponent of that latter view. "The truth is, the presence of superhumans, or whatever you want to call them, lets us believe that crime in this city is both caused and solved by them—which in turn allows us to evade responsibility for our own neighborhoods and our own city," Ridley says.

He's running for the District 4 council seat held by seven-term institution Angelo Fittipaldi, who, Ridley says, "has been part of the status quo for so long that he's forgotten how to be responsive to his constituents."

Ridley's platform consists of two planks. One, relocation of Arkham Asylum, either to one of the bay islands or to a secure and remote mainland location. Two, an aggressive push to rid the city of its shadowy demimonde of the grotesque and the deformed—and as Ridley sees it, this population includes Batman.

"Look," he says. "When Batman first came on the scene, what, two years ago? Not even, right? I was as happy as anyone in Gotham City to see the effect he had."

But recent events have changed his mind. "Merilee St. Pierre could have been an accident," Ridley says. "But why not stand up and admit it? That's what you do if you have the best interests of the city at heart."

Instead, then came Grant Street and the murder of Angela Rodriquez.

"The city can't take this," Ridley says. "In the end, Batman isn't any different from the Joker or Enfer. None of them sees the world like an ordinary person does, and what's important to us isn't important to them. We don't need them, and we can't afford to have them around any longer."

These are strong words, and although they have won Ridley growing grassroots support, he also admits that he's wondered if he should be fearing for his safety.

"My wife isn't thrilled about it, that's for sure," he says. "But she believes I'm doing the right thing."

And maybe, in the end, that will be the Caped Crusader's

parting gift to this city: by hanging up the cape and cowl, he will allow us to step out of his shadow into the full daylight of self-determination. That's what Ben Ridley is hoping, and at least in District 4, his message is finding willing listeners.

August 2, 9:36 PM

When Bud and Lou come in the back door next to the loading dock, the Joker hears them yammering at each other from his laboratory in the basement. It's typical idiotic Bud and Lou patter, and the Joker is distracted by a bemused recollection of the first time they worked for him. He needed a couple of ordinary joes, preferably with minimal scruples and a congenital predisposition toward following orders, and through the underworld connections he still had left over in the wake of his transmogrification he was able to scare up exactly what he was looking for. The fact that one of them was tall and morose looking, and the other rotund and loud, made the alliance seem inevitable. The Joker dubbed them Bud and Lou immediately, and when they protested that they wanted him to call them by their given names, he unfortunately had to get menacing. And this was before he'd polished his skills on the menacing front, so his handling of the situation had lacked finesse. "In fact," he says as he tells himself this story—him being his own favorite audience, really, especially for a story like this that falls squarely into the you-had-to-be-there category—"I believe I had to put a smile on the faces of several people before Bud and Lou understood how important it was for all of us to work together, and that for all of us to work together we would need to grant certain personality quirks, perhaps concerning monikers and suchlike verbal costuming." He laughs at the memory.

Rehearsal, rehearsal, rehearsal, he tells himself now as he putters with a complicated catalysis that will yield a new variety of Joker Juice. He can't wait to try it out. On the table next to the burners he's got a fresh set of fingernails, and the Batsuit is hanging up to dry after he treated it with a marvelous contact potion. It won't last long, but before it degrades he plans to have a lot of fun with it.

Bud and Lou bear at least partial responsibility for the failure of the reservoir gag, although the Joker isn't fool enough to absolve himself completely, and he certainly isn't enough of a nincompoop to discount Batman's role in the whole affair. The Batman problem will be taken care of soon enough, though. Already he's got the Chiropteran Crusader on the defensive, working with second-rate equipment and struggling against the tide of public opinion. These next few days will see the delivery of the punch line.

Sooner or later he'll have to do something about Bud and Lou, as well. They're not terrible examples of their kind, the aforementioned unscrupulous henchman, but unscrupulous henchmen don't last long without either acquiring some kind of scruple or succumbing to the belief that they should be moving up in the world. "There's no upward mobility in this industry," the Joker has told

Bud and Lou more than once. "How can there be? If you two suddenly became criminal masterminds, good heavens, what would the rest of us criminal masterminds do, pray tell? There's only room for so many of us. Batman's *busy*, the police are *busy*. We have to respect that and keep our ecological niche small and exclusive. Right, boys?"

Right, they inevitably replied. He believes they mean it, but he also knows that it won't last. Time to start planning for the next difficult period of training henchmen.

Later. Right now he's got all of these wonderful toys to finish off, and he's got to go upstairs and see if Bud and Lou have completed the errand he sent them on.

He's halfway up the stairs when the banter between Bud and Lou, which has become a sort of aural version of cosmic background radiation, suddenly amps up into full-blown supernova. They're yelling and screaming, there are *gunshots* for Pete's sake, and the *ping* of ricochets. "Boys!" the Joker yells heartily. "No shooting around the flammable chemicals, now!"

He takes the rest of the stairs four at a time and comes out of the stairwell just in time to see a gout of flame roar out of the open trailer backed up to the dock. Bud and Lou are standing about fifty feet away from the dock, both blazing away into the trailer. "Boys!" the Joker shouts again. "Cease fire!" He covers the distance to them just as they both run out of bullets and smacks the guns out of their hands.

"I'm terribly disappointed in you," he says, shaking an admonitory finger. "You know we're not supposed to fire guns near the piles of drums of explosive and flammable chemicals. Right?"

"But, boss . . . ," Lou begins.

"Ah ah ah." The Joker places the admonitory finger across Lou's lips. Lou gets cross-eyed trying to keep track of it.

"Um, boss," Bud says.

The Joker mirrors the finger gesture on Bud's mouth. Both of them stand stock-still, and the Joker looks back and forth between them, not even twitching when another roar comes out of the trailer.

"Boys," he says. "There will be no gunfire here. We will now put out the fire in the truck and if we have the good fortune to avoid a fire department call, we will reconfigure this space so that if anyone ever happens to show up, they will not see yon Bat-car or the magnificent collection of rusting chemical drums. Do we understand each other? You are permitted to nod."

They nod.

"Capital." The Joker removes his fingers.

"Boss," Bud and Lou say in unison, "behind you."

The Joker turns and sees some kind of spidery steel contraption emerging from the flames in the truck trailer. It pauses on the dock gate, lifts one leg, and puts it back down. "What a marvelous machine," the Joker says. "I must have one. What does it do?"

As if in answer, the robot reaches under itself with one leg, extracts a small black ball from its body, and bowls it across the floor toward the three of them. When it's about five feet away, it explodes.

There's something about being caught in the shock wave from an explosion that utterly scrambles the Joker's sense of time. He's pretty sure that he gets right back up off the floor, but meanwhile the robot seems to have moved quite some distance in the direction of the chemical drums. It's reaching for another little black ball, but it appears to have run out—or at least no more little bombs appear to skip across the floor.

So it reaches out with one arm and punctures one of the drums.

"Not so fast!" the Joker proclaims. In a jiffy he's across the floor and into the Bat-car, and in perhaps another jiffy and a half he's got it started, gunned, and squealing its tires across the floor in the robot's direction.

But the robot is fast, no question about that, and the Joker nearly runs over both Bud and Lou—Lou, in fact, twice, which leads the Joker to think in passing that since he's been thinking about it anyway, and since he is careening around the inside of a building trying to crush a marauding steel arachnid, he might as well flatten both of them while he's at it.

A marauding *pyrotechnic* steel arachnid.

"Oh ho," the Joker says as he swerves around a support beam and nearly makes jelly out of Bud. "It's you, my little upstart firebug."

He's not catching the robot, and the more he chases it, the less he finds the entire production either edifying or humorous. To relieve the tedium, he begins pressing buttons on the Bat-car's dashboard. A great number of interesting things happen: smoke pours from the vehicle's rear, some kind of visual display unfolds from the ceiling and interposes itself between the Joker's face and the dashboard, small sharp metal objects spew out from the wheel wells. He thinks there's something else, but it's hard to tell because the smoke is suddenly so thick in the room. But lo! What's this? He can see perfectly well through the display.

"Marvelous," he says, and leans into it. The robot has scuttled up one of the support beams, and as much as the Joker would just like to power the car through the beam, he doesn't suppose it's in his long-term best interest to have the building fall down on him and his laboratory. He's got plans for this place.

Lo again! A telltale on the display says TARGET ACQUIRED . . . and a tiny red square has centered itself on the robot.

"Agh!" he cries. "But once acquired, how is this target targeted, disposed of, annihilated?"

He glances at the dashboard again, and of course there it is: a blinking red button on the Bat-car's gearshift.

"Fire away! Damn the torpedoes!" he cries, and presses the button.

With a loud *bang,* a wire-mesh net appears from somewhere within the car and strikes the robot, simultaneously knocking it from the pillar and entangling it completely. Hooting with glee, the Joker accelerates and bounces the robot off the Bat-car's hood. It hits the wall with a crash, then struggles to its feet. It's able to stand, but not move.

The Joker drops the Bat-car into a lower gear and leaves a forty-foot streak of rubber between his location and the point at which bumper and wall collide with crumpling mechanical arachnid in the middle. The impact bounces his head off the display, but he's always had stars in his eyes anyway—part of wanting to be a comedian, don't you know—and he leaps with outrageous panache from the Bat-car and exclaims, "There, you infernal machine! This is what meddling with the Joker gets you! Tell your masters in your last flickers before your processors turn to sand and your wiring melts into found art!"

Then he thinks: Oops.

Because the robot has somehow gotten up, and not just up but partially free of the net, and it's dragging the net—not to mention at least four of its legs—along as it heads back across the floor.

Toward the chemical drums.

"Now come *on*," the Joker says.

It reaches the first group of drums.

"You *must* be kidding," the Joker says.

The robot detonates with a force that plants the Joker an inch deep in the concrete of the far wall. Once again he finds himself having to sort through the various ways in which he is accustomed to organize his experience: Okay, this is up, this is down. It was then, it is now now. I am somehow become one with the outer layer of this wall, although even as I realize this my weight is peeling me loose from the shallow depression my body has left. Face-first he meets the floor and counts backward from the square root of two for a while until he feels like he can get up. While still on the ground he's thinking that it won't be so bad to lose this lab, not after the way Bud and Lou's gunplay will bring the police—well, maybe—and if it's going to be blown up, well, with any luck Bud and Lou will have been blown up with it. Then he's on his feet. "Ta da!" he sings.

Well. Good fortune has indeed smiled, but in the typically ironic way of good fortune, the smile is a little crooked.

The self-destruction of the robot might well have ignited a large number of drums of chemicals, which stockpile would in turn have caused a secondary explosion that in all likelihood would have brought the entire building down around the Joker's pallid ears. But! O terrible mercy! The building is spared, because the robot—possibly deranged by the impact of the exceedingly solid Bat-car traveling at an irresponsible velocity—chose to blow itself up in the middle of a group of polybrominated diphenyl ethers.

Which, being flame retardants, retarded the holy hell out of the expanding flames of the robot's explosion. And which, by virtue of being heavy drums of fluid, absorbed a great deal of the blast wave.

All of which means that rather than being buried forty feet deep in broken concrete and bent steel I-beams, the Joker is standing more or less intact (although his chipped rib, it must be said, hurts like billy-oh) in the more or less intact ground floor of the hidey-hole. His relief at this circumstance is greatly tempered by the realization that the lovely polybrominated diphenyl ethers, for which he had such grand Enfer-negating plans, are now leaked out all over the floor and dripping from the support pillars. Their drums lie strewn about like crumpled soda cans.

He's composing an elegy on PBDEs in his head, but he keeps his voice chipper. "Boys!" he calls out. "Are you still with me?"

"Sure are, boss," Lou calls. He appears from the stairwell. Bud pokes his head in from the break room.

"Cleanup time, boys," the Joker says. His mind is already on the next thing. "Pull that trailer across the street, if the truck will still run. And find me some pieces of that marvelous little robot. I must know everything about it."

The boys, perhaps invigorated by their brush with a flaming, shrapnel-shredded death, set about these tasks with uncharacteristic alacrity. In short order the smoking trailer is backed down an alley across the street, and the Joker is sitting cross-legged on the floor with a pile of shiny steel fragments in front of him, and the number of these fragments makes it practically a statistical truism that one of them will provide cryptic clues as to the robot's maker, from which information the Joker hopes to gather information about its purchaser.

He's got this process roughed out in his head and is oddly a bit—just the tiniest bit—put out when Bud short-circuits the whole thing by saying, "Hey. Does that say Vari-Tek right there?"

Lou leans over to read the letters inscribed on one of the robot's legs. "Sure does. Is that . . . ?"

"Boss," Bud says. "You're never going to believe this. I think we just delivered these the other day."

SHERMAN STREET KILLINGS
POSSIBLY NOT RANDOM
NEW EVIDENCE HINTS AT LINK
TO GRANT STREET COP AMBUSH

Gillian O'Connor, *Gotham Globe*

Police sources have revealed to the *Globe* that evidence recovered from the Shanley house offers a possible connection to the Grant Street ambush that claimed the lives of six police officers and turned Gotham City against Batman.

Speculation about a relationship between the two crimes has run rampant since it became clear that the Shanleys were slain only hours before the Grant Street ambush, and because their house number, 1498, is the same as the Grant Street address used by Batman to plant a false tip regarding arsonist-*cum*-mass-murderer Enfer.

Speaking on condition of anonymity, a highly placed source in the GCPD told the *Globe* last night that the department is treating a Grant-Sherman connection as the leading explanation for the unlikely coincidences. A possible reconstruction of events is that Batman, or thugs in his employ, mistakenly went to 1498 Sherman instead of 1498 Grant and killed the Shanleys to avoid any possibility of tipping police to the possibility of a setup. The GCPD source would neither confirm nor deny that this reconstruction is similar to the department's understanding of the case. . . .

28

August 3, 9:00 AM

Bruce would rather be anywhere—he thinks he means this literally—than here in the press room on the seventeenth floor of Wayne Tower, looking at a sea of cynical journalists and glowing ready lights. If he ever meets Rafael del Toro in a dark alley, he's not going to be responsible for his actions.

He's been hoping that del Toro's innuendo about Wayne Enterprises would fade away, but the press office has been fielding queries by the dozen during the past few days, and it's time to put this whole thing to rest. So he adjusts his notes, adjusts his tie, and clears his throat to silence the assembled jackals of the Gotham City press. For just a moment he considers telling them that their numbers put Wayne Enterprises in clear violation of city fire codes, and that they can all just get the hell out and wait for a press release. But that kind of joke wouldn't be worth the whipping he'd get in their pages; Hell hath no fury like a journalist scorned.

So he begins.

"Thanks for coming. As you all know, in a recent col-

umn of his, Rafael del Toro stirred up what I might call
a firestorm of gossip about this company and about me
personally. Is he here?" Bruce knows del Toro would no
more come to this press conference than source a quote,
but to make his point he makes a big show of scanning
the room. "Hm. Too bad. If he was, he might be able to
come a little closer to the bull's-eye the next time he goes
shooting for juicy tidbits about Wayne Enterprises."

A ripple of expected laughter. He lets it go, then
moves on to the meat of what he has to say.

"I'm going to address Mr. del Toro's irresponsible
rumormongering with more energy and specificity than
it deserves," Bruce says, and nods to the side of the po-
dium where two of his assistants wait with armloads of
brochures hot out of the print shop downstairs. "What
you're about to receive is a complete rundown of all
nonbusiness activities funded by Wayne Enterprises, as
well as various charities, nonprofits, and research groups
to which we have lent our name. Also included in the
packet, you'll find a roster of every charitable donation
made on my behalf or the behalf of the Thomas and
Martha Wayne Foundation during the last three years.
Although this disclosure won't—can't, really—prevent
the spread of rumors, it is my hope that professional
journalists will consult it in their future efforts to char-
acterize the activities of Wayne Enterprises in nonbusiness realms.

"I know you can't assimilate all of this information
immediately, but it's my hope that you'll get back in
touch with our outreach personnel once you have. And
in the meantime, perhaps I can answer your questions
on other topics."

Immediately, the standard hubbub bursts forth as the

print journalists wave their pens and notebooks, shouting his name or just their questions, over and over. Bruce singles out Vicki Vale—she's the least sensationalist of any of them, as far as he's concerned, even though that's akin to calling her the least murderous inmate on Blackgate Prison's death row.

"Vicki," he says, and she shoots to her feet.

"Mr. Wayne." It hurts him a little that she doesn't call him Bruce. After all, they did date for a while, and for a change it wasn't him doing the leaving when it came time for someone to leave. "Are you ready to state categorically that no Wayne Enterprises money is finding its way to Batman?"

"Yes, I am," Bruce says. Pausing for a moment to arrange his full answer in a maximally quotable way, he goes on. "I wouldn't know, and I don't think anyone who holds the Wayne purse strings would know, where to deposit a check so it would get to Batman."

Vicki shoots him a glare. She knows he's deliberately joking around the question, and she doesn't like it. Tough. He answered in the first three words and gave her a chance for a follow-up. If she didn't take it, that's her problem.

From the renewed cacophony, Bruce singles out the foghorn voice of Duane Trask. Might as well get this one over, he thinks. "Duane."

"Bruce," Duane says. "If you *did* know where to find Batman, *would* you cut him a check?"

"No," Bruce says. "If you'd asked me that question a month ago, I might have answered differently. I felt then that Batman was good for Gotham City. Now, obviously, that's not as clear."

It kills him to say that. And not just him: Batman

wants out, wants to lean into the microphone and in his stony whisper tell Duane Trask that he forgives the people of Gotham City their fickleness and their gullibility, and that he will prove himself again. *The joke is currently on you, and on me,* Batman is trying to say; *but he who laughs last . . .*

Again, as he has more and more often in recent days, Bruce feels as if he is a skin worn lightly over the rage and determination of Batman. His answers are superficially direct and candid, but in truth he isn't saying anything that he wouldn't be expected to say. Batman, on the other hand, is offering shadow answers to all of the questions Bruce fields during the remainder of his availability, and it's not always easy to remember to give Bruce's responses and not Batman's.

Bruce, what's the situation between you and Phoebe Lemieux?

"Miss Lemieux and I are good friends," Bruce says.

She's a decoy, Batman says.

Bruce, does Wayne Enterprises ever feel like it's wasting money with all its support of new technology grants to the Gotham City Police Department?

"Of course not," Bruce says.

Even given the ongoing problems with corruption and poor clearance rates of violent-crime cases?

Another decoy, Batman says. *Bruce has enough money that if he doesn't throw some of it down black holes like Piskura's stable of brutally indifferent misfits, people will start to talk . . . and that's not what he wants them talking about. See previous answer about Phoebe Lemieux.*

"Wayne Enterprises offers its full support to the men and women who would keep our streets and our city safe," Bruce says.

To which Batman adds: *Vicki, did you hear that? I just answered your question.*

Did you leave the Van Gelder reception because of the news about Batman? It sure looked like you had to duck out to check on an endangered investment.

"My reasons for leaving that reception are private and will remain so," Bruce says. "If you have questions to ask about Wayne Enterprises or the public financial activities of my family or any of its trusts, I'm happy to answer those."

I left because I . . .

There has been another question.

I left because I . . .

"I'm sorry," Bruce says. "Could you repeat the question?"

Do you think Batman is valuable to Gotham City even if he makes the occasional fatal mistake that results in the death of an innocent?

"Well," Bruce says. He's shaken, and tries to force a grin, but from the way it feels on his face he can tell it's going to look awful on video.

I left because I had to know if the Joker was dead. And—if I'm telling the entire truth—because I was hoping he wasn't.

"Batman should be held accountable for his actions," Bruce says. "Just like anyone else. The truth is, though, that I think Batman's probably going to be around whether we want him to be or not. But that's more of an impression, mostly from your papers, than an informed opinion. Maybe you should ask the professor, what was her name . . . Kaplan?"

And while you're at it, ask her why I should want a creature like the Joker to live.

* * *

That question is still on his mind late that night, when out of sheer frustration he is prowling from rooftop to rooftop in the East End. The rain is gone, the moon high and clear, and his work in the cave has paid off. Finally Batman can come out. He's worked the new car (which is the old car) over until he thinks it's good enough, and Lucius's new underarmor is actually better than the stuff the Joker is currently wearing. Probably, in fact, it would have stopped Gordon's bullet cold, thus avoiding the whole DNA brouhaha. Batman pities Gordon tonight, pities everyone in Gotham City who labors under the Joker-engineered misconceptions filling the newspapers. The full scope of what the Joker has done to him only became clear earlier today at the press conference, when in the middle of an answer about Wayne Enterprises' plans to spin off its consumer-credit division Bruce realized with sickening clarity that he was paralyzed. Batman could not act, could do nothing that would reverse the damage the Joker had already done.

As quickly as the thought came, he banished it. There was one thing he could do, and that was run the Joker to ground. He had allowed himself to be suckered into defeatism, and for the son of Thomas Wayne that is an unforgivable sin. Bruce ended the press conference, re-turned to Wayne Manor, and in nine hours has up-graded his gear to the point where he feels comfortable taking on anything the Joker—or Enfer—can throw at him.

In stealing Batman's identity, the Joker has in a very real way stolen Bruce Wayne's. He had left the Van Gelder reception to discover whether the Joker had been killed because a dead Joker removed Batman's sternest test. Wanting that test to be alive is a kind of self-indulgence, a narcissistic desire to best the best in order to be the best; but, as Bruce learned in the dojos and monasteries of the Himalayas, excellence lies in competition with oneself.

Now that Bruce recognizes this, he can set about solving the problem. One way would be to give up, surrender to the impulse to end things in the traditional Gotham way: with the gun.

That, too, would be unforgivable. Bruce allows himself to have the thought, then compartmentalizes the hate and puts it where it belongs, in the reactor that drives him, where the alchemy of Batman can convert it into resolve. This isn't about the Joker. It's about Gotham City. And more than that, it's about honoring Thomas and Martha Wayne.

And more than that, it's about the imperative to uphold the standards you believe in, simply because you believe in them.

I am me again, thinks Batman, and leaps into the Gotham night.

WAYNE DENIES CONNECTION TO BATMAN
Vicki Vale, *Gotham Gazette*

In a sometimes testy, sometimes fumbling press conference at Wayne Towers yesterday, Bruce Wayne issued a strong denial that his company was in any way involved with Batman and at the same time cemented his status as one of the city's most fascinating personalities.

"I wouldn't know, and I don't think anyone who holds the Wayne purse strings would know, where to deposit a check so it would get to Batman," Wayne said in response to the first of several questions following up on *Gazette* columnist Rafael del Toro's column of this past Friday, in which del Toro speculated that Batman's activities were in part bankrolled by Wayne Enterprises or the Wayne family.

Speaking of del Toro *directly,* Wayne lamented the columnist's absence, suggesting that del Toro might be in possession of more accurate information if he attended events such as the press conference.

In answer, del Toro told this reporter that "Bruce Wayne has no interest in directly answering the question, and every interest in slaughtering the messenger. This is a conversation that Gotham City needs to have. How hand-in-glove are our business interests and the various forces operating outside the law?"

At times during the conference, Wayne appeared distracted. At several points, he asked for questions to be repeated, and more than once he gave answers that came across more like continuations of responses to other questions than direct responses to the current question. A Wayne family spokesman, speaking on condition of anonymity, confirmed that Bruce Wayne has been under a great deal of stress recently, owing to recent leadership changes at Wayne Enterprises. His health, however, is said to be excellent. . . .

29

August 4, 9:08 AM

It's good to be back in the office, Gordon thinks, even if it means that he has to spend his first day dealing with fallout from the DNA leak and—the absolute worst part of the cop's job—talking to reporters.

Scratch that. The worst part is telling someone about a death in the family. But talking to reporters is a close second.

"I sure appreciate you taking this time, Captain," Vicki Vale is telling him. "It must be difficult for you having to be the department's point person for anything having to do with Batman."

It's a transparent ploy to get him to say something controversial. "Well, Vicki," Gordon says. "I've worked on a number of Batman-related cases, and by now I've dealt with the press on Batman issues enough that the department is probably saving itself some time and man-power by doing it this way."

He's happy with that answer, but so is Vicki. Gordon starts to wonder if he's done something wrong.

"Let's talk about the DNA leak a little bit. There are

lots of questions coming up, especially since the department has done more to condemn the leak so far than to address the questions raised in the draft report."

"I think you're confusing me with Erin McNamara," Gordon says with a chuckle. "I can tell you a little bit about ways Batman has worked in tandem with GCPD before, but if you want blanket statements, you're going to have to ask Erin."

"How did it feel to shoot him?" she asks.

Conflicting feelings render Gordon speechless for a moment. On the one hand, he admires the reporter's trick of dropping the bombshell question out of the blue; on the other hand, he despises Vicki Vale for using it; and behind all that, he recognizes that the only reason for his intense response is that he does have a personal stake in this. He can't be an objective voice.

Before he answers her, Gordon takes a deep breath. "I didn't become a police officer to shoot people," he says. "But in this case the use of deadly force was appropriate. The department investigation said so, and I believed it from the beginning."

Vicki hasn't bothered to write any of that down. "You didn't answer my question."

"And I'm not going to. My feelings aren't news."

"Captain. I'm sure I don't have to tell you that anything related to Batman is news."

"I did what any police officer would have done in the same situation. I judged the use of deadly force to be appropriate given the immediate lethal threat to fellow officers, and possibly bystanders as well. That's all I have to say about it."

"Okay," Vicki says. "Then let's get back to the DNA.

Does the department find a correlation between genetic modification and criminal behavior?"

"I don't have any way to answer that," Gordon says. "We don't do DNA scans on every car thief and drug dealer who comes through."

"Well, we're not talking about car thieves. We're talking about the upper crust of criminals. It seems that every high-profile villain who has operated in Gotham City these past few years has displayed obvious characteristics of genetic modification, through either trauma or illicit medical procedures. Are there any statistics on the prevalence of black-market doctors who might do this kind of work?"

"You're out of my area, I'm afraid," Gordon says. He's wary, wondering when she's going to sneak in her next little bomb.

"Okay." Vicki snaps her notebook shut. "Let's go off the record. Between you and me, where do I go? I know this story is out there, you know it's in the city's best interest to have someone write it. So let's quit getting in each other's way."

Gordon wants a cigarette. "Vicki, if I told you about all of the bizarre things that happen in this city, you'd never get a good night's sleep again. Sometimes I think part of what cops do for people who aren't cops is keep those kinds of secrets. We know these things so you don't have to."

Some of those secrets rise to the top of his mind as he says this, but he doesn't tell her. Any big-city cop has those kinds of secrets, the things only he and other members of the force know about. The things that form part of the bond that comes with the badge and the gun. Hell, most small-town cops probably have one or two.

But journalists don't, at least not journalists like the scandal-sniffing vultures who staff Gotham City's major dailies. They don't go looking for the real stories because people don't want to read them for anything other than the kind of shivery entertainment that comes from a good horror novel. If people read those stories and take them seriously, they're going to want things to change, and on the topic of change the *Globe* and *Gazette* are studiously neutral except when making an ostentatious stand might sell copies.

"Like what?" Vicki asks, as Gordon knew she would.

He decides to give her one.

"Right after Batman took the Joker down, we were running down some of the last leads about some of the Joker's connections to the Maroons. You remember them?" She nods; any reporter would remember that particular gang. "Turns out he was using them for all kinds of errands and also squeezing them for finances. I guess he's got better money coming in now, since that was one of the first places we looked when he got loose, and none of those old sources paid off this time. Well, back then, we finally caught one of the Maroons working on the docks for Carmine Falcone. Usually the big families don't mix with street gangs; their ways of doing business are too different. But there was a history there, and we leaned on this Maroon kid until he gave up the location of one of the Joker's labs in an empty fish-processing place down on the Dixon docks."

Gordon starts arranging the pencils on his desk so he can forget about wanting a smoke. "Two things happened then. One, we crashed the fish place, and in the coolers we found thirty-seven people. Dead. Not just dead, starved to death. The Joker had kept them there to practice new kinds of Joker Juice on, and when Batman nailed him everyone forgot about those people. Except this Maroon kid, and maybe some of the other Maroons, and they didn't say anything. So I can sleep at night, I tell myself that all of them thought we'd get to the fish place before those people died. But I don't really believe it.

"The second thing is that five weeks later, we get a tip that something else is going on down at the fish place. We crash it again, and we find the Maroon kid in the same locker. Also starved to death, and with the ace of spades carved into his back."

Telling the story has made him tired. The cuts in the kid's back were so deep and wide that his rib cage showed through. Gordon has had trouble playing cards ever since. "You know what that means, right?"

Vicki doesn't answer right away. "That Carmine knew about the people the Joker had hidden away," she says eventually.

"He knew, and he wanted us to know he knew. That's the way things happen in this city, Vicki Vale. Think you could get that story in your paper?"

There's a silence between them. Gordon finishes arranging his pencils by length and debates doing it again from lightest to darkest.

"Well, that doesn't have much to do with either genetic modification or Batman," says Vicki Vale. "Are you trying to distract me, Captain?"

"No. I'm trying to tell you that yeah, there are unlicensed gene doctors in Gotham City, but I don't know who they are. And I'm also trying to tell you that I don't think they're the cause of any of this. You want that story, go find it. I can't help you."

"Apparently not," she says. "But I think it's because you're still protecting him."

"He doesn't need my protection."

"That's not a denial, Captain."

"We're off the record, Miss Vale, and in any case I can't prove I'm not protecting him, so if you're going to write it, go ahead and write it. The brass would love to see that story."

She stands. "I see. I have to say, I expected more from you than the standard cop admonition to sit on a story for the greater good."

"That's not what I'm saying, and I think you know it. Do what you have to do."

"I will." She's already at his office door. "And Captain? You, too. Take your own advice."

Then she's gone, and it's only ten in the morning, and Gordon has a stack of open case files on his desk and probably a thousand emails to delete and a couple of dozen phone messages that need listening to. Arranging his tasks from simplest to hardest, he fires up his ancient computer and accesses his department email. It's more or less what he expected, which is to say, there's nothing there he needs to read. He's copied on every department press release, and he gets the union newsletter and the homicide team morning updates and the detectives' association meeting minutes and all the other bureaucratic busywork that keeps cops from doing their jobs. Ninety-nine percent of it he deletes unread.

Before going on to the phone messages, he decides to check his personal account. There are four messages: one from a distant uncle doing genealogical research, two from Junior—who has recently begun pestering

Barbara to send Daddy emails at work—and one from a dead-drop address he has come to know well.

He opens that one and deletes it as soon as he's read the three-word text, then closes the account and picks up the phone. The day has changed around him, though; he feels as if something strong and secret and pure has reached out to him, keeping him going a little longer.

All it took was three words:

Keep the faith.

30

August 4, 10:15 AM

In his previous life, losing an expensive and useful piece of equipment like the Krawlor would have made Enfer's life miserable for days. Today, though, flushed with lingering glee over his latest message to the Joker, he's busy as a beaver getting the other Krawlors online. The fortieth is charging, and he's running a few of the others through their paces, both to see what they can do and to test his own ability to ride herd on more than one of them at a time. It's tricky, but he's getting better at it.

He's also been cooking up a whole smorgasbord of fiery goodies—mostly more Cherry Bombs, since they're so small and pack such a fine little punch, but he's had unexpectedly promising results with good old homemade napalm. He's been at this since well before the Krawlors arrived, and he's got so much incendiary potential in the back of the shop that he gets nervous every time he turns on the lights. It doesn't do any good to worry, though. Soldier on, he tells himself. Time, in the poet's words, to take it all the way. The Annunciation will be worth it.

As his sole concession to worry, though, he's relocated the rack of prostheses to the front room, where the Krawlors are milling around. For the kitchen work and the nuts-and-bolts job of activating Krawlors he's using a simple force-feedback arm, capable of stirring and turning wrenches and not much else. The other arms he plans to cache around the city for the big day, when if all goes as planned he's going to lead Batman on a merry little chase.

One other thing that has him looking over his shoulder is the possibility that the Joker will be looking for a reprisal. The two morons driving the truck obviously had done business with him before. This would of course mean removal of the Joker, but Enfer has come to accept that eventuality with surprising ease. It was never really meant to happen, he thinks of his initial infatuation with the Joker. Gotham isn't big enough for two like us.

After the Annunciation, he's going to get all of that taken care of. Ideally, it will happen as part of the Annunciation, but that might depend on whether the Joker is running around in his Batsuit that day. If so, all kinds of interesting possibilities present themselves. "I could take out both the Joker and Batman in one day," Enfer muses aloud. The Krawlors nearest him hesitate at the sound of his voice, then go on about whatever it is they're doing once they have satisfied themselves that he wasn't issuing a command to them.

He's got seventy-seven Krawlors put together, and although he hates to take the chance, it's time to be a little more aggressive about siphoning from the grid. Enfer gets his tools together, goes downstairs, and spends an hour installing a number of splices and shunts in the electrical box. When he's done, he's got enough power coming into the building to fire up all the Krawlors he can get plugged in.

And what the hell, he thinks. If Gotham Power and Light shows up, the repair guy's going to get more than he bargained for.

Two days. That's all he needs. In two days he'll have the full complement of Krawlors, each armed with combustible presents to the citizens of Gotham City . . . starting with his former GCFD brothers. They are the reason for and linchpin of the Annunciation. "Should thank them, really," he mutters as he finishes installing the rest of the outlets he's going to use to charge the Krawlors. "I might still be pulling cats out of trees."

Actually, he did that once, although Gotham City doesn't boast much in the way of arboreal variety. An absolutely stereotypical old woman called because her tabby had gotten up into the high branches of a sickly elm tree in front of her Upper East Side brownstone. They'd gotten the call, and Enfer had gone up to get the cat, which had bitten down hard on his thumb when he hauled it out of the tree. The glove, designed to withstand exposure to fire, held up under the cat's assault, but Enfer was still tempted to drop it, "accidentally," and see if the old saying about them landing on their feet was true. He'd heard somewhere that city cats never learned to do that because they spent their whole lives inside and never learned to judge distances.

Anyway, the whole job had annoyed him incredibly— had, in fact, so offended his sense of what firefighters were for that he had to warm up the old lady's brownstone a few weeks later. That was the last time he'd done

that before the warehouse ignition that had brought
Batman down on him . . .

He blinks out into a fugue of humiliated rage. He is
seventeen, about to graduate from high school, and his
chemistry teacher is standing in the doorway of the
closet where all the chemicals are kept in jars and boxes.
Enfer is at the back of the closet, one pocket stuffed with
a sulfur compound and the other with something else
that the teacher had mentioned would make the sulfur
compound go boom in the presence of water.

"Kid," the chemistry teacher says, "I told you about
this how many times?"

"I'm just looking," he says, not bothering to keep the
sullen tone out of his voice.

"I don't even care that you're lying to me," the teacher
says. "The next time I catch you in this closet, three things
are going to happen. First, I'm going to call the princi-
pal. Second, I'm going to call your parents. Third, I'm
going to fail you for the class. Actually, make it four, and
the fourth is that I'm going to call the nurse and write
up a psych evaluation request for you. How does that
sound?"

The only one of those that really bothers him is the
psych evaluation. Already he knows that people will not
understand.

"We understand each other?" the teacher says.

"Yeah."

"Then don't let me see you in here again."

The teacher stands aside, and Enfer goes back out
front into the classroom. Later that day he uses the two
powders he found to blow the bottom out of a neighbor's swimming pool.

* * *

. . . and led him here.

It takes him a minute to get his breathing under control again. Breath is important to Enfer. Fire needs oxygen, but wind will put it out; this is a lesson useful to any organism that metabolizes oxygen, and Enfer considers himself and fire both organisms. Doesn't fire eat? Breathe? Grow?

So it's important for him to keep his breathing under control, even and nourishing. He feels his heart rate come back down and some of the twitchy feeling leave his hands. "All part of the plan," he whispers, meaning not necessarily the plan for the Annunciation but the greater plan, its outlines and edges obscure, which has led him here—and which, he has no doubt, will lead him to places much higher yet.

It's time to turn up the heat on Gotham City a little more, and while he's at it to send another message to the Joker. There's a new sheriff in town, and it's time all parties concerned knew it.

BULL'S-EYE
ASYLUM HONCHO CLAIMS HE'S A SCAPEGOAT
Rafael del Toro, *Gazette* Columnist

If you were Arkham Asylum director Dr. Jonathan Crane, you'd think you had enough problems every day at work. Your clients are all dangerous lunatics, your funding is constantly under threat because upstate legislators have a bone-deep antipathy to bankrolling the treatment of a population primarily captured in Gotham City, and to top it all off you've been the target of numerous complaints about your treatment of inmates.

Now Crane can't even go to work anymore. You will all have noticed by now that Arkham Asylum burned to the ground about 10 days ago, and that since then our streets are being roamed by more than even their usual outrageous number of wackos. Somehow this, too, is Crane's fault, even though the only thing anyone can really pin on him is that he didn't stand in the ruins of the asylum with a bullhorn reading off a list of the miscreants and yahoos who escaped.

From one perspective, that's craven self-preservation; from another, it's good public policy. What good does it do us to know who's out there? Any of the possibilities, from the Joker right on down to your average stumblebum with a screw loose, are disturbing, but knowing the specifics doesn't do anything but make all of Gotham City a little edgier.

Trust me, this town doesn't need any more edge.

I talked to Crane yesterday, and it's clear that he's more than a little worn down by the controversy. "Honestly," he said, "I'm not sure why this is happening, except that it conforms to a fairly standard pattern of the public looking for a scapegoat and the media finding one."

We're good at that, Doc. Hell, if we can't find one, usually we have more fun making one up. Pin the Tail on the Scapegoat is the Gotham City journalist's third-favorite activity, right behind liquid breakfasts and manufacturing sources.

"Even if I had released the list the moment I had it compiled," Crane went on, "I'm certain most of the blame for the escapes and whatever crimes escapees might have committed would fall on me. It's the nature of the position."

Right. As if it's Jonathan Crane's fault that the Joker has gotten loose and then thrown us all a curveball by rescuing an unlucky waitress from a fate worse than death. And even then he did it by killing five other people.

You might as well blame Enfer on Jonathan Crane.

Hell, you might as well blame Batman on him.

For all we know, both of them are former patients of the good doctor's, although Crane is legally prevented from discussing such matters. Talking to him, though, you get the feeling that he knows more about both Enfer and Batman than he's able to let on.

"Both seem, from a distance, to be interesting cases," he said last night. "It would be a real professional challenge to try to help them. Perhaps I'll get the chance sometime."

That might give us all a little peace of mind. Certainly more than the release of a stupid list that most of us wouldn't have had any business reading anyway.

31

August 4, 11:01 AM

"Now, boys," the Joker says as Bud and Lou are picking up the unconscious Gotham City cop who eventually— twelve hours being an average GCPD response time in this neighborhood—came to investigate the fire and gunplay in and around the hidey-hole, "let's be careful. That's a public servant there, and we're going to have need of his particular skills."

"Whatever you say, boss," Lou grunts. The cop is a big guy, and it's a hot day in the non-climate-controlled Mormoops Central, and Bud and Lou are not in the pink of health. The Joker worries momentarily that one of them might keel over dead from the exertion. For the millionth time it occurs to him that he has chosen poorly in henchmen, at least in physical respects. Next time, he resolves. *My next henchmen will have the strength of Hercules, the morals of Caligula, and the obedience of robots.* In fact, maybe robots would be the way to go whenever Bud and Lou accidentally incinerate themselves helping to get the hidey-hole ready for the big show.

New henchmen will have to wait, though, since Bud and Lou successfully get the policeman arranged inside the entrance of what the Joker is calling Mormoops Maximus. They go back around to the outside of the building and use another entrance to come downstairs to Mormoops Central, where the Joker is standing before a bank of monitors, rubbing his hands in gleeful anticipation. He can barely contain himself waiting for the cop to awaken.

"You're sure you didn't kill him?" he asks the boys. "Our time schedule doesn't permit delays until the resurrection of the pure."

"We just gave him a knock on the head, boss," Bud says. "He'll be up and around in no time."

As if on cue the cop rolls over and begins to stir. He sits up, automatically feels for his gun, and unholsters it. The Joker gives Bud and Lou a withering look.

"You didn't say nothing about it," Lou says.

"Well, no, and of course it would never occur to you that I might not want this yahoo shooting up my best exhibits," the Joker says.

While Bud and Lou are working their way through the sarcasm, the cop gets to his feet. "Gotham City police!" he calls out, shining his flashlight around what was once the main floor of the factory. What he sees unnerves him, as it should. He's young, probably new to the force, and not yet fully acquainted with either the corruption of his new colleagues or the fiendish cleverness of their adversaries. Today will be a good lesson for him, the Joker thinks. The cop gets on his walkie-talkie and tries to call for backup, but the Joker has had the foresight to jam wireless communications in the building. The sound of static in the walkie-talkie comes over the monitor loud and clear.

"Observe, boys," he tells Bud and Lou. "If I had not taken advance countermeasures, we'd have the whole department crawling over our little bit of paradise right now."

"You sure think of everything, boss," Bud says.

The Joker toggles a switch that activates the speaker system in the nearly complete Mormoops Maximus. "Officer," he says. "It is with great delight that I, the Joker, welcome you to my latest innovation in entertainment. If you keep your head and enjoy the beneficent smile of Lady Fortune, you'll go home tonight to your TV dinner and the eleven o'clock news. If you start firing that gun everywhere and give in to your fears, I'm afraid that your potential outcomes are less salutary. Now. Let us begin."

He switches off the speakers and does a little soft-shoe before starting the show.

For a technical rehearsal, it hasn't gone badly. There are a number of glitches to work out, and the policeman, who for the most part behaved admirably, did lose his cool and ventilate an expensive feature here and there—a lapse for which the Joker is tempted to punish him. Now, however, is the time for him to take his own advice and play things cool.

Bud and Lou bring the policeman down into Mormoops Central. He's a little the worse for wear . . . well, that's an understatement, really. He was slightly the worse for wear when he went into Mormoops Maximus; now he bears a resemblance to Katatonic Kathy.

"Officer," the Joker says. "What's your name?"

He can read the man's name on his uniform, but performance is all about establishing a rapport. The officer does not answer.

"Officer," the Joker says again. He steps closer and lifts the cop's chin so they're eye-to-eye. "Do you recognize me?"

The cop nods.

"What's my name?"

The cop tries to answer, but he can't make a sound.

"Boys," the Joker says. "Get this representative of Gotham's Finest a drink of water. Unless you'd like something stronger?"

The cop doesn't respond.

"Water, then," the Joker says.

When Bud and Lou return with a glass of water, the cop just looks at it. "Officer," the Joker says, "if I had plans for you of a lethal nature, surely it's much more fun to do the deed in some of the spectacular ways possible back in the Mormoops Maximus. Like you, I ration my use of deadly force. Unlike you, I almost never can offer a rationale for my rationing. So what do you say? Are you going to worry about me *poisoning* a drink of *water* after all that? Whom would I be impressing?" He jerks a gloved thumb in the direction of Bud and Lou. "Those two? Hardly. Take a drink, wet your whistle. So we can talk."

The cop drinks the water, looking at the Joker over the rim of the glass. When he sets the glass down the Joker says, "Splendid. Now. Do you recognize me?"

"You're the Joker."

The Joker claps his hands. "Yes, yes I am. And you are . . . ?"

"Luke Harvey."

"Delighted," the Joker says, and extends a hand. The cop shakes, and for a fleeting moment the Joker is wishing he had worn a buzzer. But now isn't the time to be going for the quick gag. There's still work to be done on the Big Show. "Well, Officer Harvey, what did you think about the Mormoops Maximus?"

A glaze comes over the cop's eyes again.

"Come, now, it wasn't that bad, was it?" the Joker says. He's all solicitude as he takes the cop's hands in his and says, "Officer Harvey, we're going to have a very important guest in the Mormoops Maximus, and you are the only person I have who can tell me how to make it better. I would very much appreciate your feedback."

Trying to pull his hands away, the cop closes his eyes. His face screws up like a child's and he starts to cry. "I've got kids," he starts to say.

"Officer Harvey!" the Joker says. "Officer Harvey!"

Harvey still won't look at him, so the Joker slaps him hard across the face. "Officer Harvey, I am fully aware that my word isn't worth much around here, but you're going to have to trust me. I'm not going to kill you because I need you to deliver a message. Can you deliver a message if you're dead?"

Eyes still shut, Harvey shakes his head.

"We agree. Excellent. Now, please answer my question. What would you like to see changed about the Mormoops Maximus? Your feedback is very important."

Harvey takes a deep, shuddering breath. "I don't know," he says. "Uh, I guess the one pit toward the end, there, it's pretty easy to get over once you have it timed."

"Superb! Thank you, Officer Harvey!" The Joker

pumps Harvey's hand up and down. "Now. Here is what you are going to do for me. And I know you're going to do it, because I know you wouldn't want to ruin this excellent rapport we're developing. Am I correct?"

Harvey nods. "Yeah."

"All right, then. Your errand is in three parts. One: go and find Batman. Two: tell him what you've seen here. And three: tell him that I anxiously await his visit. Can you do that?"

"I don't know where to find Batman," Harvey says.

"Oh, but that's all right," the Joker says. "It's my understanding that among police officers, Captain James Gordon is widely assumed to have, shall we say, access to the Caped Crusader. Do you know Captain James Gordon? Fine, good. If you can't find Batman on your own, do it through Gordon. But do it quickly. This is a very important message, and I need it delivered absolutely as soon as you are able. Do we understand each other?"

Officer Harvey swallows and nods. "Yeah," he says. "We do."

"And I hardly need to add, I suppose, that disclosure of this location to anyone but Batman himself . . . or, I suppose, Captain Gordon—if you make him aware that I desire no visitors other than the vigilante himself—but in a broad sense disclosure of this location is not in your best interests, or those of your children."

"I get it," Officer Harvey says.

"Tremendous," the Joker says. "Here. If Captain Gordon is nervous about a conversation involving Batman, you may present him with this as a token of my regard."

He removes from his jacket pocket an ace of spades from a Monarch deck and flicks it expertly into Officer Harvey's shirtfront. Harvey has quick reflexes; he catches the card before it can fall to the floor.

"Boys," the Joker says, "drop Officer Harvey off back at work."

That bit of logistics taken care of, the Joker returns his attentions to the Enfer Problem. The cheek of this firebug! He must be doused.

"Must and shall be doused!" he adds aloud, just for effect. Bud and Lou were kind enough—well, momentarily sentient enough—to remember the address where they delivered the Vari-Tek robots. Soon enough, the Joker will pay a little visit and offer young Enfer a lesson in villain etiquette. When that is done he believes he might just borrow some of those superb robots, on a more or less permanent basis. He has visions of a gleaming spidery robot army popping up throughout Gotham City, each of them outfitted to deliver a special joke. Hm; he'll have to step up his lab production.

All in good time. First, Mormoops Maximus must be readied for its opening (and closing) performance. Officer Harvey is probably correct that the pit in question is a little too easily surmounted, and if an ordinary yutz like him can do it, Batman will find it comically unchallenging. That's not the kind of comedy the Joker is after, no sir.

The truth of the situation is that the Joker is much better suited to supervision of projects such as the contemplated pit expansion; so while he waits for the boys to return from their cop-delivery errand, he goes into the lab and spends an hour or so humming among his beakers and test tubes. Shame to have lost the PBDEs, but if that was the trade for discovering where the upstart firebug is nesting, then he's gotten good value for them. It would have been a kick to have a little flame-retardant fun with the boy, though. Ah, well. He sings a mournful little ditty while he's cooking up a special, easily aerosolized, batch of Joker Juice.

> "PBDEs, you've gone away
> Even though I wished you would stay
> PBDEs, you've broken my heart
> But it's all the fault of that firebug upstart . . ."

He's composed sixteen verses by the time the boys come back and he can put them to work tinkering on the Maximus. *I could have been a poet*, thinks the Joker. He's been reading this Blaise Cendrars that the firebug seems so enamored of and finds in the onetime Frederic Sauser a kindred spirit, at least where whimsy is concerned. *This was a man who knew how to make something of his losses*, thinks the Joker, turning pages while the boys sweat and curse out in the darkened Maximus.

An idea comes to him, so obvious and brilliant that he smacks himself in the head for not thinking of it before now. Frederic Sauser. "Are you hiding in plain sight, little firebug?" the Joker croons. It hardly matters, since he knows where the firebug's hideout is, but there are others who do not, and who might benefit from the knowledge. What fun it would be to provide them with it!

Delighted, he strides forth from the hidey-hole, and at the nearest pay phone he snaps the phone book off its cable and brings it back. There, plain as day in the voluminous residential listings, is a certain F. Sauser . . . but wait! The address does not match the location where the boys delivered the Vari-Tek robots!

"Better and better," the Joker giggles. He arises once more and calls out, "Back in a flash, boys!"

Then it's out the door to his favorite pay phone, voice scrambler in his pocket and a host of marvelous schemes jostling one another in his head. Not you this time, Chiefy, he's thinking . . . but who?

Ah. Perfect.

ENFER: BATMAN CATCHES JOKER
OR GOTHAM BURNS

Gillian O'Connor, *Gotham Globe*

Gotham City's newest criminal menace, the murderous arsonist known only as Enfer, has delivered an ultimatum to city law enforcement personnel and also to Batman himself. If the Joker is not apprehended by nightfall tomorrow, Enfer says, he will "announce myself in a way that will make the Arkham fire and my little joke seem like a trivial prologue."

The apparent reference is to the word HAHA, spelled out in fire across the midsection of Gotham City last week during the chaotic aftermath of the destruction of Arkham Asylum. Enfer offered no details in the message beyond a cryptic suggestion that his attack would strike "at those who have previously betrayed me."

The message, inscribed with paint thinner on the exterior of a fire extinguisher, was delivered by unknown means to the *Globe*'s news desk sometime late last night.

Professor Lindsay Kaplan of Gotham University, an expert on the tactics and psychology of the criminal mastermind, suggests that this last phrase might well be another reference to the Joker. "Enfer has lashed out at the Joker once before, by burning a number of novelty shops throughout the city," she said by phone yesterday. "It might be worth considering what other landmarks or institutions around the city he could be associating with the Joker and taking extra steps to protect them."

Asked whether Enfer's previous ambushes of firefighters might come into play here, Dr. Kaplan responded, "That could very well be. I'm sure that the mayor and public-safety administrators have already thought of that."

Gotham City fire chief Edward J. Coover would not elaborate on any extra precautions his department was taking, but in a number of interviews last night, Chief Coover said that he was aware of the threat, and that the department would be responsive. "We'll be working in cooperation with the police department to make sure that every citizen of Gotham City can feel secure that in the event of the fire department's services being needed, those services will be available and will be provided at the high level Gotham City has come to expect."

Police department spokeswoman Erin McNamara confirmed that the departments were instituting a joint security policy but declined to provide details.

The fire extinguisher was turned over to Gotham City police for examination. It is unclear whether any useful information will be gathered before the deadline.

Arkham Asylum director Dr. Jonathan Crane, at the center of a related controversy over his handling of the fire's aftermath, suggested that Enfer's ultimatum was a carefully crafted ploy to obscure an alliance between Enfer and the Joker. "It's clear that Enfer had something to do with the fires at Arkham Asylum and elsewhere," Crane said, "and equally clear that the Joker had foreknowledge of those fires."

He disputed Professor Kaplan's assessment of the situation, arguing that the Joker himself might have been either behind or complicit in the novelty-shop fires, which killed 17 people and sent dozens more to area hospitals.

"You must understand that the Joker's entire reason for existence is to sow uncertainty and chaos," Crane explained.

"Jokes are funny because the punch lines are unexpected. What better way to disguise his intent, and keep himself on the back burner until he wants to leap forth, than to stage an attack on what we would think would be nearest and dearest to him?"

And how would Enfer achieve the same effect?

"If I were a Gotham City firefighter," Dr. Crane said, "I would be very careful over the next 48 hours or so. Or, really, until Enfer is caught and we can begin to treat him."

Asked whether he thought Enfer might have passed through Arkham at some point in the past, possibly under another name, Crane said, "Speculation on that would be irresponsible at this point, given the great amount of salvage work we still have ahead of us before a complete record of the asylum's previous patients can be compiled."

32

August 5, 4:22 AM

There's a message on Gordon's cell phone when he wakes up in the morning. He wonders why he didn't hear it ring. Usually he sleeps like a stray cat, bouncing awake at the sound of a snowflake falling, but last night he slept more like a dead cat despite the heat. Barbara stirs beside him, and he pats her behind and gets out of bed. On his way to the bathroom, he flips the phone open and sees that the call is from an unknown number. He almost deletes it but figures that he might as well listen to it while he's taking a leak, since that will show about the proper amount of respect for what is probably a solicitation or a pre-recorded political message. Gordon hates election season.

When he hears the message, though, the last thing on his mind is city council races. He's out of the bathroom, dressed, and out the door in three minutes, pausing only to kiss Junior on the way.

"We've got to hit this place," he's telling Commissioner Girardeau. "It dovetails with everything we know about the guy, it's perfect."

"Captain," Girardeau says around the stem of his pipe (which makes Gordon want a cigarette). "What happened the last time we rolled out on an anonymous tip about Enfer?"

Gordon doesn't say anything. He's expected this exact question and decided before he'd gotten to his desk that he was just going to shut up and take the heat, even though it wasn't his heat.

"We lost four cops that day, and two others are permanently disabled," Girardeau says, as if Gordon doesn't know this already.

"With all due respect, Commissioner, I didn't like that tip, and I told people I didn't like it," Gordon says. He knows he shouldn't be saying it, but oh well. There goes his determination from the morning. Sometimes you can't just lie down and take other people's heat.

"And what makes this one any different?"

"That one came out of the clear blue sky, and in retrospect it's easy to see how someone with resources"—he almost adds *like Batman,* but the words *keep the faith* rise up and stop him—"could have seeded traces of common accelerants in the area to trip our sniffers. That was a plain setup, and we fell for it. And yeah, I went along, but I said at the time that there was something about the tip I didn't like. Just a hunch."

"And this time your hunch is different," Girardeau says. From his tone of voice, it's clear he's just trying to give Gordon enough rope to hang himself.

Go to hell, Gordon thinks. I'll hang, then. "Yes sir. It is. This time, we have the obvious correspondence between the name on the phone record and Enfer's well-known identification with the poet whose birth name that was. And look at the timing. The account was opened two weeks before the string of arsons started and closed two weeks after. Closed, in fact, on the day of the Arkham fire. This guy goes for the big symbolic gesture. That one screams *Hey, I'm starting a new bigger phase.* It *screams* it."

Girardeau thinks. Gordon waits.

"And you don't think Batman could have set all of this up," Girardeau says when he's done thinking.

I don't think Batman set the first one up, is what Gordon wants to say, but he's not dumb enough to be quite that plain-spoken at this particular moment. "No sir, I don't. The last tip was clearly thrown together at the last minute. The house's occupants had been dead for less than a day when we showed. The time frame of this one, and the approach, is completely different. If this was a setup, why go to all the trouble to set it up before anybody knew that Enfer was going to be a problem? The only way that makes sense is if Enfer was setting it up and deliberately arranged all of this so that we would run across it at some point. But again, why? If what he wants is to start fires and kill firemen, he's doing fine at that, and he's already gotten some cop notches on his belt, too. This whole thing isn't his style, is what I'm getting at."

"Style," Commissioner Girardeau repeats.

"Yes sir. I can call it modus operandi if you like that better, but what I'd mean was style."

"Then whose style is it?"

"I don't think it's anyone's style. I think what it is, is a genuine tip. I think Enfer is at that location at least some of the time, and if we don't go get him we're going to be sorry about it later."

"So who called it in?"

Here's where Gordon has to tread carefully. He's got a theory, but the department brass tend to dislike his theories, and knowing this, he has gotten closemouthed. This one, though . . .

"I believe, sir, that what we might be dealing with here is a case of there being no honor among thieves."

Girardeau looks at him.

"By which I mean, I think another criminal called in the tip."

"On what basis?" Girardeau asks.

"On the basis that it would be just like the Joker, for example, to see Enfer working in the city, having some success, drawing Batman's attention, and get . . . I guess the word is jealous."

Girardeau puts down his pipe. "Captain Gordon. If I understand you correctly, you're suggesting that the Joker has dropped the dime on Enfer because he's jealous that Batman's attention isn't fully directed at him. Do I mischaracterize your assertion?"

"Maybe more of a speculation than an assertion, but no, you're not mischaracterizing it."

"Well, then. If the Joker is behind this, how in the hell can you think anything about it is on the up-and-up?"

"Because in this case," Gordon says, "the Joker gets the best laugh out of playing it straight."

"Gordon, you might be right. But you might be wrong. I'm going to have to run this one past some of the higher-ups. After Grant Street, the rules are a little different. I'm sure you know what I'm getting at. Hang tight." Girardeau stands, indicating that the conversation is over. "If it's any comfort to you," he adds as Gordon walks to the door, "I'd be willing to go, but not all of us are as free and easy with our careers as you are."

* * *

Two hours later he's still waiting for Girardeau's go-ahead. He hasn't eaten, he's ignoring the phone, spontaneous combustion is no longer a question of if but when. He passes part of the time by calculating the potential fallout if he rolled out on his own, or with a small unit of uniforms he can trust. Probably, he concludes, he'd get fired, or at least busted back to patrol duty. The Gotham City Police Department can tolerate various forms of corruption and brutality, but it comes down hard on failure to follow the chain of command. Is it worth it, if I nail Enfer? Gordon wonders. Would that make losing the job worthwhile?

It might. If he lost this job, he could take Barbara and Jim Junior out of Gotham City, maybe back to Pittsburgh or maybe somewhere small, where Junior could have all the things both his parents had when they were kids. A yard, a school where the playground wasn't all asphalt with lines painted on it, a sky with stars . . . maybe it is worthwhile.

If he nails Enfer.

He's about to do it, his hand is reaching for the phone to find out where Vasquez and Tyler are, when there's a knock on his door. "Come on in," Gordon says, and a uniform sticks his head in.

"Captain Gordon? I'm Luke Harvey, and, ah . . . you got a minute?"

"Nothing but, right now," Gordon says.

Harvey steps in and shuts the door behind him. "This is going to sound crazy," he says, "but I've got a message for Batman, and I was told to bring it to you."

"Kid, you turn yourself around and get the hell out of my office," Gordon says.

"I can't do that, sir," Harvey says. "It was the Joker who gave me the message, and he didn't sound like he'd be happy if it wasn't delivered."

Gordon takes a second look at Officer Luke Harvey. There are discolorations visible on the dark blue of his uniform, both of his hands are busted up like he's just come from a brawl, and now that he's been in Gordon's office for more than a few seconds Gordon can tell that he smells like he's been at a fire.

"Harvey," he says, "there are a lot of people in this department who could get me fired for even admitting that I knew how to get a message to Batman. Truth is, I don't know if I can or if I can't. But if I'm going to take a chance on you, you've got to give me a reason."

"Only reason I have is this," Harvey says, and lays an ace of spades on Gordon's desk.

Gordon eyes it for a long moment.

"You need to play the lottery, kid," he says.

"I don't know if I'm lucky yet or not, sir," Harvey answers.

"If you walked away from a conversation with the Joker, you're lucky. And from the looks of it, it wasn't just a conversation. Am I right?"

And Harvey sits across the desk from Gordon and tells him about the Mormoops Maximus.

TAKING THEM TO TRASK
Duane Trask, *Globe* Columnist

First he was everywhere, then he was a little too much everywhere, now he is nowhere to be found.

Where is Batman?

In the midst of the direst criminal assault in this city's history, our self-appointed guardian angel has gone AWOL. Joker to the left of us, Enfer to the right, and what with the fires and the dread of whatever the Joker has up his sleeve, Gotham City might—just might—be willing to forgive Batman his recent sins, if only he would snap back to his previous form and do what he's been doing over the past 18 months or so.

I wouldn't. I'm done with Batman. There was a time, right after he appeared, when I was taken with the utopian dream that he would ride into town and flush the city clean of its various manifestations of vice and corruption—but after Grant Street and Merilee St. Pierre, I realized that a costumed crackpot is a costumed crackpot.

All the same, if Batman wants to come back and take care of this Enfer-Joker mess (and yeah, I think they're related), I'm willing to pick up my pom-poms and cheer for as long as that takes.

After that, though? Far as I'm concerned, you can put all of them in a sack and throw them in the river. And not because of this DNA sideshow; count me among the skeptics in that area. I want all of them gone because the one useful thing that can be learned from the trumped-up DNA controversy is that the people of Gotham City aren't really served by the idea that there are these superhuman figures out there, either as threats or as salvation. I have no more use for guardian angels than I do for monsters under the bed, and as soon as Batman gets his courage up and appears to do battle with the Joker and Enfer, I'm hoping they all disappear to wherever it is that bogeymen go when children have grown up and learned not to believe in them anymore.

33

August 5, 5:22 AM

Bruce awakens before dawn with a single thought chiming in his head. He flings back his covers and is out the bedroom door and down the hall without even putting on his robe. Ten minutes on the computer, interrupted by a ten-second phone call from the untraceable line in the study, is enough to tell him what he needs to know, and by the time Alfred has appeared in the doorway with his morning coffee Bruce is awake enough to accept it and say, "Why, Alfred, does it always take me the longest time to figure out the most obvious things?"

"I confess to some difficulty in selecting an answer, Master Bruce," says Alfred.

It's too early in the morning for Bruce to appreciate Alfred's dry wit. "We ran the search on Cendrars, came up with all the biographical correspondences, the Kropotkin link, all of it," he says. "And it never occurred to us to do this."

He points at the computer screen, on which Bruce has pulled up telephone listings for Gotham City. The name F. Sauser sits highlighted in the center of the display.

"He's even listed his phone number," Alfred says with mild surprise.

"Which almost makes you think it couldn't be him," Bruce says, "but I tried a call and the number's disconnected. I tapped Gotham Bell's records, and the number was apparently only active for a month, starting not too long before the fires began. Long enough for him to use the bill to get other utilities started, right? Then I wormed around in the postal records for a while, and there's an F. Sauser with a post office box in the same area."

"The data are indeed persuasive," Alfred says.

Bruce is too distracted to be annoyed by Alfred's characteristic insistence on using the plural verb with the word *data*. He's already planning angles of approach to the house, and he's also thinking how strange it is to have the feeling that a solution has been broadcast into his head. It's not the first time that his subconscious has done this to him—or, to use another psychological framework, the first time that Batman has told him something he couldn't quite figure out himself—but it catches him by surprise every time. Which is how it should be, he thinks. If that kind of revelation doesn't take you by surprise, it's because you don't spend most of your time thinking in a linear way, and if you're not doing that there's probably something wrong with you.

"I'm taking him out tonight," Bruce says.

"Then it seems," says Alfred as he lifts Bruce's coffee cup back onto the serving tray, "that we should adjourn to the cave."

Batman simmers close to the surface all day. When Alfred reminds Bruce of appointments he's scheduled for lunch and immediately after, it's Batman who answers. No jokes about who's going to say what in the papers, or which fat-cat donor is likely to have his nose put out of joint—just a flat, distracted *Cancel it*. First, Bruce puts the finishing touches on the car. He's got an intuition that he's going to need it tonight, and he wants it in top shape. He doesn't have time to install all the features he had on the other one, but by early afternoon he's got it customized for smoke and he's stiffened the driver's harness for better impact absorption. This car is a little heavier than the other one, and he hasn't driven it nearly as much, so he isn't certain what kind of performance deficit he'll face in the event of a flat-out chase with the Joker. He is certain, however, that he's a better driver than the Joker, and that will have to cancel out any deficiencies in his equipment. Ingenuity trumps gadgetry; that was one of the principles drilled into him by all of his teachers. To a man, from Ducard to al Ghul, they would frown on the extent to which he's surrounded himself with shiny mechanical toys.

His answer, were he ever to have the conversation, would be that one can employ the toys as an extension of, rather than a substitute for, the skills of the body and the mind.

"Have you seen the *Globe* this morning?" Alfred asks.

"Glanced at it."

"Miss O'Connor got quite a scoop."

"If she's in the right place tonight," Bruce says, "she might get another one. Strange how she keeps getting the inside word on all of this stuff before anyone else knows about it."

Although it isn't all that strange. Enfer wouldn't be the first villain to pick a media contact person and start an ongoing conversation. Even the Joker has been known to do it, which may be where Enfer got the idea.

Thinking of the Joker again pushes Bruce to broach a topic he's been avoiding so far. "Alfred," he says. "I want you to lie low tonight."

"I beg your pardon?" Alfred has been running a software diagnostic to make sure that all of the car's subroutines are communicating properly. From his response Bruce isn't sure whether he means he hasn't heard or wants an explanation.

"Take a night off," Bruce says. "Get out of the house. Go see a movie, visit friends in the country."

"That would feel uncomfortably like dereliction of duty, Master Bruce," Alfred responds.

Bruce puts down the last of the Bat-shuriken he's been sharpening and balancing. Two dozen will have to be enough. "Alfred. I don't know whether the Joker will come back here. I don't know whether he'll get involved in whatever happens when I go after Enfer tonight. There are too many things I don't know, and I don't want to add your safety to the list."

"Touching, Master Bruce," Alfred says. "All the same, I think the best course is for me to stay on here."

"I'd hate to have to order you to do it," Bruce says.

Alfred looks him in the eye. "I would equally hate having to refuse such an order."

Bruce gets a utility belt and fills three of its compartments with shuriken. Eight each, a perfect double handful. He breaks open the rest of the utility belt's pockets and straps and sets about filling it with a full complement of gear: six gas-fired grapnels, a longer rope with grappling hook designed to be thrown, a dozen smoke grenades, another dozen flash-bang grenades. In a pocket by themselves he sticks twenty magnetic homing devices, and he fills the last pocket with three of the sensors Lucius has sent from Applied Sciences. He also packs three ampules of an antivenin he's put together that according to lab simulations should mitigate the effects of Joker Juice.

"If that doesn't do it," he says to himself, "nothing will."

Then to the suit. He checks the underarmor for tears or other defects, then looks at the cowl. Thinking about Enfer, he's added a pair of retractable polarizing lenses that should be ideal for seeing in conditions that would otherwise either blind him with smoke or set his eyes watering from heat. He doesn't like the idea of having anything between his eyes and the world, but he knows this is a crutch. There are four other senses, and in any case having lenses in the cowl is better than having his eyes boiled in their sockets by one of Enfer's surprises.

He has a mental image of Tsunetomo sardonically raising an eyebrow, to which he silently responds: *Extension, not substitution.*

"Eight hours, Master Bruce," Alfred says. "Time to eat, at least, if you won't take a break."

Bruce takes his lunch in front of the computer. He's been considering whether he should tell Gordon about the tip, and he's still not sure. If the police act on the tip immediately, another Grant Street could result, only this time there wouldn't be a disguised Joker there to spring a trap. In addition, a police action could easily tip Enfer off and make him harder to find later.

On the other hand, what is his responsibility to Gotham City? Does he dare wait until nightfall—five hours away—and take the chance that Enfer won't kill before then?

Maybe it's true, he thinks. *Maybe we don't think like they do.*

Close on the heels of that thought, he thinks: *but wait a minute. Am I* we *or am I* they?

Bruce hasn't devoted much thought to the question, but abruptly it comes to the front of his mind. He has taken the pure human about as far as it can go, possibly far enough that he has more in common with the deformed or metahuman criminal class than he would like to admit. It isn't the first time he's thought this, but the media frenzy over the DNA results has hammered home to him the fact that no matter what he does—no matter how many lives he saves or how many catastrophes he averts or how many villains he puts behind bars—to much of Gotham City, he will always be one of Them. They will want to have him around as long as they find his actions useful, as long as they can rock their children to sleep with Batman stories; but they consider him a useful freak.

"What the hell," he mutters. "I am a useful freak."

"Beg pardon?" Alfred says from over near the car.

Bruce looks over at him. "Alfred. Are you washing the car?"

Chamois in hand, Alfred gives Bruce his best patronizing-butler look. "That would seem to be evident, Master Bruce."

And Bruce is laughing, not at Alfred but in pure unexpected joy at the knowledge that he isn't as alone as he is always so ready to assume.

Nightfall is five hours away. Bruce sends Gordon a short message and gets back to work.

JOKER: GOTHAM PD LETTING ENFER BURN OUT OF CONTROL

Vicki Vale, *Gotham Gazette*

In a highly unusual move, Gotham master criminal the Joker contacted this reporter shortly before today's *Gazette* went to press. He accused the Gotham City Police Department of failing to act on a tip related to the whereabouts of his villainous counterpart Enfer and further alleged that city officials had been conspiring to protect Enfer since his appearance in the city.

During the course of an extensive conversation—his part of which was conducted in rhyming couplets, none of which are printable in this newspaper—the Joker displayed considerable familiarity with the workings of Gotham City's official and unofficial hierarchies. In addition, he offered tantalizing insights into last week's disastrous Grant Street raid and related events, which claimed the lives of at least nine people, including four police officers.

Claiming direct knowledge of the events, the Joker said that the unsolved murders of a Sherman Street family less than a block from the Grant Street address were obviously a bungled first attempt to execute the setup. He further alleged that Gotham City police have known this for some time and have suppressed the information lest it swing the pendulum of public opinion back in Batman's direction. . . .

34

August 5, 7:21 PM

According to the almanac, sunset in Gotham City comes at seven twenty-one post meridiem, and at exactly that moment Enfer enters the command that sets his army of Krawlors loose on the city. They line up and troop out the open bay door like a well-drilled militia, which is what they are, and he is their field marshal, safely installed at a remote location.

He's broken them up into thirty teams of three each, with five held in reserve here at the command post. His initial instinct was to pair them off, but what with all the media hoopla surrounding his little message he's opted for thirty sure things instead of forty-eight strong possibilities. Besides, once each team has achieved its initial objective, he can redirect them. Gotham City has lots of fire stations.

Keeping an eye on thirty monitors at once—each divided into three subscreens—starts to make him feel kind of like he's a fly. Ninety perspectives blend into a kaleidoscope of cityscapes. As an act of ocular self-preservation, Enfer whips up a little program to put the estimated time until destination up on each monitor, so he can pay attention to the ones that count.

Phase One is going to be a lot of fun, just by virtue of the amount of stuff that will burn, but for the first time in years Enfer is actually looking forward to something more than a fire. As soon as he spots Batman, Phase Two is going to begin, and then, as Enfer's grandfather would have said, we'll see who's leather and who's lace.

Let's not get ahead of ourselves, though, he cautions himself. Hunker down here, watch the Krawlors do their thing, and venture out only when the potential reward of that venture demands it. The successful grand scheme demands a certain dexterity in risk analysis.

So, Phase One. He's got the Krawlor teams numbered in order of their arrival at their targets, and as the fur begins to fly, it's all Enfer can do to keep up with the mayhem. If he were a cartoon character, his eyes would be dividing into ninety little rectangles.

Team 1 hits the closest fire station to the command post. It's one of the oldest in the city, built back when there was still open land on all three islands. The firefighters who work out of this station take pride in still using the pole to get down to the engines; they're a throwback bunch, hardy and profane, veterans of the worst a neighborhood filled with old and crumbling buildings can throw at them.

The first two Krawlors, 1.1 and 1.2, go around the back, down an alley, and surprise a detail of Gotham City police standing guard. Enfer has programmed them to take immediate action against a number of patterns, including police cruisers, and they immediately roll Cherry Bombs in the direction of the police detail. Krawlor 1.3, utilizing the diversion, has come around the other side and is climbing the back wall of the station. At about the same time that the Cherry Bombs go off under the front end of the first cruiser, 1.3 is breaking a window and raising hell in the fire station kitchen. Through its monitor, Enfer sees Joysticks twirling in the kitchen and down the hall.

Abruptly the news becomes rather mixed. In the alley 1.1 and 1.2 have done a bang-up job of scattering the police detail and are now heading into the station's ground floor, but through 1.3's monitor Enfer sees two firefighters appear shoulder-to-shoulder in the kitchen door. They level shotguns; as 1.3's feed goes out, Enfer flinches at the sudden white noise.

Downstairs, he sees 1.1 and 1.2 heading into the garage. Krawlor 1.2 goes dark just as 1.1's monitor registers a blinding light, and the view is momentarily upside down. Then 1.2 rights itself and, responding to an emergency subroutine invoked by the loss of its other two team members, unloads its jellied-gasoline payload and torches the garage in a consuming orange cloud.

Score: three Krawlors lost, one fire station well on its way to full combustion. Call it a draw.

The first half an hour passes in repetitions of that scene, with slight variations. Enfer tinkers with his approach, with the result that after the first five or six assaults he's getting at least one Krawlor extracted every time. Knowing that the firefighters are armed makes a difference; it puts a premium on timing, for one thing, and also necessitates some softening up from a distance before the Krawlors invade each station.

After his first dozen teams have executed their missions, he has fourteen surviving Krawlors, but all twelve stations are merrily ablaze. An expanding ring of glorious destruction spreads across a graphical map of Gotham City on his main display. "Beautiful," Enfer murmurs. "Beautiful." As each team completes its mission, he leaves the survivors to execute their automated responses and concentrates on the next wave of seven teams, which is due to arrive over the next two or three minutes.

He's creating an expanding ring of both fiery destruction and inability to respond to that destruction. Burning Gotham from the center out, and he'll stop when his thirty teams have reported back from their missions and he can point out to the Gotham powers-that-be how precarious their position will be if he decides to reload and do another thirty missions. Can they stop him? No, they cannot. What does he want?

He wants two things.

He wants the Joker, and he wants Batman.

If he doesn't get them, there won't be a cop or a firefighter left on the three islands, and then the people of Gotham City will find out what it's like to be at one another's mercy . . . and at his.

Enfer first sees Batman when Team 13 is making its approach to the fireboat docked at Rogers Marina. "Figures you'd show up where the rich people's toys are, Mr. Civic Hero," Enfer sneers into the feed of 13.2, which is taking evasive action by running along the deck of a sleek black fifty-foot yacht with sails emblazoned with the initials KYK. Krawlor 13.2 flips a few Joysticks into the air as it runs, and they spin across the marina channels, burning their way through sails and rigging. Now, that's improvisation, Enfer thinks; he hadn't even considered torching boats. This is one of those times when the robots seem more innovative than humans.

Through 13.3's feed, Enfer gets a look at Batman up close and personal. Unfortunately the view doesn't last, because Batman does something so quickly that the feed can't keep up, and the next thing Enfer knows 13.3's feed is white noise. "Shit," he says. Krawlor 13.2 is still flinging Joysticks all over the marina, though, and Krawlor 13.1 has made its approach to the fireboat by creeping along the underside of the pier. It springs across the gap and clings to the fireboat's hull. Gunfire erupts all around it, as a police speedboat bristling with sharp-shooters opens up. Krawlor 13.1's feed herks and jerks as some of the bullets ping off its chassis and legs, but the Krawlor itself seems to be doing fine. It gains the deck of the fireboat and rolls four Cherry Bombs, one after another, down the stairs that lead belowdecks.

As it turns to make its escape, a *chunk* comes over the audio and suddenly the Krawlor can't move. It looks around, and the cause becomes apparent: Batman has pinned one of its legs to the deck with the pick end of a fire ax. He leans into the display and says, *"À très bien-tôt."*

Then he's doing a backflip over the fireboat's railing onto the pier as the Cherry Bombs go off and 13.1's feed dissolves.

À très bientôt? Mr. Civic Hero offers a witty threat and makes it insulting by saying it in abominably accented *French*? Enfer is inflamed. He will not just kill Batman, he will disperse his ashes across the city's fire hydrants to be pissed on by dogs. He will stuff and mount the Hero's scorched costume and display it on the roof of his car. He will strike the word *bat* from the city's lexicon and replace it with *chauve-souris*. He will . . .

No. Of course. That was the Joker. Banter like that is much more in the Joker's character than in the Hero's. And of course the Joker would play the Batman role tonight, the better to thwart Enfer—momentarily—and the better to go on with his own mad plan to turn Batman into a symbol of violent caprice and unreliability . . . a symbol, in short, of the Joker himself. The real Batman is elsewhere, doing something inscrutable, scheming invisibly until he can . . .

"Excuse me. Mr. Sauser?"

Enfer turns to see Batman, his heart lurching in surprise and confusion. *How did he know about this place? And how did he get here so* fast?

Then Enfer realizes that the death's-head grin is not Batman's, and the wisps of green hair curling from under the cowl are not Batman's.

"My upstart firebug," the Joker says. "The time has come, the Joker says, to talk of many things."

EXTRA!: ENFER ON EARTH
PYRO-VILLAIN SPREADS DESTRUCTION ACROSS
GOTHAM; FIREFIGHTERS, POLICE TARGETS
Gillian O'Connor,
Special to the *Gotham Globe*

Details are sketchy, but arch-arsonist Enfer is apparently making good on his threat to spread havoc across Gotham City. Reports coming in from all over the city paint an apocalyptic picture of fire stations and other city facilities under siege from an army of mobile robots armed with bombs and incendiary devices. The swath of fire is spreading from the Rogers Marina to the Upper East Side, and the most recent eyewitness accounts claim that fire stations as far south as the financial district are under siege as well.

Of Enfer himself there has been no sign, but Batman sightings are pouring in, indicating that the Caped Crusader has joined the fight to save the city.

Mayor Hill has mobilized the National Guard to assist in firefighting and disaster-relief efforts, and unconfirmed reports indicate that Gotham City will soon be declared under martial law. . . .

35

August 5, 8:53 PM

The firebug is out the door in a jiffy—oh, how the Joker wishes he knew the French word for "jiffy," but the gift of languages is, alas, not his—and the Joker casually strolls to the Bat-car and heads out after him. There's no hurry. The game will play out as the game will play out.

Also, he stuck a little Joker Detector on Enfer, in what was even for him a scandalously ingenious manner: simply by entering the house and planting a few on each doorknob. So easy. If the firebug wipes his hands, the little fake boogers will stick to his clothes, et cetera . . . but he won't. He's in too much of a hurry for that. He hasn't even taken his black fireman's hat.

While the Joker looks at the Bat-car's GPS to see where the firebug is going, he glances in the rearview mirror to make sure Bud and Lou are taking care of their end of the operation. It shouldn't be possible for them to screw it up, but they wouldn't be Bud and Lou if they didn't at least try to find a way.

"All I want you to do, boys," he said to them earlier, as they were planning this escapade, "is go into the house after I'm gone. Plug the servers into the big battery pack on the wheelbarrow. Then wheel the whole shebang out to the van and take it back to the Maximus. Are we clear?"

"Sure are, boss," the boys said.

"Repeat it back to me," the Joker said.

They did, and now as he sees them coming out of Enfer's little bungalow hideaway the Joker has a flush of pride in his boys. To all appearances they are actually transferring a useful and delicate piece of machinery without wrecking it. "*Vaya con Dios,* boys," he says. "Great start. I'm so proud." He wishes he had a hankie to wave out the window. The fact that they can't hear him makes the occasion all the more poignant; the Joker is brought nearly to tears by shame at how he almost employed this very Bat-car as an instrument of double henchmancide. Then he's brought nearly to tears by the hilarity of remembering Lou trying to bounce his considerable self out of the Bat-car's way. *Hahahahahaha-haha . . .*

But wait! There's a firebug to catch, and exterminate! "After you, firebug menace!" he cries out and squeals away down the street, one eye on the road and the other on the little red bug icon creeping across the GPS grid of Gotham City streets.

"Firebug, firebug, oh, fire, firebug . . ." The Joker's singing at the top of his lungs as he tests the Bat-car's cornering ability, in addition to the agility of local pedestrians. There aren't as many of them as there might be, since large parts of the city appear to be under siege by vaguely arachnid and pyromaniacally violent robots, and the large numbers of sirens and nervous, trigger-happy cops help to keep the good citizens of Gotham indoors. So the Joker has the streets to himself, at least compared with what Gotham traffic is usually like.

He wonders where the firebug is going. "Where aa-aa-aa-re you, firebug?" he sings out the window, momentarily regretting his lack of discretion but realizing that the Batman Impostor Gag (BIG) is probably nearing its climax. Its punch line, the point at which it will pass from gag into history remembered in the natterings of old men around barbershop chairs, et cetera, et cetera. So discretion is not a quality of tremendous value at this juncture.

The firebug's icon has come to rest inside a building near the corner of Mulligan and Schuyler—not all that far from McGee's, in fact. Remembering that slaughtered icon of his youth renews the Joker's resolve. He furrows his brow, tightens grin into grimace, and brings the Bat-car to a rocking halt at the point nearest the bug icon on the dashboard GPS. The storefront in front of which he has double-parked is Safari Sports and Outdoors. "I say," the Joker says. "Is there to be gunplay?"

He starts whistling the theme from *The Good, the Bad, and the Ugly* as he approaches the store's glass front doors. Trying to fling them open like spaghetti-Western saloon doors, he accidentally shatters both of them, and then all of a sudden he's a sheepish Bullwinkle. "Don't know my own strength," he confides to a terrified stockboy huddling under a pile of clearance parkas. "Oh. Here, kid. Mind putting these back in the car out front? You'll know the one. But don't take it anywhere, okay?"

"O-okay, Batman," the kid stutters, scrambling out of the pile with the Bat-car's keys. For a moment he has trouble getting purchase on the slippery parka shells, but when his sneakers finally touch carpet, he's gone like the hope of heaven.

"And see someone about that stutter," the Joker calls after him. "Doctors can do wonders nowadays!"

Then it's on into the vast retail savanna that is Safari Sports and Outdoors: thousands of square feet of outrageously priced clothing and accessories, artfully arranged around dioramas of African wildlife. The clusters of fleeing and hiding customers add to the sense of being on the hunt. Such an abundance of game! Such an abundance of consumer goods! There's an athletic-supplies wing with racks, bins, and piles of everything from lacrosse sticks to bocce balls; and in the back the store at last becomes true to its name, with a full-service firearms counter and a shooting range in the basement. The Joker isn't a betting man—or in the strictest sense of the word, a man at all—but if he were, he'd put his hard-earned money on the firebug being down there.

As he's heading toward the gun counter, it becomes vibrantly clear to the Joker that he'd have lost the bet. The firebug pops up from behind the handgun display case and lofts a pair of what look like paper-towel rolls in the Joker's general direction. At about the midpoint of their journey, both of them blaze into flaming life at either end and spin fast enough that they start flying in wide loops through the store, igniting whatever they come close to. One of them hits a stuffed antelope and starts skipping and bouncing along the floor under hanging racks of outerwear and sport shirts; at about the same time, the store sprinklers kick in and suddenly it's monsoon season in the Serengeti. Briefly nonplussed by this change in circumstance, the Joker isn't quite ready when the second spinning missile bangs squarely into the back of his head. Only Batman's superb craftsmanship spares him a quite uncomfortable burn, not to mention a probable concussion. He grabs the missile and flings it away toward the front of the store, where it gets stuck in a herd of zebras and slowly fizzles out in a haze of steam and burned fur.

"Firebug!" cries the Joker. "We haven't had our chat, and already you're so hostile!"

The firebug responds by leaping over the counter and charging toward the Joker, who is surprised enough by this turn of events to be still laughing when Enfer crashes into his midsection. They go down together, and the Joker rakes the spines of his gloves across the firebug's face while the firebug delivers a series of extremely damaging punches to the side of the Joker's head. For a moment there are two firebugs—the Joker really isn't cut out for this kind of work—and then the real firebug is standing over him. "Okay, hey," Enfer says. "Let's remember which side we're on, here. The enemy of my enemy is my friend, right?"

"Well, sometimes," the Joker says. "Sometimes they're all just enemies. Let's not make things any more complicated than they have to be. Simple joke, funny joke."

"No wonder you didn't make it as a comedian," the firebug says.

"You dare?" the Joker shrieks. He reaches into one of the Bat-pouches and throws whatever it is he finds there, which as it turns out is a fistful of little bat-shaped and sharp-edged metal things. Most of them sail off into the wilds of the savanna, but one plants itself in the back of the firebug's right hand.

"Aren't you the strong, silent type," the Joker marvels when the firebug issues not a whisper of pain.

"I make my own kind of noise," the firebug says. "Now seriously. Let's both work on the Batman problem tonight and then settle what's between us."

The Joker affects towering and wounded pride, which is no mean feat from a sitting position. "Before you went to the papers, I might have considered it. Now how can I trust you? And that's even if I were to forgive you for that atrocity you perpetrated on our city's novelty shops."

"Was trying to get your attention," the firebug says.

It comes to the Joker's attention that despite the sprinklers, the fire burning on the retail floor of Safari Sports and Outdoors is getting fairly intense. All that cotton. All those taxidermied animals.

"You being a professional in this field and all," he says, "how long do you think we have to get out of here?"

"Figure we should be moving toward an exit," the firebug says. He extends a hand. "Come on. You don't want to talk now, we'll talk outside."

Against his better judgment, the Joker takes the firebug's hand . . .

. . . and it comes off in his.

"*À très bientôt,*" the firebug says. "Suck-aire."

The firebug's dismembered hand is squeezing quite a bit harder than it seemed to be when it was still attached to his body. Marvelous, the Joker finds himself thinking. He considers elective amputation, then recovers his faculties and leaps to his feet. It's not as easy as it should be with his balance thrown off by the prosthesis attached— in a friendly kind of way—to his right hand. In the few seconds it takes him to get his balance back, the firebug is gone out the back door.

The Joker shakes his arm. The prosthesis won't come off.

He shakes it harder. The prosthesis still won't come off. Sparks suddenly fly out of the shoulder joint, followed by a cloud of nauseating black smoke.

The Joker picks the Bat-shuriken out of the back of the prosthesis's hand. Then he can't help it. He starts to laugh, and he's still laughing when he gets back to the Bat-car.

"A dud, hoo hoo," he gasps. "A purely ornamental *arm*ament . . . *hahahahahahahaha* . . ."

With that he's off after the firebug again, driving with his left hand and banging the shifter up and down with the wrist of the prosthesis. His fingers are numb, and if he were a regular guy, the Joker figures his metacarpals would be ground into meal fit for the giant at the top of the beanstalk.

He passes a fire station, which is now a fire station in the same way that his lab is a crime lab, which is to say it is a station in which fire happens. A number of police officers are blazing away at something unseen but al-

most certainly a Vari-Tek Krawlor. Overhead, a helicopter hovers. The sound of heavier gunshots is heard
above the general hubbub.

Spang! A bullet skips off the Bat-car's roof.

"Delightful!" the Joker exclaims. It's worked! At least
some of the local yokels in blue are shooting at Batman
on sight!

"What a little . . . misdire-e-ection . . . ca-a-an . . .
dooo," he croons.

Spang!

It's the helicopter shooting at him. Well, at Batman,
but at some point—well, this point right here, when the
bullets are bouncing off his roof instead of Batman's—
the mistaken perspective becomes meaningless. "One of
those semantic disputes," the Joker lectures the prosthesis. "For example: Are you an arm, now that you're no
longer being used for that purpose? Or are you now an
arm-shaped collection of gears and latex? What's the
difference?"

Spang! Spang!

What's the difference, the arm wants to know, *between Batman and another individual dressed as Batman and driving Batman's car in such a manner as to
suggest he is Batman?*

"I'll tell you what the difference is," the Joker retorts.
"I am me. No more, no less. Not who I used to be, but
me. Batman, he's . . . I'll tell you what Batman is. He's a
sufferer. Whoever he calls himself during the day, this is
a man so in love with his own pain that he's created an
entirely new identity just to indulge it."

He's still arguing with the arm when the boys call in
to let him know that the server is up and running back
in Mormoops Central. "Fabulous," he says, and hangs

up to make another call. He waits, and waits . . . ah. "Yes, hello. How are you, Doctor Crane? Oh, you recognize me; how wonderful of you. Well. I have a simply irrepressible desire to make use of some of your, ahem, therapeutic materials . . ."

36

August 5, 9:22 PM

From the marina Batman fights robots all the way across the East End, and then south toward the address of one F. Sauser. He feels not just as if he's on the horns of a dilemma, but that the dilemma is literally propelling him. Take out as many robots as he can, or sacrifice the lives and property the robots will destroy while he makes a beeline for Enfer and cuts the head off this beast? When there are no robots in sight, he leans toward the second option; but as soon as he sees one, and the havoc and pain it spreads, he knows that option one is the only choice.

The sun has been down for two hours, and in that time he has personally wrecked twenty-one of the Krawlors. He's trying not to think of the irony that Wayne Enterprises had one of the research contracts to develop the Krawlors' pattern-recognition software. One of these days, when his control over Wayne Enterprises is more complete—and, to be frank about it, when he has the energy to devote to the enterprise—he's going to rebuild the family business along more responsible lines. Maybe that's a utopian goal, but it's surely not any more utopian than thinking he can single-handedly make a lasting difference in the civic life of Gotham City.

Or any more utopian than thinking that he can single-handedly destroy what seems to be an army of Krawlors, remotely controlled. In the middle of a pitched battle with three of them twenty minutes ago, he saw all three freeze, just for a moment, before launching back into their coordinated assault on one of the Bowery substations. That's when he knew they were slaved to a single user somewhere, and that makes it all the more important that he get to that nerve center.

The address in the Gotham City phone directory is burned into his forebrain. He's less than half a mile away, running the wrong way up a one-way portion of Henry Boulevard, when something explodes in a building on the south side of Henry and much of its façade slumps into the street. Instantly Batman's out of the car and clambering over the wreckage, hearing gunshots and registering the distinctive click and whine of the Krawlors' servomotors. When he gets a look into the building, he sees that it's an ordinary office that shares a back wall with a fire station. Now both buildings are burning—the office not as aggressively because it just collapsed—and there's a running battle between Gotham City police, armed firefighters, and two Krawlors. He can't see the third and wonders if it was the source of the explosion that wrecked the office building.

Suddenly the air is full of the spinning missiles Enfer threw at him during their first encounter. The two Krawlors, bullets ricocheting off their legs, are throwing them up in the air as fast as they can retrieve them from chassis storage compartments. The missiles break windows and start burning inside several buildings on the block, and they've got the police detail pinned behind a GCPD cruiser just to the west of the fire station.

As Batman watches, one of the missiles sails in through a half-open cruiser window and begins to pinball around the inside of the car. Knowing what's going to happen, he starts fighting his way straight through the burning, shifting rubble from the collapsed office building to the other side of the block. His cape catches on protruding rebar, and he tears it free; something burns his feet, and he leaps ahead. Then he's on the street, four shuriken flashing out of one hand to punch two of the spinning missiles out of the air.

How long before the ammunition in the cruiser cooks off and takes the gas tank with it?

He's across the street, spreading his arms. A bomb goes off somewhere behind him, the blast wave throwing him forward just as he jumps, clearing the cruiser, and at the apex of the jump he pirouettes in the air, stiffens the cape, and settles like a shroud over the three cops pinned down on the other side.

"What the—?" One of them starts to fight him, and Batman draws the cape tight, restiffens it, and hunkers down like a mother bat over her babies as the shotgun shells and flash-bang grenades in the cruiser begin to cook off. He can feel the struggles of the three cops and hopes against hope that one of them doesn't lose it and start shooting. This isn't the way he wants to find out if Lucius Fox's special underwear is all it's cracked up to be.

The roar of the gas tank exploding is at first too big to be a sound. It's a feeling, a sensation of being violently

compressed, of having the parts of your body rearranged so that you are no longer three-dimensional.
Then comes the sound, but by then the heat is already
almost unbearable, and Batman smiles fleetingly as he
imagines the collective media orgasm were he to be
found dead sheltering—*or was he?*—three cops from
the detonation of their cruiser.

He has thoughts like that when his brain is cooking in
the pan of his skull, and when the wave of heat has
passed he has the good grace to be embarrassed about
them.

Standing up, he releases the cape. The three cops, two
uniforms and a ranking coat-and-tie, spill away from
him.

One of the uniforms immediately stands and levels his
gun at Batman. He's wild-eyed, panicky. His hands shake.
"Freeze!" he screams.

I could take the gun before he thought to pull the trigger, Batman thinks. But cops don't like it when you take
other cops' guns.

"I'm not going to freeze while Gotham burns," he
says calmly. "If you need to take a shot, take a shot."

The second uniform doesn't say a thing. Looking
around, Batman sees that the Krawlors have gone on to
their next target, wherever that is.

"Maybe you shouldn't shoot him right away, Tyler,"
the plainclothes cop says. "It's a little soon after he
saved our lives, don't you think?"

Batman looks and, sure enough, it's Jim Gordon.

"Tell your man here to shoot someone else, Captain,"
Batman says.

"Shoot someone else, Tyler."

"Captain, there's a department order—"

"Tyler, if you shoot Batman right now, I will do one of two things. Either I will shoot you myself, or I will have Vasquez do it and get him promoted afterward." Tyler's eyes pop out of his head. "You don't think that happens around here?" Gordon goes on. "Kid, I've been at this game a long time. You don't know what you're getting into. Aim the goddamn gun at the ground."

After a long moment—long enough, Batman thinks, that later he'll be able to convince himself that he could have done it and chose not to on his own terms—Tyler lowers his sidearm.

"Captain," Batman says. "A word?"

Gordon steps away from the uniforms. The two of them lean their heads close. Batman is about to ask him why he didn't follow up on the tip when Gordon says, "Your message. I got a call saying the same thing at the crack of dawn this morning."

Batman remembers waking up with the thought in his head, at about the same time when Gordon would have been getting his message.

"From who?"

Gordon shrugs. "You want me to handicap it, I'm going to say the Joker. But who knows how these people think? Hey. Speaking of the Joker, I've got a little message for you."

He hands Batman an ace of spades. On the back, in a florid script: *Your presence requested at the Mormoops Maximus! Don't delay!* And below that, an address.

Mormoops Maximus. Very funny.

"I'm going there soon as I take care of Enfer," Batman says. "Keep up the fight here."

Gordon cracks a smile. "Keep the faith, right? You, too."

* * *

Keep the faith, indeed, Batman is thinking. Keep believing that the average Gothamite isn't like Officer
Tyler, ready to shoot him as soon as a disembodied
policy crosses his desk as a memo.

There's no good reason to have that kind of faith in
this city; yet he does.

He's a block from the address where F. Sauser has his
phone bill sent, or did until the line was disconnected recently. He guides the car into the alley that bisects each
block in this neighborhood lengthwise, flicks off the
lights, and switches from the gas engine to the electric.
Silent except for the crunch of tires on gravel, he ghosts
up behind the house.

It's dark, and the back door is open. Batman gets out
of the car and walks through the open door, up two
stairs, and into a linoleum-and-Formica kitchen. He
smells something odd, a chemical smell, and after a moment of mental wheel-spinning puts it together with the
scent Enfer gave off the first night they tangled. He
walks into the living room, which is unfurnished save
for a single chair, a folding table, and two large metal
shelves creaking under the weight of . . . he counts . . .
thirty computer monitors. On the folding table is another monitor, a keyboard, and a mouse, all cheap mail-
order brands. He doesn't find a processor.

Something is stuck to one of his gloves. He looks at it
and almost flicks it away in disgust before he has a moment of investigative synergy, and everything in the
house falls together into an obvious narrative. "Ah,"
Batman says. Holding the fake booger between thumb
and forefinger, he heads back out to the car and opens
up the code that runs the car's dashboard tracking ter-

minal. It only takes a minute to splice in the dozen lines of code that allow it to search a spectrum of frequencies and see what other homing devices are operating in the immediate vicinity, and it only takes a minute after that to isolate the booger's frequency.

Then it's just a matter of pinging that frequency until he finds out where Enfer has gone, and whether the Joker has gotten to him yet. Possibilities ramify on the other side of that event. If Enfer still has control of the server, and therefore the Krawlors, then once Batman has run him down the problem will be solved. If the Joker has gotten control of the server, locating it will be more of a trick. It might be at the so-called Mormoops Maximus, but where the Joker is concerned it's rarely a good idea to trust logical deduction. If necessary, he will wring the location of the server out of the Joker; and if necessary, he will find it in whatever burrow the Joker's dug into since he got out of Arkham.

First things first, he tells himself: track the homing beacon and find Enfer.

But something about the knowledge that he and the Joker hit on the F. Sauser solution so nearly simultaneously has him wondering if maybe the Joker is expecting exactly this.

37

August 5, 10:14 PM

Nobody with any pride in himself would run around Gotham City with a prosthetic arm stuck to his real hand, Enfer tells himself. And the Joker, whatever else you might say about him, has some self-esteem. So he thinks he's got a few minutes before the Joker shows up, and he plans to use that time wisely. Okay, he's lost the server, and therefore probably lost control over the Krawlors in the field. But now that he's back in the old factory, he's got some goodies in reserve, and what kind of host would he be if he didn't prepare a welcome?

First he sets his five Krawlors in a perimeter near each entrance to the building. Second, he puts on his long coat and loads it with goodies. Third, he sets up a dead-drop switch, keyed to the buckle holding his arm into its harness, that will trigger the boomification of his spare arsenal in the back room. And fourth . . .

But that's when the Joker makes his appearance, signaled by the sequential thumps of several Cherry Bombs going off just outside the door at the far end of the building. Enfer puts on his oxygen mask and tanks, gets his spare hat on over the getup, and buckles his coat. He's ready. He wasn't sure which arm to use, but now that the event is upon him he's happy with the one he's got. The only thing he worries about is that he designed the nozzle for a less viscous liquid than the runny version of napalm he's currently tanked it up with. But if it works, even for a minute—the right minute—then hot diggity. That's taking it all the way.

More booms, and then a rising electronic squeal from the back of the building. Enfer doesn't have time to wonder what's making it, although his initial guess is that he's just borne aural witness to the demise of yet another Krawlor. God, he's spent a lot of money tonight. Never mind; by now it should be clear to the powers-that-be in Gotham City that they can't afford not to deal with him, and the deal is going to be a tough one.

"Did you learn?" he mutters to himself. "You didn't do what I wanted, and what did it get you?"

"Hellloo-ooo," comes the Joker's voice, drifting through the vast floor space of Enfer's soon-to-be-former residence. After tonight, he's going to have a real house. A town house. A penthouse. With fireplaces.

Still in his Bat-disguise, the Joker swaggers into view, his caped and cowled profile backlit by the glow of fire from the darkened rear portion of the building. "Well, there you are, my upstart firebug," he says warmly. He holds up his right arm, and Enfer sees that the prosthesis still dangles from the Joker's right hand. It's somewhat the worse for wear, though. The latex hangs in strips, and clusters of wiring and sprung springs gleam in the firelight as well as the harsher glare from the trouble lights hanging around Enfer's workstations. The titanium humerus appears to have snapped off entirely.

Enfer decides to make a joke. "I trust you with my body, and this is how you treat it?"

"My deepest, most rueful apologies," the Joker says. He regards the mangled limb. "But those Krawlors are robust indeed. I had to keep hitting it. Them."

When he looks back up at Enfer, the light in his eyes seems brighter than the fire slowly spreading from the back door. "I do hope to conclude our business with a touch more finesse. More . . . what's the word . . . éclat?"

Where are the rest of the Krawlors? Enfer starts moving laterally away from the Joker, who keeps the distance between them constant. "Come now, little firebug," the Joker says. "Have you no pyro-pranks for me? No incendiary interventions? I perish—perish, I say!—in anticipation of your innovation." With a flourish the Joker produces a handful of shining steel, little bat-shapes spread like cards in his hand. He snaps them one after another at Enfer, and before Enfer can move three of them have bitten through the coat and sunk into the flesh of his upraised left arm. The fourth embeds itself with a *clang* in the prosthesis.

The Joker stalks more aggressively now, and Enfer circles him, shutting the Joker's taunts out of his mind. "I do so appreciate the gesture, you know," the Joker says. "Arkham's an abominable place. Your adoration was touching. The truth is, though—and I've told the boys this a thousand times—the truth is that the ecological niche, if you will, of the criminal mastermind, the archvillain, is a small one indeed. Small enough that only I can occupy it." Another salvo of steel bats whickers toward Enfer, biting into his legs; one pings off the oxygen tanks. "The boys have taken this lesson to heart.

There's nothing wrong with ambition, but like anything else, misdirected ambition becomes a liability, don't you think? I do."

Now, Enfer thinks. He flips a switch attached to his belt and the five prostheses he hasn't used start to spew gas vapors into the air. Now there isn't long; with an open fire at the back of the building, boomification of the premises is a foregone conclusion. The only question is whether the timing will be right.

The Joker wrinkles his nose. "Dear me, firebug. Must we pollute this, our final conversation, with foul odors? Is that not eau de skunk I smell, the common tincture added to municipal gas supplies so Auntie Mormoops doesn't incinerate herself when she forgets to turn off the oven after the cookies are done? Why, I think it is! From which I can only infer, Enfer, that you mean to do me harm by the ignition of said gas. Has it come to this? Do you not know that this marvelous Bat-getup encasing my precious flesh is superhumanly fire-resistant, perhaps in that regard superior even to your delightful fireman's regalia?"

Behind the visor and inside the oxygen mask, Enfer can smell himself. He's keyed up enough that if he snapped his fingers right now, the building would come down around them. There's a way to fix the timing issue that has worried him. The only question is whether the building will withstand the explosion. He never did have a chance to do a thorough investigation of its structure. Concrete, I-beams, he thinks. Pretty strong. Wouldn't be surprised if parts of the upstairs come downstairs, though, and it'll be best if I'm not here when it happens.

His mind is wandering, and as if he's snapping out of a dream Enfer realizes that the Joker must have doctored the little steel bats. I'd be dead right now if I were a regular man, he thinks. Probably my alterations are causing some pretty interesting chemistry with the Joker Juice.

That interesting chemistry is making him feel stoned, stoned, stoned, is the truth of the situation. Also, his feet are numb and the stump of his arm is itching fit to drive him nuts. *Ma main coupée brille au ciel dans la constellation d'Orion,* he quotes in his head, wishing he could see Orion from in here.

Whoa; what was that?

The Joker's right *there,* right *over* him, which means that at some point Enfer hit the floor. He doesn't remember doing it. He raises his right arm and squeezes the fist. This is supposed to cause a jet of slightly thinned napalm to coat the Joker's head and torso, but what happens is that a stream of slightly thinned napalm courses down the arm to pool inside the sleeve of his coat.

Grinning, the Joker plucks a steel bat out of the arm. Gasoline gel drips from one of its wingtips. "Dere *zeems* to haff been a *vailure* off pressurization, Herr Firebug," he says.

Enfer's head is buzzing. He takes off his oxygen mask, and the helmet with it. The smells of gas and smoke sting his nose, along with the acrid chemical tang of himself.

"*L'univers me déborde,*" he says softly, so softly the Joker's grin gets slightly quizzical and he leans closer to hear. "*Je sais aller jusqu'au bout . . . et j'ai peur.*"

"Oh," the Joker says, in mock sorrow. "Don't be afraid, little firebug. You haven't done all that badly. The bit with the firemen at the beginning showed promise, and the Arkham hijinks was, I must admit, inspired. *Haha,* indeed. But misdirected ambition . . ." He shakes his head. "I will enjoy using those little robots, though. Thank you for making me aware of them."

Enfer feels as if he is already vaporizing. With the prosthesis he reaches slowly across his body and takes off his left glove.

"*Je n'ai plus peur,*" he whispers.

"Beg pardon?" the Joker asks. The Bat-mask leans even closer.

"Now I'm not afraid anymore," Enfer says, and—

And the only flame in the universe is a poor thought . . .

—and snaps his fingers.

38

August 5, 10:37 PM

Well, that is an experience I hope never to repeat, the
Joker is thinking as he staggers out of the smoking ruin
of the firebug's incinerated headquarters. The first *boom*
was bad enough, what with all the gelid and/or va-
porous hydrocarbons—but the second, not funny at all,
not a bit. What on earth did the firebug have stored up
back there in the rear of the building? "People shouldn't
be trusted with that sort of ordnance," he sniffs, brush-
ing soot and flaming skeins of napalm from the Batsuit.
At the same time he's thanking his lucky stars for the
superhuman reflexes—and let's not forget the inspired
speed of thought!—that allowed him, in the fraction of
a second between the birth of the flame between the firebug's thumb and forefinger and the annihilation of the
ground floor of the building, to duck under the Bat-cape
and trigger the hardening response that transformed it
into a personal bomb shelter. Even with that protection,
he's a little deaf and feeling more than a little singed.
Flash-fried, even. Seared in the manner of a Cajun
steak . . . thinking of which makes him hungry.

Of the firebug there was no visible sign after the explosion, which was just as well. When the Joker is hungry, he has little desire to view detonated firebugs.

However, he does always enjoy the sight of a little carnage, especially if he had a hand in its creation, so he allows himself a few minutes to stand, arms akimbo and Bat-cape blowing in the fire-accelerated breeze, on the street in front of the collapsing remains of the firebug's nest. The night sky is full of sirens and spotlights. At street level the only illumination comes from the few working streetlights and the great many working fires.

"Gotham City," the Joker says with pride. "My city, my love. Who could live anywhere else?"

He seats himself in the Bat-car and roars off, noting with passing interest the lack of traffic on Gotham streets. There is no lack, however, of columns of smoke. Or sirens, or helicopters, or—"Incoming!" he sings out as bullets ping off the Bat-car's chassis—trigger-happy police officers. He blows smoke just to give the boys in blue something to think about, then reverses direction and accelerates back through the smoke.

Just as he's coming out of the cloud, the Joker experiences an odd moment of cognitive dissonance. Why, isn't that car in front of him, its matte-black finish swallowing the sweep of his headlights, a *Bat-car*? How can that be when he is driving the onliest Bat-car in all of Gotham City?

Or perhaps he is thinking that thought after he T-bones the other Bat-car at a speed that can only be considered excessive and only thinks he had the thought before the collision because of the way that blunt trauma to the head scrambles his sense of time. Either way, he is still curious about the phenomenon when he wrenches the Bat-car's door open and leaps out onto the street. His foot catches on the harness and he lands flat on his face, the Bat-cape settling over him like a parachute.

How humiliating.

Up on the feet, quick, take a bow. People love pratfalls. "Thank you, thank you, I'm here all week!" he proclaims, and standing up out of the bow he notes that in fact there is another Bat-car, which can mean only one of two things. Either there is a copycat out there who is enamored of the idea of being an impostor Batman, or Batman himself has managed to acquire a new car.

Of the two, the Joker—even in his state of temporarily diminished mental capacity—finds the second to be more likely. Still, he feels it necessary to confirm his intuition. He walks up to the other Bat-car, the driver's side of which is quite spectacularly stove in.

"Well. Shut my mouf if it ain't dat ole Batman!" the Joker says.

The Chiropteran Crusader glares at him with a look the Joker recognizes, having directed it at so many people himself. It's a look that promises murder.

"I do hope this little incident, fatal as it was to our dear little firebug, won't prevent you from attending the grand opening of the Mormoops Maximus," he says with grandly inflated solicitude. "I'd assist you in exiting your vehicle were it not for my concern that you might presume upon my altruism by provoking some sort of fisticuffs. So here's what let's do: I'll toddle off to await you at the address I'm sure Captain Gordon has provided you, and you come along whenever you're ready. Sound fine? Fine. Ta ta."

The entirety of this little soliloquy is made possible by the fact that Batman's Bat-car, having received the force of the Joker's Bat-car, is rearranged and wrinkled in such a way as to prevent the Chiropteran Crusader's immediate egress.

What a lucky ducky I am, the Joker thinks.

He executes an imaginary tip of the somewhat battered Bat-cowl and exits in the manner of a classic vaudevillian, soft-shoeing it back to his Bat-car. Once he's around the corner and out of sight, the Joker starts planning. Batman won't be long, no sirree, and there are things to do. One cannot entertain, not really, unless all of the doilies are dusted and one has changed out of these charred Bat-things and into proper garb for hosting important guests.

Plus there's the little matter of those Krawlors, which are in dire need of a meticulously Jokeriffic reprogramming.

"To Mormoops Central, Jeeves!" he cries out, and floors it.

Not too long after that—which expression has even less meaning than it might, given the Joker's somewhat tenuous grasp on time—he's charging through the alley door at Mormoops Central, offering a tip of his sooty cowl to the lingering memory of Katatonic Kathy. "Boys! Our hero approacheth!" he announces. "And the firebug will send no more spiderbots to trouble us! A red-letter day indeed!"

Bud and Lou are sipping from brown paper bags. The Joker stops.

"Now, really," he says.

The foamy splatter of beer on concrete momentarily drowns out the various mechanical and hydraulic sounds coming from the direction of Mormoops Maximus.

"I go forth to change," the Joker says. "Pinstripes or the solid purple?"

"Pinstripes," Lou says at the exact moment that Bud opines in favor of the purple.

"Thank you, boys," the Joker says. "I'll be back in a jiffy."

Exactly one jiffy later, he is back and sitting in front of the fine array of monitors the boys have liberated from a dockside warehouse. They've also been kind—or lucky, in the way that simpletons are often lucky— enough to wire up the server in such a way that it actually performs its function of command and control over the forty or so surviving Krawlors.

"Exemplary work, boys," the Joker says, and is surprised to find that he means it. Either Bud or Lou apparently has a touch with computers. He doesn't want to ask which of them, because the question would clue them in to the fact that he thinks they've done something right, and once they know that, anarchy and rebellion are bound to ensue.

Being no slouch at the keyboard himself, the Joker wastes no time revising the primary instructional matrix governing each Krawlor. "No longer, my pretties, will you randomly assault and destroy GCPD black-and-whites," he promises. "Such a waste of your potential. Why don't you come back to Mormoops Central, rest up a minute, and recharge those wonderful cargo spaces?

Then, once you're full up with Joker Juice, you may venture once more into the Gotham environs and show the ghost of our dear departed firebug how this archvillain game is truly played."

"Great speech, boss," Lou says.

39

August 5, 10:44 PM

In any conflict, Bruce Wayne has read, there are a certain number of intrusions of simple randomness. Often these are decisive.

Batman does not want to hear this. The collision of the two cars and the intersection of the real Batman and his deranged impostor do not interest him as expressions of military history or chaos theory. Batman's entire being is subsumed within the imperative to get out of the car, track the Joker to this Mormoops Maximus, and end things. The car, designed to remain functional after impacts with anything up to and including concrete walls, could possibly still drive, although the left front tire would scrape itself to pieces on the collapsed portion of the fender and the steering would be about as sensitive as a sedated mule. Fighting his way out of the harness, Batman has no intention of finding out whether he could drive to the Mormoops Maximus, and how long it would take; his body and his anger will get him there much more quickly.

Free of the harness, he rolls across to the passenger

door and opens it. It comes up short against a mailbox
on the curb, and in a burst of fury he swings his legs
around and slams both feet into the door panel. The
rusty bolts holding the mailbox to its concrete base snap
and the box skids off the base and topples onto the sidewalk. Batman pauses just long enough to refresh his
equipment from the glove compartment and console of
the car. Then he's like smoke, blending into the shadows
of firelit Gotham City, seen only when he wants to be,
invisible even to the daylight version of himself.

The address, in a decrepit and largely deserted industrial area of the East End, announces itself by a flashing
orange neon sign: MM, MM, MM, MM, against the background outline of a bat. It's the only light on the block.
The Joker must be feeling bold. Batman wonders what
his plans are for the Krawlors, two of which are just
now skittering around the back of the building.

Mormoops Maximus.

The Great Ghost-Faced Bat? That's one interpreta-
tion. The other, more in keeping with the Joker's style, is
a killing floor with a bat theme. It's not worth thinking
about. What remains is a last obstacle; the details of that
obstacle will not be important until he encounters them,
and they will not be knowable until then.

Another Krawlor appears briefly on the street before
following the previous two around the corner. Batman
considers going after it and gaining access to the building that way. That approach brings an excess of variables: the Krawlors might already be reprogrammed to
attack him, or they might be headed down into a holding area with no direct access to the Joker, or . . .

Admit it, he prods himself. You want to go in the way

the Joker wants you to. You have accepted the terms of the game because it is a game you enjoy playing, and you enjoy playing the game because you have long since lost both your fear of death and your belief that anyone in Gotham City can outsmart you—but at the same time, you know that if that person exists, it's the Joker, and you just have to know what challenge he's laid for you this time.

This is the self-indulgent shadow cast by the monolithic dedication of Batman to the betterment of Gotham City. It's true. No point in denying it.

Maybe we are different, he thinks.

He is across the street and in the front door before a fourth Krawlor, just pushing a manhole cover out of its way as it comes up from below the street, can register his presence.

Inside, the darkness is so complete that even his hyperacute eyes can barely discern any patterns. He waits, still and silent, until his vision is as normal as it's going to get. Outlines of a broad, open floor supported by naked I-beams slowly emerge from the even black. An abandoned factory floor, he thinks; but he knew that when he walked in. Across the room, the right angles and straight lines crumple into less distinct shapes.

A dim light, smoky orange in color, appears on the far wall. Above it, letter by letter, a message spells itself out: THIS WAY TO THE MAXIMUS.

He goes toward this darkly carnivalesque invitation, bearing first almost all the way to the left-hand wall, conscious at every step of the smoothness of the floor under his boot soles and of the possibility—the certainty, really—that the Joker is observing him. No visible-spectrum camera that he knows of would return a useful image of him in the minimal ambient light, but his face and breath will be beacons in infrared, and a standard night-vision lens will pick him out as a silhouette. He'd be a fool to assume he is invisible, but there's no sense making himself obvious, either. Even though it's the Joker's show, the best way to throw a wrench in the works is to look like he's doing exactly what the Joker expects while he's actually scoping out ways to make those expectations work against the Joker. Tactical judo.

Now that he's closer to the door, he sees that the room has been remade to look like a cave: I-beams have become flowstone columns, and in the ocher glow from the sign he can see old light fixtures redone to look like stalactites. Ah. So what we're looking at here is a joke on the partially transformed cave below Wayne Manor. Batman's mind runs through possibilities of what might await on the other side: water, invisible holes, rockfalls . . . spiders, crickets, fish . . .

Bats.

He takes a breath, holds it in until he can feel the tap of his pulse in his throat. Then a slow exhalation, centering and preparatory. His body, trunk and limbs, muscle and bone and brain, stands ready.

What he needs to know, more than specifics of what awaits him on the other side of the orange-lit door, is the location of the Joker's control room. A setup like this one requires fairly rigorous surveillance and real-time control, and that's not even taking into account whatever the Joker's got cooked up for the Krawlors.

That last thought—and memories of what nearly happened to the reservoir last year—spurs him forward. If the Joker's previous behavior is any indication, he'll be timing Batman's progress through the Maximus and hoping to synchronize it in such a way that at the very moment Batman gets through the Maximus, he'll realize that it's just a moment too late. That was the point of the Alfred joke, Batman thinks. This is the same thing, only with more than Alfred's life at stake.

He walks through the door.

"Welcome, Caped Crusader," comes the Joker's voice through unseen speakers. "As you can see, I was so inspired by my unexpected visit to your sanctum sanctorum that in addition to paying my own little homage to your presence in our fair city, I had to re-create your subterranean hideaway . . . only with a few little twists whose artistic merit I'm sure you'll be able to appreciate."

This must be a cue, since as the echo of the words dies away Batman can hear the drip of water, an effect not present before.

"Is this a guided tour?" he asks.

"Consider me your Virgil," the Joker says.

"Right," Batman says, and moves forward.

Under his feet, the feel of rough stone. In his ears, the drip of water and a quiet rumble that puts him in mind of the furnace in the oldest part of Wayne Manor. In his eyes, the dimmest reds and oranges. In his nose, traces of petroleum and another, earthier smell he can't identify. Ahead of him, a fork in the trail between piles of boulders and thick forests of stalagmites.

"But bear in mind, you don't have the leisure of Dante," the Joker goes on. "I have plans for those Krawlors, and those plans are under way. I'd hate to have you miss their grand send-off. It's going to be quite a *juicy* spectacle."

Juicy, Batman thinks. Right. Put together a couple of dozen Krawlors—or however many are still operational—and a quantity of Joker Juice, and what you have is disaster.

"Juicy in here, too, I'll bet," he says, fishing a little.

"Oh, I'll keep you interested," the Joker says. "Now you have a decision to make: right or left?"

Batman goes left.

"Marvelous," the Joker croons. Ahead, Batman sees the trail slope downward beneath a lowering ceiling. He's just shifting his weight to take the next step when he feels something shift in the floor. A spring; his weight is already committed forward, and he flexes down, then out, diving forward into the descending tunnel. He passes into blackness, and the quality of the sound in the cave changes. Behind him the roar and glow of fire throws his shadow against the opposite wall of the room he's leapt into. It's much farther away than he'd anticipated, a broad chamber rather than the narrowing passage he'd expected. Just as he understands this, he also senses that there is space below him. Tucking into a somersault, he catches the corners of the cape and partially stiffens it, relying on the strength of the fabric to absorb the landing he believes is coming.

Lucius, he thinks, here's some useful product testing for your bulletproof underwear.

Shielded by the cape, Batman at first doesn't realize that he has fallen into water. The impact knocks the breath from him, and then he registers that his body has made a *splash* rather than the meaty *thud* he's gotten too used to over his short career as a crimefighter. The water closes over his head, and he lets go of the cape, kicking back to the surface.

The suit and cape absorb no water and are reasonably light, so swimming is no problem. The water is moving, though, and that is a problem. Where is it going?

"Oh, Batman?" the Joker says. His voice doubles and redoubles in the room. "The Krawlors are almost ready. I'd hate to have you miss their grand debut because you were floating out to sea."

The current picks up, and Batman floats on his back, spreading his limbs. His sense of smell has caught up with the other four, and he detects small amounts of oil in the water. His hands and feet slap small bits of debris. A wastewater cistern, he thinks. It must drain into a pipe, and probably at some point there's a screen for large debris. If I get pinned against that, I won't be around to see the Krawlors for sure.

His left foot jars into a wall, then skids into a stronger current. Batman sends the maximum charge through the cape's fibers, stiffening it into a sail—or, in this case, a rudder. It sweeps into the current, pulling his upper body with it, and then jams in the mouth of the drain-pipe. Good thing the electrically stimulated fibers are insulated by the exterior layer of the cape, he thinks; but it's a mixed blessing, because as his body is caught in the rush of water, Batman is strangling on his own weight. Far too much time has passed since he drew a full breath. He reaches up over his head and catches one hardened edge of the cape in both hands; then, turning himself on his side, he flattens himself against the inside of the pipe and slowly belly-crawls back toward its mouth. The pressure on his neck lessens, and his head breaks the surface.

Quiet, he thinks. Let him think you're gone for now.

"Yoo-hoo, Batman!" the Joker is calling.

Batman gets first one hand, then the other, on the protruding lip of the drainpipe's mouth. He reaches up and finds that the wall is made of large granite bricks, slippery but imperfectly cut so that they offer more than enough finger- and toeholds. Hand over hand, he pulls himself out of the water until he can get one foot out of the current. Then he relaxes the cape and takes twenty seconds just to breathe.

"Yoo-hoo! Do respond, Crusader. This won't be nearly as much fun without a Bat-witness." The Joker has adopted a comically insincere pleading tone.

Not yet, Batman thinks. He climbs the wall, brick by brick and seam by seam. When he is eight feet or so above the surface of the water, he looks around. Whatever trap he sprang in the outer room is still burning brightly, and in the light from that fire he can see an opening in the wall above him. Ninety seconds later he is hoisting himself through it.

He's in a tunnel, less than thirty inches high and slightly wider. Its floor is dry, and it rises gently away from the storm-water cistern. He bear-walks for maybe fifty feet, pausing every few steps to listen. The tunnel is full of noises, all indistinct except his own breathing. Periodically the Joker's repetitions of *yoo-hoo!* echo behind him. He starts to wonder if they're recorded, but before he can waste too much energy wondering, he sees light ahead and turns his entire focus to the end of the tunnel.

Almost there, he stills himself to listen. Light flares and dies above him in time with a repeated hissing and thumping; and behind that, a mechanical squeaking. Covering the last few feet to the end of the tunnel, he encounters a heavy grate bolted across its mouth. He tests it, and feels it give a little.

Well, he thinks, I was always going to be noisy at some point.

Lying on his back, he spreads his feet to brace them against the tunnel walls. Then he works his fingers into the grate and pushes, slowly and steadily increasing the force until he feels the ghost of movement in one corner of the grate. Shifting one hand so his center of pressure is closer to that movement, he breathes in . . . holds . . . and with the exhalation snaps the grate loose.

He slides it out of the way and lifts himself out into a room that makes him understand the Joker's *bon mot* about the *Inferno*. Flames belch from the walls and ceiling, and chaotic showers of what look like molten rock spray up from the floor. Batman stays where he is, waiting for the pattern to become apparent. He lets his eyes unfocus, mapping each of the separate cycles onto a collective timeline and waiting for the common denominator to reveal itself. Bit by bit, it does. There is a path, to what he doesn't know. With some agility and timing, he should be able to traverse it. The problem is that if the path is just an artifact of the way the Joker put the puzzle together, he won't be any better off at the end of it than he is now.

"Oh, Batman?" the Joker calls over the grunt of the flames. "I heard something in there. Where are you, most worthy adversary? You're a little off track, I think. Understandable, of course. Tell me where you are and I'll extend an invitation. In all honesty—I'm crossing my heart this very moment—I'd hate to have you fail before you can join me in watching the Krawlortante Ball I have planned for . . . my goodness, look at the time! Ten minutes from now. Do hurry. I'm waiting."

He's sweating inside the suit and wreathed in steam coming from the cape. Ignoring the Joker, Batman watches for the entry point to come around again. There . . . it . . . is.

He steps, rolls, freezes as he comes up out of the roll and a tongue of fire shoots across the path; runs a dozen steps, squats, and ducks under the cape as little flecks of molten rock spatter from the closest lava shower. Again and again—until he reaches the wall, and a small oasis where he can stay still and catch his breath again. As much as he hates to do it, he slips the lenses in place behind the cowl's eye openings. The heat in the room is drying his eyeballs in their sockets. Breathing, too, is a problem; his throat is seared and his nose burning.

When he has blinked some tears back into his eyes, he can see across the room again, and he understands two things: one, he has come into the room via a route the Joker did not anticipate, and two, he is less than twenty feet from what must have been the way the Joker wanted him to emerge from the room.

Here's where he can spring a little surprise. Putting his head down and wrapping the cape around his upper body, Batman charges straight through a belching cloud of fire and under the lintel of the finished doorway marking the exit. He catches part of the inscription over the door just before he passes beneath it: . . . YE WHO ENTER HERE.

A little late for that, he thinks. Anybody who makes it this far either never had any hope or is incapable of losing it.

He's not sure which category Bruce Wayne would belong to—or, really, how you would tell one from the other. In close proximity to a fiery death, hope and desperation look much the same.

Quiet.

That's the first thing he notices. No gouts of flame, no hungry swirls of water. Just silence, textured ever so slightly by the squeaking noise he hears from the tunnel mouth.

"Virgil symbolizes the intellect," he says out loud. "Thanks for the tip."

A pause.

Then he hears a slight *pop* as the speaker comes on. "Good gracious. There you are. Six minutes, you know. Can't hold the curtain, even for such a VIP as yourself." There is a soft hiss somewhere in the room, and the smell of something astringent. "Here's a little something to spur you on," the Joker says. "Courtesy of Arkham Asylum."

Then the room explodes in bat wings, precisely at the moment when Batman's brain spasms with cold, unreasoning animal fear.

From the rustle and whir of bat wings, patterns resolve themselves.

"Bruce."

His father's voice, cold and distant. It's dark, but as if he's viewing a stereoscope Bruce can see the silhouette of his father, resolving itself from the churning background of bats.

"This is not what I raised you for, Bruce."

I honor you, Dad. And Mom.

"No, you don't. You honor your pain. Your life since the night we died has been one long effort to dissociate from and displace your guilt, masquerading as a crusade against crime. That's the only superhuman thing about you. I don't know how to put it any more clearly."

Somewhere, part of Bruce's brain knows that it's the Joker doing this; but it's the part of the brain that talks ineffectually when you're in the middle of a nightmare and only succeeds in adding more torque to the horror of the experience because there's no way to know if it's true. All that he has is this tiny, tiny voice against the looming presence manifesting from the bats.

"You can't be eight years old forever, Bruce. You can spread all the fear you want, but . . ."

His mother's voice this time, closer than his father's but still flattened by disappointment. Bruce *is* eight years old, maybe forever, and maybe he will be wrestling with these specters forever.

". . . but you can't make yourself less fearful by spreading that fear to others. As long as you're creating more outside, there's always more inside you to replace it."

It's for good, Mother. I bit down on my fear; I held it; I subdued it. And now I make it work for me. Fear is my engine.

The bats are raining flaming guano. Batman sinks to his knees, every muscle quivering with the effort of keeping his mind in one piece.

His father again. "Bruce, what else needs to happen for you to understand this? If you hadn't put on that

damn outfit to begin with, what would the Joker have
had to steal? How many people would still be alive if
every criminal misfit in Gotham City didn't suddenly
have a measuring stick that he wanted to test himself
against?"

*They don't need a reason, Father. They are how they
are.*

"You mean we, don't you?"

No. Yes.

We are how we are.

Fire all around him, and he isn't going to be able to
hold it together much longer. It's the Joker doing this,
the tiny voice repeats. And if you let him, you're going
to die here and the Krawlors are going to hose Joker
Juice all over Gotham City—because you're still grieving Mama and Daddy. You're still grieving the decisive
intrusion of randomness into your life.

A *snap,* in his mind. Maybe something breaking,
maybe something falling together like the last piece of a
model, a perfect fit. Through the storm of bat wings and
fire he catches a waft of clean, air-conditioned air across
his face. *There.* Randomness intervenes. Some of the
fear evaporates . . .

"There," he growls, and *knows* where this current of
air has come from, knows how it was torn and twisted
by the beat of a million bat wings and the mushrooming
convection of a thousand fires.

Or maybe it's intuition.

Either way, when he lunges to his right, both fists together, he crunches through a double sheet of drywall
and the room is flooded with light.

* * *

The Joker sits, old-fashioned microphone in one hand and an unlit cigarette in a long holder dangling from two fingers of the other. He looks up at Batman and says, "Dear me. Decided to cut the Gordian knot, have we?"

The fear drives him like the pain that sinks a trapped coyote's teeth into its own leg. He flexes his shoulders and snaps the wall studs on either side of him, jerking pieces of them loose with either hand as he steps through the opening into . . .

"Welcome to Mormoops Central, Batman," the Joker says. He puts the microphone down. "It appears I'll no longer need this."

"I don't think they let you smoke in prison anymore, either," Batman says.

"The city's concern for my health is touching." The Joker starts to reach for something—maybe a squirting carnation, maybe exploding fake dogshit, who knows—and Batman is across the gap between them before the Joker's arm has moved six inches. He snaps a punch into the Joker's overbroad mouth, just by way of introduction, and before the teeth have finished falling out he has the Joker spun around to the floor, an elbow in his neck and one of the broken wall studs raised over his head.

"That's another one of those things that's only funny when it happens to someone else," the Joker says. His eyes are wide, and the blood running into his mouth takes some of the insouciance out of his grin. "Fear. And that's what you're after, isn't it, you humorless stone-faced ghoul? You just want to scare people. Well, fine. I'm scared. But the joke, my faux-chiropteran adversary, is still going to be on you."

Batman looks up and sees that he's holding the piece

of two-by-four with the pointed end down, as if he's about to stake a vampire.

Bruce Wayne once read a work of philosophy in which it was written that when you look into the abyss, the abyss looks back.

This is one of those moments.

Batman raises the stake and with all of his strength throws it like a spear over the Joker's head, where it buries itself squarely in the mail-order corporate logo that decorates the center of the server taken from the home of the recently departed F. Sauser.

Sparks shoot out of the server's vent, followed by a slow, steady little orange flame that gutters out after a few seconds. The array of monitors goes a flat blue. Looking around Mormoops Central, Batman counts thirteen Krawlors in his field of vision. All of them are still except three, which are slowing to a halt.

"You probably would have disguised yourself as me when you did your grand proclamation about the Krawlors, wouldn't you?" he says.

The Joker's smile is oddly dreamy. "Yes," he nods. "I would have."

I will not kill, Batman thinks—and putting everything he has into each one, he drives three straight right hands into the Joker's head.

With each of them, he feels a little of the fear drain away. He stands over the unconscious Joker, feeling the vibrations of those punches die away up and down the bones of his arm. He senses eyes on him and turns to see two ordinary working stiffs coming in the door from a side room. Behind them he can see a laboratory setup, and various vessels filled with fluids and gases in the

Joker's favored shade of green. Henchmen, he thinks. Probably the ones who killed the Shanleys.

"You didn't have to do that," one of the henchmen says sorrowfully.

Batman picks up the battered Joker and slings him over his shoulder in a fireman's carry. "I didn't have to let him live, either," he says, before carrying the Joker up and out into the smoky, siren-split Gotham City night.

BULL'S-EYE

Rafael del Toro, *Gazette* Columnist

Okay, I was wrong.

Read that last line carefully. Savor it. It'll be a while be-fore you see it again.

But I write it with no regrets, because being wrong about Batman means that I have a profound sense of all-is-right-with-the-worldness. The Caped Crusader is in his hideout and I am at my keyboard, the Joker is on his way to wherever we're going to warehouse the crème de la deranged, and things are as they should be.

Who knew the Joker would have been able to pull off a Batman-in-disguise joke for so long? Makes you wonder if deep down, we all *wanted* to believe that the Batman dream, this vision of a nocturnal Lone Ranger, was going to go sour on us eventually. We sure didn't waste any time buying what the Joker had to sell.

I'm no psychoanalyst, but that explanation feels true to me. As Gothamites, we're incapable of believing the best about people. Confronted with pure examples of human self-lessness and devotion, we shuffle around like we've got rocks in our shoes.

Maybe Jonathan Crane could tell us why. If he's in the mood to tell us anything, which is rarely the case . . . and speaking of it, perhaps I should be repeating the first line of this column with respect to Crane as well as Batman. But more about that later.

For now, it appears that Batman was the victim of a cruel joke played by the greatest of jokers, which is to say the Joker, and that the rest of us were equally victims. Especially Merilee St. Pierre, the other unfortunate pedestrians, and the Shanley family.

So it looks like I need a new rant.

Hm . . .

Ah. Got it.

There's this guy. He's been widely quoted in the papers because he's been at the center of a controversy lately. It appears he didn't handle the dissemination of information with great skill or concern for the public well-being. It also appears that he might have deliberately misled the public about the method of the Joker's escape, thereby causing numerous fatalities among the citizens of our fair metropolis.

But what the hell, that's Gotham City officialdom, right?

Right. Sure. I had a thought, though. If Batman can teach us any lesson, maybe it's this one: we don't have to stand for this kind of crap. Can anyone—and I mean *anyone*—tell me why the hell Jonathan Crane still has a job?

EPILOGUE

December 1, 7:16 PM

"Once," says Jim Gordon, "there was a crocodile who could fly . . ."

James Junior wriggles deeper into his bed. Just a month ago Gordon and Barbara moved him from a crib into a bed. It was one of those bittersweet occasions; Gordon is proud of his boy for making the transition and sad that Junior will no longer be in the crib with the dinosaur mobile turning over his head.

Gordon has told this story maybe a hundred times in the last four months—told it to Junior, that is. He's told it so much that he catches himself creating new versions of it in his head while he's on the phone, or filling out reports, or doing any of the million other tasks that still seem to be dropping out of the sky in the wake of the Enfer Inferno, as a nameless *Gazette* headline writer dubbed the events of August 5.

Once there was a man who could fly, or at least everyone thought he could. We all called him Batman . . .

Once there was a crocodile who took the shape of a man and lurked underground waiting to . . .

Once there was a man who burned, and then was burned, and then survived to burn again, and then died in a fire of his own making.

He won't tell that to Junior, but that's the one that's been rattling the loudest inside his head for the past few months. Gordon has managed to tease part of the Enfer story out of sources from the East End all the way across to North Africa, but there's too much he doesn't know. He's got his suspicions about Jonathan Crane, who after the initial uproar seems to have survived with his position intact—and who also looks to be getting a fat line item in the state supplemental budget to rebuild Arkham Asylum right where it's always been. Thinking about the political horse trading that went into that makes Gordon tired.

Until Arkham is rebuilt, its inmates—including the Joker—are going to be housed in a mothballed state prison a hundred miles or so from Gotham City. Gordon will sleep easier knowing that, but he knows that as soon as the new Arkham is built, all of the psychopaths and deranged lunatics will be right there at Trigate again. Even if they don't escape as often, he can't help but feel that their presence has an effect on the city.

Two weeks after the Inferno, Wayne Enterprises announced a multimillion-dollar grant program to assist in the reconstruction and improvement of firefighting and police facilities in Gotham City. Cynical meatheads like Duane Trask grumbled about Bruce Wayne throwing his money around so he could interfere with Gotham City politics, but Gordon is of the opinion that Gotham City politics need a little interference. A billionaire do-gooder would be a welcome change of pace from your run-of-the-mill graft and corruption. On

Election Day the Ridley guy took out Angelo Fittipaldi, and other incumbents had closer races than they'd experienced in years. Maybe a new breeze was blowing. Gordon's too cynical himself to actually believe that, but he's not too cynical to want to.

"The crocodile flew all the way to the moon," Gordon says, "and when he got to the moon he decided to see what kind of flowers grew there."

Junior's eyes are closing.

Flowers, Gordon thinks. The seas of flowers at all of the funerals following the Inferno, the rows of cops and firefighters saluting their fallen.

"There were moon-roses, and moon-lilies, and moon-daffodils," Gordon says softly. "And the people who lived on the moon were building . . ."

He trails off. Junior is asleep. Gordon sits next to his son's bed, tired but steeping himself in the pleasure of being just a dad for a little while. Until tomorrow morning, when he has to get up and be a cop again. He looks out Junior's bedroom window into the darkness of early winter. Batman is out there somewhere. It's good to be able to believe in him again.